BOOK OF THE DEAD

"What is it?" the woman asked.

"A book—one that will give a man any dream or wish he might desire. It will make the weak strong, the poor wealthy, the stupid brilliant. No matter the wish, it will be granted." He chuckled malevolently. "It will give me much pleasure to witness the corruption of human beings with this little device."

"But, Master, if they get their wishes, how will mighty Lucifer gain his end? Is there a consequence?"

Mirthless laughter echoed through the cavernous room. "Of course there is a price. There is always a price. They who own the book and use it will become *of the dead.*"

Other Leisure Books by John Tigges:

EVIL DREAMS
VESSEL
KISS NOT THE CHILD
VENOM
UNTO THE ALTAR
AS EVIL DOES
HANDS OF LUCIFER
GARDEN OF THE INCUBUS
THE IMMORTAL

BOOK OF THE DEAD

JOHN TIGGES

LEISURE BOOKS ▇ NEW YORK CITY

For all the book lovers in the world, such as
Art Furlong
and
David McGhee
and
Bonnie Hearn
Read and enjoy Book of the Dead

A LEISURE BOOK

September 1989

Published by

Dorchester Publishing Co., Inc.
276 Fifth Avenue
New York, NY 10001

Copyright© 1989 by John Tigges

Printed in the United States of America.

. . . but they that have done evil (shall come forth), unto the resurrection of judgment.

Book of John; Chapter 5, verse 29

And these shall go into everlasting punishment . . .

Book of Matthew; Chapter 25, verse 46

. . . and yea, there is a book, and if thy name is in the book, thou art doomed to be of *The Dead*.

Book of Ahama; Seventh Book, Lago 3

PROLOGUE

The black filled every corner, seeping into the open space where the figure sat hunched over, thoughtfully stroking his grizzled chin. His eyes, the pupils dilated to accept the meager light, jerked from side to side. Batlike wings, folded against his back, twitched spasmodically. Agitated, he stood, his tail with a spade-shaped tip lashing frantically back and forth.

"I don't know what to do with you." His words rang hollowly through the Stygian dark. "It's almost too early. I didn't think I'd get anyone so soon."

A figure stepped from the blackness and approached the demon. "I do not wish to be a burden, mighty Lucifer. If you do not wish me here, but speak the words and I shall be gone.

I have mothered thousands of demons, and I can always find a priapus for my own use. There are many about."

"You do not wish my priapus? My cock? It is the mightiest of all, woman."

"I know this. The others have told me of it."

"Then why be satisfied with something less?"

"Because of the stuff from which I was made —the slime of the earth and the mud and filth of vermin—I am the way I am. Because God thought I would be perfect, made from his handiwork, he created me for Adam, but Adam wanted me to be subservient and lie beneath him."

"And with your high spirit and willfulness, what did you do?"

"At first nothing. I coupled with Adam, and we produced monsters—demons and devils that would have populated the garden. But I wanted to mount his priapus as much as he wanted to mount me. I have the muscles to milk a man of all his seed if I so choose. But he would have none of it. He was the master—I, the lesser creation! So I left him."

"And went where? There is not that much on earth yet."

"I found our offspring and coupled with them, producing more monsters and demons." She threw her head back and laughed mirthlessly in the darkness. "God sent his angels to bring me back to Adam. When I refused to go with them, God banished me here—to be with you. He said I would be henceforth known as the *night hag* and prowl the wastes with beasts and demons."

"And here you shall be. But I have no time for you now. I will give you the power to gather unto yourself men of weak character and powerful cocks. You shall milk their seed as well as their very essence, leaving nothing more than a shell. Their spirits shall be unto themselves and have no contact with anyone or anything once you have finished with them. You will toy with them, tease them and give them what they want, but at a price no one would be willing to pay if they knew at the time what the charge would be."

"My lord and master," the woman said, "show me how to accomplish this."

"Are you considered beautiful?"

"I was made beautiful by the Almighty. My beauty is such as to lure anyone to do my bidding, no matter what I ask."

"Let me see." The shadowy figure swept his arm in an arc before him and a blinding light shone brilliantly, centering on the woman.

Waves of raven black hair cascaded over bare shoulders, half covering her large, firm breasts. Alabaster skin reflected the light, accentuating the triangle of black pubic hair. Dark aureoles, tipping each breast, stood out in stark relief. Her round, black eyes stared up at Lucifer.

"Yes, you are beautiful and, I'm sure, alluring to men. That is the way you shall appear to them for all time. You shall roam the earth forever doing what you want, winning souls for me. When I summon you, you shall appear as this—" He made another sweep of his arm and instantly changed the woman's appearance. The luxuriant hair stiffened and stood out at right angles to her head. The deep penetrating eyes changed shape, one growing to three times the size of the other, widening and growing rheumy with large tears dripping from them. Her nose broadened, flattening against her face, while her red lips drew back in a grimace, exposing broken teeth and a lolling tongue. Her breath came in labored puffs and grunts as her breasts sagged into pendulous globs of flesh, hanging over her protruding belly. Sores popped open, spewing forth an oozing pus that dripped along her blotched skin.

The thing looked up at him and grunted. "Why? Why should I look like this?"

"The other way you do not look like a night hag. Let's not disappoint the one who made you and thus named you. When men see you or dream of you, you will be beautiful, but in reality you will be thus!" He turned and returned to the rock on which he had been sitting. "I have plans that will change the earth. My plans will disrupt His puny plans and you will help me. Among other things is this." He pointed to an object lying on a rock near him.

The misshapen figure hobbled over to it, limping on one leg that was much shorter than the other. "What is it?" she asked.

"A book—one that will give any man any dream or wish he might desire. It will make the weak strong, the poor wealthy, the stupid brilliant. No matter the wish or desire, it will be his or hers. Since I order you to be responsible for it, I assume more men than women will be exposed to it." He chuckled malevolently.

"Of course."

"It will provide much glee to witness the corruption of human beings with this little device."

"But, master, if they get their wishes, how will mighty Lucifer gain his end? Is there a consequence?"

The mirthless laughter that answered the question echoed through the cavernous room. "Of course there is a price. There is always a price. They who own the book and use it will become *of the dead*."

When he didn't continue, the misshapen woman waited for a moment and then said, "And that price is?"

Again, Lucifer laughed. "What is your name, Adam's equal?"

"God called me Lilith, my Lord."

"In time, my dear Lilith, you shall see the horrendous price that will be paid for the use of my little book. Has God replaced you yet?"

"You mean as a mate for Adam?"

Lucifer nodded and stroked his chin.

Lilith shrugged. "I do not know."

"I will look into it." He waved his arm, and

she resumed her former appearance. "Study you well, *The Book of the Dead*. Through it, you will bring me countless souls."

She bowed and he disappeared, plunging the room back into its former darkness.

CHAPTER ONE

April, 1951

A brisk spring breeze wound through the hills of northeastern Iowa, carrying a promise of growth in the near future. Birds that had just recently returned to the area flitted here and there, gathering the makings of nests. The scent of newly opened flowers clung to the wind, announcing their readiness to be pollinated. The grass had turned green during the last few weeks, and a progression of showers and thunderstorms had cleansed the countryside, making it sparkle anew.

The previous night's storm had blown down dead branches and even injured some healthy limbs, which hung sadly. Here and there, the rain had washed rocks down the hillside, creating small landslides.

The smell of the Mississippi River in the east carried a fragrance all its own. The crest of the springtime flood had passed the previous week, and the mighty river flowed onward toward the south and the Gulf of Mexico.

A thin, frail man wearing a cap walked along the floor of the tiny valley. A fishing rod rested on one shoulder while he seemed to struggle with the weight of the tackle box he carried in his opposite hand. Emil La Motte moved in quick, nervous steps, his shallow face twisting in what might be interpreted as anger by one who didn't know him. An acquaintance would recognize immediately the expression of disgust and inhospitality which were his hallmarks.

He stopped and lowered the box to the ground. Catching his breath, he ran a hand through his graying hair. He shouldn't smoke so much—it seemed to affect his breathing—but what the hell! He was 62 years old and not in the best of physical shape. Smoking and a little whiskey each day seemed to be his only diversions, other than trying to exist in a community that didn't give a rat's ass for anyone who didn't seem to fit. Emil had lived in Nowaupeton, Iowa, since 1942. He had moved there with the idea of getting a job in a defense plant some 30 miles away in Dubuque, but when the job didn't come through, Emil had taken to fishing commercially in the river to support Magdalene, his wife. His son, Edgar, had been drafted and sent overseas.

Maybe Emil had been wrong to stay there. There had been plenty of jobs available in the nearby towns and cities, even a big paying job in Savanna, Illinois, at the armory. But that was over 100 miles away. He had disliked the idea of commuting there every day, and he didn't want to stay in Savanna during the week and just come home on weekends. Workdays ran ten hour shifts, and even work on Saturdays and Sundays wasn't out of the question. He had considered moving his wife there but shipping their possessions would have cost too much.

So he stayed in Nowaupeton, fishing. In 1944, just when the war seemed to be going the Allies' way, Magdalene died and Emil felt alone, as if a part of him had died as well. When the war was over, Edgar came home to Nowaupeton, but he had changed. He'd been shell-shocked and acted peculiar, sometimes frightening Emil half out of his mind. The townspeople, especially the children, mocked Edgar, and a seething hatred for the townspeople of Nowaupeton began fomenting in Emil. Less than a year after he came home, Edgar left one day and never came back. He took nothing with him and, for all practical purposes, simply disappeared from the face of the earth.

Emil repositioned the faded cap on his head and sighed. Picking up his tackle box, he made his way through the valley again, avoiding small trees and wild evergreen shrubs. The path he was taking would save him almost half a mile to reach his favorite fishing spot. It wasn't like fishing commercially with nets and trotlines. All he wanted to do was drop a line in the water and wait for a channel cat or a bullhead to take his bait. When he'd caught enough, he'd take them home, clean them and eat them. The next day, he'd do pretty much the same thing, unless he caught more than he could use in one day, which had happened frequently. Now, with the water level back to normal, fishing should be good.

The valley, which had been formed when the last glacier had inched its way across the face of the earth, was surrounded by low-lying hills. For some reason the glacier had split, moving around a goodly portion of northeastern Iowa, northwestern Illinois and parts of Wisconsin and Minnesota. The vale turned this way and that, leading toward the Mississippi River.

Emil stepped around a rock outcropping that had been bared thousands of years before and stopped dead in his tracks. He stared long and hard at the rusted plate lying against the hillside. What was it? He strained his eyes, trying his best to identify the plate's seemingly rectangular shape. For all the years he'd come this way, he'd never seen it before.

He set his tackle box and rod and reel on the rock and stepped toward the piece of metal. Maybe it was from a flying saucer. He'd heard about a pilot out west someplace who'd seen a spaceship or something and called it a flying saucer. Emil shook his head. He didn't know if such things could exist.

When he stood in front of the plate, he realized it wasn't just a plate but a door of some sort. A door? What would a door be doing on the side of a hill? The earth around the bottom of the door and covering the edges was muddy and soft. Maybe the storm had washed the ground away, exposing the door. Maybe it had been there all the time, waiting for someone to find it. But what would be the purpose of a door, in this valley? Did it hide something? Was there something behind it? Or was it merely lying there against the hill, once having been covered by earth and now exposed?

Emil dropped to his knees and wiped away some of the soft, muddy earth covering the bottom part of the door. When he finished, he stood and looked down. Sure enough, it was a door all right. Even had a peculiar looking handle.

He tentatively reached out and tried turning the latch, but it didn't move. Rusted tight. Emil shook his head. He assumed the door was made of iron and might be worth something as a piece of scrap metal, but he'd have to figure out some way to move it and get it into Dubuque to a scrap dealer. He could use the extra money but he didn't want to spend more to get it there than its possible worth.

Then he noticed the hinges. They didn't stand

out from the door itself nor had he felt them
when he saw he was wiping the dirt away. Now,
because the sun reflected off the surface, he
could see the distinct outline of hinges, three
of them, along one side.

Looking around, he spotted a large fallen
branch. He'd try prying the door up. If it
moved, it meant it had just been thrown there
sometime in the past. But if he couldn't budge
it, it might mean the hinges actually held the
door in place and might be hiding something
of even greater value than the door itself.

After getting the branch, he moved a rock
into place to act as a fulcrum and began
wedging the tip of the limb under the bottom.
He pushed down. The branch bent dramatically
but nothing happened. He tried again, but the
door remained in place. Maybe he could move
the door by jacking the branch under the top
edge and lifting instead. Trying the new tactic
brought nothing for his efforts.

He had to do something. The door was his.
He didn't care whose land it was on. He found
it, and it was his. He had to open it somehow.
Maybe if he had tools, he could get the damned
thing open. What would he need? A decent
crowbar to act as a better lever than the
branch. Dropping to his hands and knees, he
studied the handle. It appeared that it should
move without much effort. There was no
evidence of a lock of any sort, and he couldn't
figure why anyone would put a door with a
latch on it in the side of the hill and not have

some way to open it. If it wasn't locked, maybe all he had to do was free the rusty handle. There were seams along which he could squirt some oil. Did he have any? He wasn't sure. He could always get some at the service station or at the store.

Heaping the muddy earth back over the door, he laid the branch across it to hide any signs of his digging in the event someone came by before he got back. Just to be on the safe side, he'd bring back a flashlight in case there was something behind the door—something like a room. There had to be a room of some sort. Why else would the door be there?

Satisfied that he had sufficiently camouflaged the door, Emil turned and picked up his rod and tackle before hurrying back along the path.

Two hours later, Emil returned to the valley and hurried to the spot he'd covered over. He'd had no difficulty in getting the necessary items to open the iron door. The crowbar and small tool box he carried now had replaced the fishing rod and tackle box.

Ever since Magdalene had died and Edgar had decided to leave without so much as a goodbye, Emil had been looked on by the residents of Nowaupeton as the village oddball. Well, he'd show them. He was certain he'd find something well worth the effort he'd expended to open the rusty door; then they'd change their attitude toward him. For the most part he had no friends in the small community and kept to himself, avoiding all but the most necessary human contact. He had no influence nor money nor power and therefore would revel in the chance to show those bastards just how smart he actually was.

When he reached the door, he quickly threw aside the branch and once again scraped away the wet earth.

The iron plate rested at a 45° angle against the side of the hill and obviously had been exposed to the heavy rains of the night before, washing away the covering that had kept it hidden. Emil shook his head, wondering how long it had been covered.

Once the door was totally exposed, Emil took the can of oil he'd bought at the service station and squirted it around the seams of the handle. He breathed easier when the oil didn't simply run down the door, knowing he'd managed to get it inside the workings of the door latch. He sat down and waited. If the oil was going to do the job, it would take a few minutes for the lubricant to seep around the metal and free it. When five minutes had passed, he stood and reached out for the handle.

It moved a bit, grudgingly squealing as he jiggled it. Reaching down, he picked up the can and squirted more into the seam. After waiting several more minutes, he tried again and to his delight found that the handle moved freely.

But the door refused to budge. Taking the can once more, he squirted the remaining oil along the seam between the door and the frame. Rust held the plate securely in place, but with the help of the oil and a heavy hammer, he knew he'd be able to be free the door. How long it would take remained to be seen.

He patiently waited for the oil to do its work before starting to hammer along the seam of the door. When he figured enough time had elapsed, he stood and picked up the three pound hammer. Gripping it firmly in one hand, he hesitated, then brought it up over his head. He stopped and slowly lowered the hammer. Maybe he should try the latch first.

Gingerly reaching out, he grasped the handle and moved it. When it had gone as far as it could, he pulled out, and to his amazement the door swung open.

A foul smell of stale air, decaying matter and dampness washed over him. Squinting, he peered into the darkness that lay beyond the small pool of sunlight that illuminated the entrance. It wasn't a room after all but what appeared to be a tunnel, lined with supporting timbers. He reached out, grasped the nearest shore and tried moving it. It stood solid, unyielding. He checked the one on the opposite wall of the narrow passangeway and found it to be equally strong.

Should he enter? Why not! He'd found the door and managed to open it. Whatever lay beyond might be worth a fortune, and it was his—all his.

He turned back to the tool box, pulled out

a silver barreled flashlight, turned it on and directed it into the black maw before him. All he could see were more shores holding up the tunnel. Whoever had built this passageway had taken more than enough time to do a masterful job. Still, he cautiously checked each set of braces as he came to them, but he had nothing to fear from a cave-in. The tunnel would last a thousand years considering the manner in which it had been constructed.

Tentatively going inside even farther, he took step after step, slowly making his way along the passage. Because he was walking so cautiously, he knew that he had moved no more than perhaps 100 yards.

What lay ahead? Jewels? Gold? Silver? Who had left it there for someone to find by accident? There couldn't have been pirates this far north. Indians? Were Indians capable of building something like this? If so, why? There were legends about Vikings who had made it as far west as Minnesota, which lay to the north. Had Vikings created this remarkable tunnel? And if they did, why?

All he could do was follow the tunnel and find out the answers by exploring and investigating himself.

Suddenly he stood facing an earthen wall, studded with rock and roots from trees overhead. Why did it end here? For what reason had it been dug in the first place? To simply build a tunnel for no obvious reason and have it end at the barrier in front of him?

He coughed. "Goddamnit, anyway. Nothing," he muttered aloud. "Shit!"

He turned on his heel to start back and stopped. Something lay on the floor of the tunnel, something he hadn't seen when he walked over it the first time. Still, he should have kicked it. He hadn't lifted his feet more than an inch or so with each step. Why hadn't he seen it or felt it?

He lowered the flashlight, directing a pool of light on the object. It appeared to be a piece of leather, covering something else that stood perhaps two or three inches high. It lay in his tracks in the dust. Emil squatted down and studied it, noting the peculiar tooling in the leather cover.

Slowly reaching out, he touched the piece of hide with the tip of his forefinger. It looked like leather and felt like leather, and he moved to pick up the item, whatever it was. It was heavy, and he struggled to tip it far enough to slide his hand underneath it. It was no larger than a paperback book in size but decidedly heavier. Once he had a firm grip on it, he lifted it.

He played the beam of light over it but couldn't quite figure out what it was he held. He had to get outside where he could examine the thing in the light of day. The tunnel seemed to be closing in on him, and he gasped for air. He hurried along the excavation, no longer cautious.

Emil made his way out of the tunnel into the sunlight and plopped down on the grass to look at the object he held. It was shaped like a book of some sort, but the pages were thick, as if they were made from metal. That made sense since the thing was so heavy in the first place, but who would have made a book with metal plates for pages? He narrowed his eyes, lifted the leather covering and gasped.

The sunlight reflected dully off the golden page that lay in front of him. He lifted it and looked at the next page and the next. Each one was made of what appeared to be gold. Certainly that would explain the weight of the book. Leather thongs held the golden plates together and were attached to the leather coverings in front and in back.

A sinister smile crossed Emil's face. He wondered what it weighed. At $32 an ounce, the 10 or 12 pound weight would yield a pretty nice sum, but perhaps it had an intrinsic value for what it was rather than its gold content. That he didn't know. He knew he held something of value in his hands and felt his luck was finally about to turn for the better.

He packed up the tools and closed the door. He hesitated for a moment, wondering if he should recover the door with earth. Why should he? He took what was of value. No one knew there had been anything of value inside, except him. It would only delay him in getting home if he stopped to cover it now.

Deciding against it, he struck out across the valley, back in the direction from which he had come, toward his home in Nowaupeton. There he could examine it and weigh it and find out just how much his treasure was worth.

When he left the valley, a zephyr whipped down from the trees on the surrounding hills, gusting toward the open tunnel. The door shimmered in the sunlight and slowly vanished. When the door was gone, the tunnel covered over and grass quickly grew where the opening had been. A dry, hoarse laugh rode on the wind and slowly died out.

CHAPTER TWO

September, 1989

Rob LaMotte opened his eyes. They burned. They usually did if he didn't get enough sleep. His eyelids felt sandy and rough whenever he blinked, and he tried opening them again. This time he rubbed them, and the pain lessened. He could see sunlight squeezing in around the edge of the drawn shade. He wished they had at least one more window in the bedroom, but that was just another drawback to their one bedroom, cold-water, walk-up apartment.

He turned to look at his wife, Sherry. She lay on her back, mouth partially open as she quietly snored. Her large breasts and bloated belly rose and fell slowly. Her blond hair fell away in a tangled disarray, framing her face. She hadn't removed her makeup from the night before, and she looked like hell.

Rob ran his hand down his own body, feeling his nakedness. At least he'd remained somewhat slim despite not being in shape. His penis jerked when his hands brushed the top of his pubic hair. He smiled. Although he was 40 years old, his sex drive hadn't diminished one bit. He'd heard that once a guy passed 35, it was all downhill. Well, he hadn't found it to be that way. He could still get an erection almost by willing it. The slightest stimulation usually resulted in firm proof of his virility.

He rolled closer to Sherry and ran one finger along the edge of her nightgown. Slipping his hand inside, he moved slowly, toward her breasts. Just as he was about to close on one of the nipples, she moaned and turned away. He let his hand ride along with her heaving body and pulled himself up behind her, letting his erection press against her bare ass.

Just then, the alarm went off.

"Why do you get horny every morning? You know I've got to get to the restaurant by 7:30. We haven't got time," she said, stiffling a yawn and sitting up at the same time.

"You're never ready in the morning, and I'm too goddamned tired at night. Can't you be late just once?"

"No!" She threw her legs over the edge of the bed and stood. Lazily stretching, she pulled on her old kimono and shuffled toward the bathroom, which was next to their bedroom.

"Some marriage we got," Rob said, sitting up.

"What do you mean by that?" She turned, framed in the doorway, an ugly expression of distaste and anger on her face.

"Look at us. We're both forty, living in a cheap dump like this. Christ, it's got to be the last apartment on the goddamned face of the earth without hot water. Do you like living like this?" He got out of bed and stood, facing Sherry across the bed.

"Of course I don't. Why don't you do something about it? Why don't you get a job that pays something?"

"I make pretty good money selling hospitalization."

"When you work—and when you sell a policy. But I've noticed that's happening less frequently. What's wrong?"

He shrugged. "I don't know. It's tough out there. There's those that got it and those that don't. Maybe I don't anymore. I don't know."

"If you feel that way, why don't you quit and get a decent job?"

"Sure. Right away. Jobs are growing on the goddamned trees, waiting to be plucked. Besides, who'd hire a guy in his forties?"

"There's a lot of people in Davenport and the other cities around with good jobs. Why can't you get one? Christ, Rob, you could get a job sweeping up someplace. At least you'd bring home a regular paycheck. I do. Why can't you?"

"Shit! If your tips aren't good, you don't bring that much home. Look at you. You're getting fat. How can you expect people to tip a fat waitress?"

Sherry glowered. "Fat am I? You little piece of shit! I've got more gumption in my toenail clippings than you have in your whole body. When was the last time you sold a policy that was paid for?"

Rob looked away. Business had been awful the last three or four weeks. They had no money in the bank and had been living on Sherry's income during that time. He had to get something going or they'd be in real trouble once the first of the month rolled around. He frowned. When had he last sold a policy? He couldn't remember. He shrugged again. "I don't know."

"There you have it. A real winner, aren't you? Unless you get something going real soon, Buster, I'm taking a hike. And I'll take the kid with me. You'll never see us again."

Rob looked up. "You don't mean that, do you?"

"Try me. If you don't sell something today, you've had it. If your boss doesn't fire you, I will—as a husband. You're worthless."

"It isn't my fault. Ever since that jerk in the White House was elected everything's gone to hell. He's—"

"That's typical of you, Rob. Blame somebody who's a thousand miles away for your own shortcomings."

Rob looked up to find his wife gone and heard the bathroom door slam shut. She'd be in there for an hour, trying to make herself look young. She should give up on that as a losing battle. He pulled on his underwear.

"Daddy?"

Rob ran his hand through his brown, thinning hair. He didn't need a kid asking questions as to why they were fighting again, but he had to face up to some responsibility. "What do you want, Jeremy?"

Jeremy appeared in the doorway and yawned. "Why are you and Ma fighting again?"

"We just had a little disagreement. Get dressed for school. You'll be late."

"It's not even seven o'clock. I don't have to be there for another hour and a half. Why were you fighting?"

"None of your business, Jeremy. Get dressed."

Jeremy turned and trudged back to the living room where he slept on the couch. At 11, he was bright and sensitive. There were times when Rob questioned how he and Sherry could have produced a child like him. He was nothing like his parents. In a way, Rob felt they should be thankful for that. Maybe Jeremy would fare better in the world than his mother and father. At least Jeremy had a father. That was more than Rob could say. Oh sure, he'd been sired by somebody, but he'd never known his father. When Rob was only a year old, his father had taken off and deserted his mother and him.

When he'd been old enough to ask questions, he'd found out that his father was probably insane, a casualty of World War II, a shell-shocked veteran who'd married his mother. When the pressure became too much, he'd simply walked away and left the two of them without anything. How could anyone expect Rob LaMotte to amount to anything without some sort of father image to emulate? He'd drifted from job to job after dropping out of high school and flunked his physical for the service because of a combination of little things that kept him from going to Viet Nam. For the only time in his life, he was thankful for the couple of allergies and high blood pressure he had had most of his life. At least he wouldn't turn out to be a looney like his old man. But then, his old man had left his wife and baby son. If Rob did that, he wouldn't have to put up with Sherry's incessant complaining anymore. Maybe being a looney made sense.

Rob grinned crookedly at his illogical thinking. He put on his pants and went to the kitchen and made a pot of coffee. He lighted the burner on the stove with a wooden match. No hot water and a gas stove that needed priming. He shook his head. Maybe it was Sherry who had dragged him down to this level of not caring about success or anything else that mattered. He didn't know and frankly didn't care.

"Hurry up and get dressed, Jeremy. You'll be late for school," Rob said roughly.

"Ma's in the bathroom."

"Get dressed and eat your breakfast. By that time, she'll be out of there and you can use it."

Jeremy moaned and sat down on the lumpy couch. After dressing, he went to the kitchen and looked longingly at his father.

"What's the matter?" Rob asked.

"Where's my breakfast food?"

"Je-e-e-sus Kay-ryst! Do you need somebody to wait on you hand and foot? You're eleven. Get your own goddamned cereal." Rob left the kitchen and went back to the bedroom.

Jeremy pulled down a box of corn flakes and dumped some in a bowl. After sprinkling sugar on it, he emptied the milk carton into the bowl and sat down. He spooned in every last flake as if he were starving. He looked up to find his father tucking his shirt into his pants.

"If you're finished, you can leave for school after you use the bathroom. Understand?"

Jeremy nodded but said nothing.

Just then, the bathroom door opened and Sherry came out, her makeup on, her hair brushed and combed. She stepped into the bedroom and shut the door.

Rob nodded to his son, and Jeremy hurried to the bathroom. After a few minutes, he came out and headed for the door.

" 'Bye, Dad."

"So long, Jeremy," Rob said quietly without looking up. He poured a cup of coffee and went to the refrigerator just as the front door closed. Bending down, he looked about for the milk carton.

"Sherry, where the fuck is the milk?"

No answer.

He slammed shut the door and picked up the cup. He'd made it strong and found it almost too bitter to drink. When he lowered the cup, he found Sherry standing in the doorway, dressed in her waitress uniform.

"What did you say?"

"I asked where the milk was."

"Probably gone. Christ, I can't afford a half gallon of milk every day or so, you know."

Rob cringed at the reference to her paying for the milk. The bitch! She took every opportunity to complain about his sales slump. He'd show her. He'd go out and sell as many policies as he could. Then he'd decide what he'd do. He'd either share with her the up-front money he got for commission, or he'd stash it and put together a nest egg to get the hell away from her. He couldn't stand much more of her nagging. Ever since he went into a slump, she'd been riding him, trying to egg him on to do better. The last couple of days she'd gotten downright nasty about it. He'd carried the memory of her cutting remarks with him to the office and out into the field where he couldn't concentrate on closing a single case. It was all her fault. He knew it. He was susceptible to such criticism and reacted accordingly.

He looked up and away from his wife. Maybe Jeremy got his sensitivity from him. Certainly Sherry was anything but sensitive when it came to making the man in her life feel needed and appreciated. When he turned around, he found her lifting a cup of coffee to her lips.

After sipping it, she set it down and stared at him. "That's about the worst coffee I've ever tasted. If you decide to get out of the insurance business, don't ever consider going into the restaurant racket. You'd be arrested for poisoning people."

She stormed from the kitchen and went to the front door. Whirling around, she faced him once more. "Sell a policy today and bring some money home, or don't bother coming home. Understand?"

Before Rob could respond, she'd opened the door and left, slamming it after her.

Rob sat down at the kitchen table. Picking up the cup of coffee he'd poured for himself, he sipped it. It wasn't that bad. Sherry would have griped about anything and everything, no matter what he'd done. He was glad she was gone. At least he'd get a little peace and quiet before he had to leave for the office.

After he finished his coffee, he went to the bathroom and shaved with cold water, just to remind himself of the predicament in which he found himself. When he came out, he put on a tie and spun about to face the door when he heard a key being inserted. The door opened slowly and Jeremy walked in.

"What are you doing home?"

"I've got time. I waited until Ma left. I wanted to talk with you."

"Talk to me? What about?"

Jeremy closed the door behind him and walked over to the couch. He sat down and looked up at his father. "Are you and Ma going to get divorced?"

"What?" Rob stared at his son.

"Divorced? You know, break up?"

"Why do you ask?"

Jeremy looked away, his light brown hair flopping over his forehead as he turned. Then he said, "You and Ma yell at each other an awful lot."

Rob walked over and sat down next to his son. "I know. I'm sorry for that. I really am. Things haven't been going well for me lately and your mother is upset and sort of . . . well, trying to prod me to do better. Do you know what I mean?" He hated making excuses for his wife, but he had to tell his son something.

Jeremy slowly nodded. "But you say some pretty terrible things to each other. Do you know that?"

Rob nodded, and he felt a rush of warmth. Here was an 11-year-old kid, trying to act as marriage counselor. Unbelievable! "You can believe this or not, Jeremy, but your mother and I love each other. At least, I love her. And I sure do love you. You aren't afraid of us not loving you, are you?"

Jeremy shook his head. "I don't know. I guess I might have thought of it a couple of times."

Rob took Jeremy by the hand and helped him stand up. When he faced him, Rob took him by the shoulders and peered intently into his son's eyes. "I love you. I guess your mother loves you, too. We're having some pretty rough times right now, and we yell at each other and say things we probably don't mean. That doesn't mean we don't love you or want you around. I never knew my father. I guess I remember that whenever I get angry with you and try to hold up on any punishment. Do you understand that?"

Jeremy nodded. "Who would I live with if you and Ma did get divorced?"

Rob felt shaky inside. His life wasn't much to brag about, but unsavory as it might be at the present time, he felt comfortable knowing what to expect when he came home. He didn't think they could afford a divorce lawyer at the present time. He felt certain that an attorney would want his money up front, just like he did when he sold a policy.

"I . . . I don't know, Jeremy. I can't answer that question, but I don't think you have anything to worry about. Okay?" He lifted his son's downcast face and forced himself to smile.

A tear fell from Jeremy's blue-green eyes, and he managed a weak grin of sorts and reached out to hug his father. Rob folded him into a tight embrace, and for a long minute the father and son communicated silently on the same plane.

"Want me to walk to school with you?" Rob asked when they parted.

Jeremy shrugged. "I don't know. The other

kids might laugh."

"Laugh? Laugh at a couple of pals walking down the street?"

"Okay. Can I wash my face first?"

"Sure."

When Jeremy came back to the living room, he looked up at Rob who had slipped on his suit jacket. "How come you can't drive me to school?"

"Normally I would, son, but my gas tank is pretty low and I've got to be sure I can get to the office for our meeting this morning."

"Oh," Jeremy said quietly. "Things really are rough, huh?"

"That they are, my boy." Rob opened the door and closed it after his son passed under his arm. "I guess I can afford the time to walk with you to school and then come back for my car. Besides, the exercise will do me good."

They hurried down the steps to the ground floor and exited onto the street. In seconds they were at the corner, heading for the pubic school five blocks away.

Two men stepped back into the doorway when the man and boy came out of the building across the street.

"How long you been watching them?" the shorter man asked.

"Just a couple of days now."

"You think it's him?"

"It must be. The name is the same, but I haven't contacted him yet to ask him questions."

"I don't think you should. I'd let Mr. Zwotney talk to him. I think the fact that he has the same name is good enough to contact the boss and let him decide. You might blow whatever the boss' deal is with this guy."

The taller man tugged at the seat of his pants and nodded. "I guess. You got a cigarette?"

"Hell no. You know I quit. You should, too."

"I know."

"Let's follow him and see where he goes."

The two men stepped from the shadows of the doorway in which they had concealed themselves and started after the man and boy.

CHAPTER THREE

April, 1951

The main street, which never had been named, roamed along the base of the hill that lorded over Nowaupeton, Iowa, population 276. The decision to incorporate the small village had been made when fishermen, tourists and campers began flocking to the Mississippi River. The reason was to guard the towns-people against the outsiders with police protection and maintain a semblance of law and order. Also, if the town was incorporated, the town council could seek state and federal funds for improving their lot in life and make Nowaupeton that much more appealing to the tourist.

Emil LaMotte walked slowly, doing his best to look normal and natural despite the leather-bound stack of plates he carried. No one seemed to pay him the slightest bit of attention, and for that he was most thankful. He felt like screaming out, telling the whole town that he had found something of great value and that he'd soon be looked up to and admired by the very people who had treated him like so much dirt under their feet.

He followed the contour of the hill and the road, first walking up a slight incline, then down a steeper one, only to struggle against the next grade which was even more sharp. A car drove past him, sliding over the top of the hill, and Emil muttered under his breath, "Outsiders. Goddamned outsiders and their money." Well, he'd soon have money, too. Then he could buy what he wanted and do what he wanted, and no one would ever question him again. Not that they had ever done so in the past, but Emil felt that each time he went into the grocery store and bought a few food staples, everyone knew about it before he got home.

After reaching the peak of the hill, he passed Ferguson's Grocery Store and kept his attention fixed straight ahead. Since he'd left earlier to go fishing, he didn't want Dot Ferguson to notice he wasn't carrying fish and wonder why he didn't stop in to buy something. Instead, he clutched his prize tighter and hurried along. After passing the gas station, he turned his head away from the Catholic Church that clung to the side of the hill. He didn't go to church and didn't care much for the hypocrites who did. They'd go there every Sunday and pray their fool heads off, making amends for all their transgressions against God and man and then go out on Monday and repeat their same deeds. Emil spat on the road and shook his head. He hated people, but he hated those who were hypocrites the most.

He passed several homes that had been built around the turn of the century and continued toward the river where his own house stood, close to the Milwaukee Railroad tracks that separated the town from the river's bank. The small three-room house was the only thing Emil LaMotte owned, and when he approached it, he didn't see the squalor or the decrepit state of disrepair. The last of the paint had peeled off long before he bought it, and he'd never taken the time to do anything about brightening up the exterior. The roof of a one car garage rested on the ground next to the house, covering the shattered walls that once had supported it.

Emil opened the front door and closed it behind him in one motion. He pulled the window shade and a gloom filled the room that befitted the spartan furnishings of table, three chairs and sofa. Clouds of cotton stuffing puffed out here and there on the couch, accentuating the lumpy pillows.

After leaning the crowbar against the wall

next to the fishing rod and putting his tool box on the floor, he sat down at the table.

"Now," he said quietly, "let's see what we have here." He pulled back the leather coverings and felt his mouth fill with saliva when he saw the dull glint of the plate on top. Digging in his pants' pocket he brought out a jackknife and opened it. Scratching the surface in one corner, he stifled the whoop of joy he felt rushing to the surface. The bright golden color contrasted sharply with the surface. It *was* gold! All the way through. He hefted the stack of plates again and estimated the weight to be probably 12 pounds.

What if it wasn't gold? What if it were brass? Or copper? He shook his head. It couldn't be brass. Didn't brass tarnish? Of course it did, and this wasn't tarnished, just dull. A good cleaning would bring out the golden luster just like the scratch he had made on the surface of the first plate.

But what about copper? Wasn't copper sort of a golden color? A little more red but sort of gold nonetheless. But copper turned a greenish color if it wasn't cared for properly, and this wasn't green. Far from it. Was there anything else that could look like gold and not be gold? He pinched up his whiskered face in thought for a long moment. There was nothing. There was something called "fool's gold," but he didn't think anyone ever made anything out of it. And if the leaves were gold-plated, the gold-plating was thick since he'd scratched into the soft surface at least a 64th of an inch.

It had to be gold.

Picking up the book, he examined it closely. Each page was made of the same material— gold. Then he noticed the writing. Had that been there when he looked at it closely after he'd brought it out of the tunnel? He didn't know. Perhaps the bright sunlight had obliterated the scratchings. Now, in the half light, he could definitely see something that resembled writing, but it didn't look like any writing he'd ever seen.

He stood and crossed the room to the window, lifting the shade a few inches and brightening the room considerably. That might help. Resuming his seat at the table, he picked up the book again and held it at an angle to the window, letting the light shine on it obliquely. The writing stood out clearly. Emil found it strange that the writing wasn't embossed but stood up in relief to the page itself. That meant that someone actually wrote with gold on gold pages to leave a record of some sort.

But why? For what reason? Where had it come from? Who had left it there in the first place, and why had they used gold? Emil shook his head and studied the writing more closely. The peculiar characters fascinated him. What did they mean? Was there some message contained that would make him wealthy? Or powerful? He'd be satisfied with either one. But what good would it do him if he couldn't determine what the message was? To whom could he take it? Was there anyone around who was smart enough to decipher something like this?

Maybe the priest would look at them. Sure, he'd look at them and then try to figure out how to get them away from Emil. Emil shook his head. That would never do. He had to keep his discovery a secret from everyone. But then how could he make use of the knowledge or information contained within? Dare he risk going to Dubuque or Cedar Rapids and consult a stranger? He didn't think that would be any more wise.

What should he do? He looked across the room. The semicircular wall table caught his attention, and he studied the two pictures standing on it.

"What should I do, Mag?" he asked, standing. He crossed the room and picked up the picture of his dead wife. The oval face stared at him in a firm yet gentle way. Her hair clung tightly to her head, making the curls and ringlets seem like a cap. "What should I do with this stuff, Mag?"

He set the picture down and looked at the other without picking it up. Edgar, looking solemn in his army uniform, stared obediently forward for the photographer. None of the passion he'd displayed after his discharge could be seen. When he'd come home from the service, he had fallen into a routine of eating and sleeping and dreaming of the nightmare he'd been put through as a Nazi prisoner-of-war.

"You wouldn't know what to do with a million bucks if somebody had handed it to you, would you, dummy?" Emil asked bitterly. He turned his back on the pictures and went to his chair.

He had to get a grip on himself. First, he had to see what the book would be worth just for the gold content. Since he didn't have a scale, how could he weigh it? Maybe he had something in the kitchen that could be used to compare the weight of the plates.

Once in the small kitchen, he opened the only cupboard and peered inside. There were three cans of condensed soup and two cans of peeled tomatoes and a can of corn. Why didn't he own a scale of some sort? If he went to the grocery store and asked Dot Ferguson to weigh his find, she might cheat him. The weight on the can of corn caught his attention, and he pulled the tin down. 16 ounces. One pound. He pulled down the cans of tomatoes. Each weighed one pound. The soup cans each weighed 10 3/4 ounces. Scooping the cans up, he went to the table in the other room and searched for a pencil and paper once he'd deposited them next to the plates.

An idea was forming, but he had to do some figuring first. When he found paper and a pencil, he sat down and added the weights of the cans in ounces. He quickly totaled 80.25 ounces. Scratching out the quarter ounce, he jotted down 80 and divided it by 16 ounces to the pound. The cans weighed five pounds, forgetting the quarter ounce. Now he had a five pound weight that he could balance against the plates, which he estimated to weigh between ten and twelve pounds.

Rigging up a seesaw balance arrangement with several boards he found outside the back door, he put the cans on one side and the plates on the other. The cans immediately lifted up, showing the plates weighed considerably more. He had to take the book apart. Turning it over, he winced. The thongs on the back were undone. Had he untied them? Had they been untied the whole time? He couldn't remember. Maybe they had been. What difference did it make? There were ten pages or plates. He'd try half of them first.

After putting the cans on the left, he placed five of the gold plates on the opposite side. The cans slowly raised the board on which they and the pages rested, teetering on the fulcrum Emil had set up. When he repeated the action with the other plates, the same thing happened. He had ten pounds of gold. Narrowing his greenish eyes, Emil worked feverishly on the multiplication, sat back and realized he had over $5,000 in gold. He was rich. There was a lot he could do with that much money. He'd maybe get a new house—or a new car. He could buy a new car and pay cash and have a lot of money left over. Maybe he'd even try to buy back the small acreage he and Magdalene had bought when they first came to Nowaupeton and eventually sold. When the defense plant in Dubuque didn't pan out and he had decided against going all the way to Savanna to work, they'd sold it for next to nothing after their house had burned down.

He didn't like to think about the fire. He and Magdalene had liked their home and land, a small house on five acres. The land lay across the bottom of the hill that was to the west of Nowaupeton and right below the Newton mansion. The Newton mansion had been Magdalene's idea of luxury, and she had often wished the two of them could have been lucky enough to live there or someplace like it. But the Newton widow still had been living then, and now the place was deserted.

Emil smiled, licking his lips. What if he could buy the Newton place for the money he'd get from selling the book? He laughed. Wouldn't that be great? He wished Magdalene was still alive to share in his good fortune, but she had died shortly after moving to the house by the tracks in which Emil now lived. That goddamned fire! That's what had taken such a heavy toll on his wife.

He remembered the night too well. He wished he could forget it and how they'd gone to bed, after deciding to look for work around Nowaupeton as opposed to moving away. With Edgar in the service, they had just each other, and they were still in love after over 25 years of marriage. He didn't have to worry about being drafted since he was over 50 when the war began.

JOHN TIGGES

They had gone to bed and were in their first, sound sleep when Magdalene awoke, coughing. She had screamed that the house was burning. Once Emil had awakened and smelled the fire himself, he had grabbed her by the hand and pulled her through the house to the front door and the safety of outside. They had barely escaped with their lives.

There was no nearby fire department that could have helped, and along with the curiosity seekers, they watched their little home burn to a pile of charred ashes.

Within the next week, while still in a state of shock, they sold the five acres of land for a pittance to Mayor Dan O'Malley and moved into the house by the tracks. Though they bought it, neither wanted to expend much energy fixing it for fear their work once more would go up in smoke. Their spirits broken, Emil and Magdalene became reclusive, ignoring the other townspeople, wanting only to be left alone.

After Magdalene died and Edgar came home from the service, shellshocked and devastated, Emil withdrew even more. When Edgar left without a word, Emil felt relieved. He didn't want to be responsible to or for anyone.

For the longest time after his son left, Emil felt he wanted to die and get it over with. Life held nothing for him. His wife and son were gone, and he had felt his own mental capabilities slipping away from time to time. Now his attitude was bright, buoyed by the discovery of the plates in the tunnel.

He had to devise a plan. First, he had to get an accurate weight or somebody would cheat him. He knew that. Hadn't the mayor tried to cheat him a second time? The Mayor of Nowaupeton had tried to buy his house by the tracks with the idea of putting in a facility for storing gas once the war was over. That sonofabitch! Ever since he'd practically stolen those five acres, Emil had hated O'Malley. For all Emil cared, Dan O'Malley could drop dead and go straight to hell. Now things would change if Emil had money. He'd improve his own lot, and maybe people would show him some sort of respect. All he'd had his entire life were hard times and bad luck. The only decent thing had been Magdalene.

Emil picked up the plates once more. He wondered what was written on them. He wondered if anyone could tell him what the writing meant. Maybe the book itself was a means to unknown riches. Maybe it contained the secret to life or wealth or fame or anything else that ordinary people wished for but never attained. Where could he take the book? As far as he knew there were a couple of colleges in Dubuque and one up in Decorah. Neither place was that far that Emil couldn't put together the bus fare and just go. It might be better to put his mind at ease and know what it was he actually was selling. What if the person who wanted to buy the book knew what was written on the golden plates and cheated Emil out of another fortune by getting the pages away from him?

Emil rapped his fist on the table. First thing he'd do after accurately weighing the book was take it to one of the nearby colleges and have some professor tell him what it was. Then, based on what he learned there, Emil would either sell it for what he could get or use it, if it was meant to be used, to make a fortune for himself. No matter which way he turned, he was bound to profit by the book.

He grinned. Then maybe he'd try getting even with some of the people who'd wronged him over the last few years, and Dan O'Malley would head the list. Emil would figure out some intricate plan to settle his old score with the mayor. Emil picked up the book and gasped. Underneath, a small pool of blood had congealed. Where had it come from? He looked at his hands. They were uncut. Where had the blood come from? The book, which had been lying face down, was smeared with blood. At least, to Emil it looked like blood. He sniffed the cover of the book. It had the distinct coppery smell of blood to it.

His hands trembling, Emil stared at the book. The book couldn't be bleeding and he wasn't cut, so the blood had to have come from someplace else—but where?

Suddenly he heard an automobile stop outside. Probably some goddamned fisherman.

Emil went to the door and peered through the dirty glass in the window. The car, a new

Chevy, was black and shiny. No fisherman would take a new car fishing, not to Nowaupeton at least.

Squinting, Emil tried to see who was behind the wheel but couldn't make out the man's face. When the car door opened, Emil sucked in his breath. The man was dressed in a suit and tie and a new hat. Who the hell could that be?

When the man pulled out a briefcase and started toward Emil's front door, Emil panicked.

Somehow, somebody already knew about the book with the golden pages and was coming to take it away from him. Emil would never allow that. Before he gave up his treasure, he'd fight to the death for it.

He had to hide it, but where? Where could he hide it?

Emil looked around the small, squalid room. There wasn't any place he could put it to assure its safety. The bedroom? Under the mattress? He ran to the third room in the house and, after looking at the bed, decided that would be the first place anyone would look.

He ran back to the living room.

When the man knocked on the door, Emil jumped, squealing as he did.

He had to get rid of the book and do it now. The man must know he was inside the house.

Emil ran to the kitchen and saw the open cupboard. He threw the book onto the shelf where the cans had been and slammed the door shut. When he returned to the living room, he suddenly realized that if the man were looking in, he could have witnessed Emil hiding the book, but he didn't have time to run back and look for a better place. He stood transfixed. What should he do?

The knock came again, and Emil worked his way toward the door.

His hand shaking, Emil reached out for the knob and turned it. The sound of the latch opening seemed to explode in his ears. He inched the door open a mere slit.

"I'm looking for Emil LaMotte? Are you he?" the man asked.

Emil nodded, his throat parched, his tongue stuck to the roof of his mouth. Then he realized the man couldn't see him nodding and croaked, "Ye . . . yes."

"I've got to talk to you about a mix-up on some property and taxes that are due. May I come in?"

Emil stared at the man through the crack in the door. What should he do? Taxes? Property? What did he know about any mix-up? He'd paid his taxes every year. At least it didn't have to do with the book. If it did, the man was awfully clever in the way he didn't even mention anything about the book.

"Do . . . do I have a choice?" Emil managed to ask.

"Only if you want to lose your property."

Emil thought for a moment. Even if he did have the means to get some money now, he wasn't that rich that he could afford to lose his house and land—not again.

Emil opened the door. "Come in."

CHAPTER FOUR

September, 1989

A hush fell over the smoke-filled sales room of the Inter-American Health and Accident Insurance Company. Ben Arnette, the district manager, perused the men and women sitting in front of him before finishing his morning pep talk. When he felt he had milked the quiet moment for all it was worth, he said, "All right, then, let's get out there and hit 'em. Everyone meets his or her quota today. Right?"

A half-hearted chorus responded, "Right."

"I can't hear you," Ben said in his best drill instructor manner, even though he had never spent a moment in the service.

"Right." The single word was followed by

subdued mumblings from the older sales personnel who disliked Arnette's old-fashioned sales pitch.

This time the response seemed to satisfy him, and Ben grinned.

Rob stood and moved slowly toward the door. If today proved to be the same as yesterday and the day before and the week before, he might just as well turn in his brief-case and call it quits. He couldn't figure out what he was doing wrong. If he asked Ben for help, it would be a sign of incompetence considering Rob's length of time in the business.

"Hey, Rob, how's it going?" a voice called from behind him.

He turned and saw the heavily jowled face of Clarence Tearmuth split into his best "winning sales" smile. Clarence was a good enough person, but Rob felt he bordered on being totally phony. Perhaps the man believed everything he said when he was out pitching for business. If that were the case, then Clarence would soon be lying about everything everytime he opened his mouth.

"Hi, Clarence, how's it going?"

"Great, simply great. My ratio of closes per call is climbing every day. Currently I'm getting eight sales for every ten calls. Not bad, huh?"

Rob wanted to throw up. He hadn't had a sale in weeks, and Sherry was about to throw him out. And here was this phony bragging about selling to 80% of the people he saw. There just didn't seem to be any justice in the world for

Rob LaMotte. Maybe he should ask Clarence what he was doing to be so successful. "Got a minute, Clarence?" he asked suddenly.

"Sure, Robbie, what's up? Want to buy some insurance?" Clarence threw his head back and laughed in a nasal, braying way that reminded Rob of a jackass clearing his sinuses.

"You've been having a pretty good run lately, haven't you?" Rob asked.

"Sure," Clarence said, sobering when he realized that Rob was talking business. "Why?"

"You're not having any trouble at all, are you?"

"None. It's like shooting fish in a barrel."

"Maybe you can help me then."

"Why not ask old Ben? He's got all the answers if you need help."

"Ben is full of bullshit and pat answers. You're actually doing it."

"What's your problem?"

"I'm doing everything by the book and not missing a trick. Still I seem to be shooting blanks when it comes to getting any sales."

Clarence grinned broadly. "Come on, Robbie. You know the business is run by the law of averages. Things'll change."

Rob turned away. He might have known he couldn't count on a hotshot like Clarence to help him, and he was damned if he'd go to Ben Arnette for help. Arnette would interpret his asking for help as a sign of weakness and probably can him on the spot. Rob had experience and had been successful for years as a salesman. He'd always managed to weather the rough spots, and as Clarence said, the business was run by the law of averages. If Rob hung in there, in time the pendulum would swing back and he'd start selling a high percentage again. But would Sherry tolerate the present state of things for very long? He doubted it very much.

"Hey, Robbie, what's wrong? Come on, you can tell me."

Rob turned back. For a change, Clarence wasn't wearing his shit-eating grin and seemed genuinely concerned. "You got time for a cup of coffee, Clarence?"

"Sure have. In fact, I'll buy."

Rob wondered if it was charity. Clarence probably thought that he should buy since it must be apparent that Rob was down on his luck. "Where do you want to go?"

"Well, since I'm buying, let's make it the Busy Bee around the corner. It won't take either one of us out of our way."

The two men walked down the flight of steps from the second floor of the Cushing Building and out into the cool September air. A minute later they entered the yellow-fronted Busy Bee Cafe and headed for a booth.

A flat-chested, pimply-faced girl about 20 years old walked up to them and placed menus in front of each one. "Coffee?" She looked out the dirty window of the restaurant without paying the slightest bit of attention to her customers.

"Yeah," Clarence said. Turning to Rob, he asked, "You want anything to eat?"

Rob shook his head. He felt like a bum taking a handout from some generous soul who felt sorry for him. Even if he were hungry, Rob wouldn't take a bite of food from Clarence. A cup of coffee was somehow different. It didn't seem like charity.

When the girl walked away to get the coffee, Clarence said, "All right, what's up?"

Rob gazed around the small room, taking in the two men who sat hunched over coffee at the counter. The thin, emaciated man who owned and managed the Busy Bee was framed in the window that opened between the kitchen and the counter, looking as if he should try eating some of his own food. Maybe it was because he knew how it was prepared that prevented him from eating enough to look healthy. The smell of grease hung in the air, ladened with the stench of cigarette smoke and the aroma of strong coffee.

"I . . . Well," Rob began, "I haven't been hitting lately."

"I noticed there was nothing beside your name on the sales sheet at the office. What's the trouble?"

"If I knew, I'd fix it. That's why I wanted to talk to you. Is it me? The people I'm calling on? The product? What? What the fuck is wrong with me?"

The girl returned and placed a steaming mug of coffee in front of each man.

"Hey, come on," Clarence said, ignoring the

waitress, "you're a good salesman. I've seen what you've done in the past. Besides, we all hit dry spells every once in a while. Is something bothering you other than work?"

Rob shrugged. "My wife has been pretty bitchy lately. She's complaining because I'm not bringing home the bacon."

"They can be tough but it's not unusual. Broads have a knack for cutting a guy's balls off with a word or two, don't they?"

Rod nodded. "The thing is, I'm afraid she'll leave me."

"Shit, you might be better off without her."

"That's not fair, Clarence. We've got a kid."

"I forgot. It's a boy, isn't it? How old is he?"

"Eleven."

"That could be tough, all right. Courts can be pretty rough on child support and late payments and what have you."

"If I could only sell a few cases this week, she'd back off. I know she would. I just wish to hell I could be successful and she wouldn't have to work at that goddamned Greek's place."

"Where's that?"

"Frank's Place. Frank Yearnall."

"He's Greek?"

"Naw, but the sonofabitch looks like one. He's got bushy eyebrows like Dukakis."

"I suppose if you got her to stop working, she might change her mind all right. But hell, she hasn't got reason enough to file for divorce or leave you, has she?"

"I dunno. Between her riding me and business being lousy, I feel like shit. Real nervous."

"Nervous? You? Christ, Robbie, you're a dyed-in-the-wool salesman and that type doesn't get nervous. You know what I mean?"

Rob managed a half-smile. "I feel really nervous today."

"You do, huh? About what?"

"I don't know. It's just—well, an uneasy feeling. Like I'm paranoid or something."

Clarence laughed. "Paranoid?"

"Yeah. Like everybody's watching me."

"Why would everybody want to watch you?"

"That's just it. I don't know. It's a creepy feeling."

"It's crazy."

Rob looked up abruptly only to find Clarence lifting his cup to his mouth. Had he meant that Rob was actually crazy, or did he mean that the situation was crazy, wild, unreal?

"You know, Clarence," Rob said quietly, "you might have a point there. Maybe I am going nuts."

"Bullshit! No way. Get out there and sell. That'll take your mind off of things. The more you call on people, the closer you'll get to a sale. Believe me. I know."

"I know you know. I know it, too, but the well's gone dry, Clarence. I've had it. I think I'll call on these today and call it quits." He threw his lead cards, which had been handed out at the sales meeting, onto the table.

"Let's see what kind of people you're calling on today." Clarence picked up the yellow cards and thumbed through them. "Jesus Christ, are these the kind you've been getting lately?"

Rob shrugged again. "I guess so. I didn't look at them very closely yet. Why?"

"Well, shit, you got rotten addresses. I know this town like the back of my hand, and I'll guarantee you one thing. Christ Almighty himself couldn't sell salvation at these places. The people are too old to buy and poor— fucking dirt poor! If this is the type of people you've been calling on, I can understand why the well's run dry. There's never been any water in it in the first place."

Rob pulled the cards away from Clarence and studied them for a minute. "I wonder if Arnette's been giving me these on purpose?"

"I doubt that. He should be spreading the shit around just like he does the sugar. It's probably just a goddamned goof-up. Tell you what, we'll bring it up at the meeting tomorrow morning and nail the sonofabitch. Okay?"

Rob smiled bitterly. "Sure. And in the meantime, I go out, have another rotten day, and my wife gives me the heave-ho when I get home tonight. Right?"

"Wrong! Tell you what. I'll give you a couple of my goodies here and take a couple of your baddies. Okay? That way, you should score and tell your old lady that you clicked today. Make sense?"

Rob brightened. "I appreciate that, Clarence.

I really do. I'll owe you."

"Hey, I'd expect the same thing from you if I were in your shoes. Just remember it and help the next guy you run into who's in the same situation."

When Clarence stood, Rob did the same and followed him to the counter where he paid for their coffee. The girl took the dollar bill from Clarence and rang it up on the register. She dropped two dimes onto the counter.

"Keep the change, honey," Clarence said magnanimously.

Rob followed him out the door, ready to hit the sidewalks and make a sale.

Sherry leaned on the counter of Frank's Place, staring into space. The owner, Frank Yearnall, walked up behind her and patted her rear end.

"Stop that," she snapped.

"What's the matter? Grumpy this morning?"

She turned to face him. Frank stood five feet ten inches tall and weighed well over 200 pounds. His face, although full, appeared youthful in spite of his 45 years, and his handsome features still showed through the corpulence he had allowed to accumulate over the years.

"I'm just not in the mood."

"That time of the month?" He grinned wickedly.

"No, it's not that time of the month. I'm just in a pissed-off mood this morning."

"Your old man bugging you again?"

Sherry looked away. She wished she had never confided in Frank. He stored away every detail in his mind and seemed capable of dredging up conversations, word for word, from weeks ago. Still, she had no one else in whom she could confide—certainly not Rob. That weakling seemed to care for nothing the last few weeks. Maybe she should leave him. She could take Jeremy and move away from Davenport. Who the hell needed a river town that rolled up the sidewalks at ten o'clock every night? Life was quickly slipping away from her, and she felt she was being cheated out of so many things, like a house—a real house that could be their home. There was no way they'd ever be able to afford one now with interest rates up and property values sky high. They had no money to waste on an evening of fun, just for her and Rob. What the hell was a girl to do? Hang around and grow old with a goddamned failure?

"What makes you think Rob's at fault?" She narrowed her eyes, refocusing her attention on her employer.

"Well, you haven't got your period, and you don't want me smacking your butt. So it must be your old man. Is it?"

"Yeah," she said grimly. "The bastard's a loser. He hasn't brought home a dime in the last two or three weeks."

"I thought insurance men made a lot of money."

"Some do, I guess. But Rob's with this fly-by-night operation and he's . . . well, he's just not cutting it anymore as a salesman."

Frank shook his head and reached down, patting Sherry on the arm. When she didn't withdraw, he let his hand rest on her shoulder.

"See, all we've got coming in is what I'm making. I appreciate the fact that you pay me the minimum. I know normally you wouldn't have to do that, and since the trade is mostly college students, the tips aren't that great either."

"What can I say?" Frank said, feigning modesty. "An old friend needs money, I'm willing to pay. After all, we've been through a lot together, you 'n' me, haven't we?"

Sherry bit her lip. Frank had raised her salary to the minimum wage from the $2.10 he'd been paying her and the other waitresses after she had weakened and accepted his proposition of a night at a motel. It hadn't been for the whole night, and Frank had closed up the restaurant an hour early just to allow them enough time to get to the Shady Inn and get a room. She'd been curious. She'd had a few men in her life but never one like Frank. She'd been real curious as to how he would perform. He'd done well, and later when he asked, she had to admit that it had been the best sex she'd had in a long time.

The peculiar thing was that it hadn't bothered her when she went home. She'd been certain she'd feel guilty when she saw Rob but she hadn't, and the meetings with Frank became more frequent. When he told her he loved his wife and would never leave her for anyone, Sherry accepted it. Now, she felt she should leave her own husband for reasons that she knew were sound. They were wilting and dying on the vine as a couple. They didn't love each other any more. She knew that. Jeremy was the only reason they were staying together, and at best that was a poor reason.

"Yeah, Frank, we've been through a lot, you 'n' me. What should I do? Leave Rob?"

"If he isn't producing income and isn't producing in the bedroom, you should leave him."

"What about my kid?"

"What about him?"

"A boy needs a father, don't he?"

"Sure. But you can get anybody to be a father if you work it right."

"You want to be his father, Frank?" She narrowed her eyes in a mischievous way.

"Hell no," Frank said without hesitating. "You know how I stand where my marriage is concerned. I wouldn't leave Rita for nothing."

"I know that but that's not what I meant. Would you be a big brother to him? You know, take him places and be a sort of father figure to him?"

"I doubt it. I got my own kids to worry about, you know."

"Then it wouldn't be quite as easy as you said, would it?"

"Well, what I meant was, you're a good-looking woman. You shouldn't have any problem finding a guy to, well, you know, do what you want him to."

"You mean whore my way through life?"

"I didn't say that." He wiped a hand across his face, rumpling his dark bushy eyebrows.

"What did you say then?" Sherry glared at him. He had no right to suggest anything like that. She never should have allowed him to become intimate with her.

"Let's forget it. Tell you what. I know how you can make fifty bucks real easy, if you want."

Sherry knew what he meant. "Yeah? When?"

"How about when you're finished with your shift. You don't have to go straight home, do you?"

"You know I do pretty much what I want."

"That's what I thought. Could you use fifty?"

"Goddamnit, Frank, you know I can always use money. Especially now."

"Okay, okay, don't get feisty on me. We'll go someplace, and afterward I can drop you off close to your home. All right?"

"Yeah, sure. That's great." She looked up when the door opened and several college students walked in. Taking enough menus to go around, she made her way through the tables toward the booth the new customers had chosen.

Frank grinned slyly and walked over to the cash register. He opened the cash drawer and lifted the tray. Removing a 50 dollar bill he found there, he folded it and put it in his pocket and closed the drawer.

Sherry walked back to the counter after giving the students the menus. Fifty bucks would come in handy. It wasn't always that Frank offered her money for the time spent with him in a motel, but at best she felt it would be only a stopgap measure. It wouldn't change the way she felt about Rob, but she couldn't afford an attorney. She wondered if Frank would consider lending her the money for a lawyer. It wouldn't hurt to ask.

Suddenly a frown crossed her face. She was doing the very thing she had just told Frank she'd never do—whore her way through life. Well, once or twice could hardly be construed as a way of life. Besides, she desperately needed the money. Rob sure as hell wouldn't bring any money home today and probably not even in the near future.

She filled three glases with water and carried them to the booth.

Rob swallowed. He'd purposely made a few of the bad calls just to kill time and give himself something to look forward to by keeping the cards Clarence had given him in reserve. Clarence had been right. The people he'd been calling on didn't have the ability to pay even the first premium on a policy. Why hadn't he seen it himself? Maybe he'd been trying so hard, he felt anybody would be a good prospect. The product itself wasn't that good, but as he usually said in his sales presentation, "Bad breath was usually a whole lot better than no breath at all." But the people he'd been calling on couldn't and didn't buy.

He looked up at the house before him. It was an ordinary two story, tract house that was probably 70 or 80 years old, but it was well kept, the lawn and yard neatly trimmed. That showed him that the people inside took care of their property and probably themselves as well. People like that could be sold.

When he walked up to the front porch and rang the bell, an older woman answered. After he told her who he was and why he was there, she opened the door. She called her husband into the living room, and in minutes Rob was giving his sales presentation.

"I know," he said as a way of concluding the talk, "that hospitals are very expensive and anyone can find himself there for any reason at any time. Isn't that true?"

The couple nodded.

Rob picked up their existing policy they had shown him and opened it. He pretended to be studying it and shook his head every so often. After a few minutes had passed during which he hadn't spoken, he looked up and smiled apologetically. "I have to say, Mr. and Mrs. Wilson, that this policy isn't worth very much. Have you had occasion to use it?"

Mr. Wilson shook his head. "No, thank God, we've been in good health."

"Then," Rob said, closing in for the sale,

"let's be practical and do something about your coverage before either one of you has to go to the hospital. The coverage you have now isn't worth the paper it's written on. If you went into the hospital today for, let's say, ten days, your bill could be well in excess of three to five thousand dollars. Of course, that's just the hopsital and not the doctor's bill. If you have to have surgery, the costs will be that much higher. Your present policy would pay about fifteen dollars a day. I assume you have Medicare and maybe Medicaid. The policy you're going to buy today would pay everything that the coverage you get from the government wouldn't. Surely you wouldn't like to owe the hospital and doctor a whole lot of money, would you?"

The Wilsons slowly shook their heads.

Rob walked back to his car. He felt good. He felt vindicated. He'd done a good job of selling, and he had the application and the money for an annual premium in his pocket. Now, he could hold his head up and face Sherry when he got home that night.

After he started the car, he felt the hackles on his neck move. There was that feeling of being watched again. He reached up and adjusted the rearview mirror but could see nothing behind him. Glancing to the left, he could see nothing suspicious there either. Well, whatever had made him react like that could go to hell. Rob LaMotte's dry spell was over.

He pulled away from the curb and checked his next appointment. It was only a few blocks away. He felt hot. He felt good. He felt like a salesman again.

He didn't notice the car turn the corner behind him and follow from half a block away.

Sherry adjusted her bra and slipped into her waitress uniform. Frank had finished quickly, and she felt relieved that she wouldn't be that late in getting home.

"Where you going?" Frank asked from the doorway of the bathroom.

"Home. Where else?"

"Just once? Is that all I get for fifty? Just once? That's pretty expensive nooky, isn't it?"

"You can be glad you got that. I'm not in the mood for a lot of sex right now."

"Shit. You're no fun when you're got problems. You open to a deal?"

"A deal? Like what?"

"I've got this little apartment over a garage downtown. It's got a nice private entrance, and I . . . well, I use it from time to time, let's say, to entertain people."

"How come you've never taken me there?" Sherry asked, knowing full well the implication of Frank's entertainment.

"I've had my reasons. You know me too well for one. At any rate, what I'm saying is this. Suppose you leave your old man and use my apartment for a while. You know, until you can get on your feet, financially that is. I wouldn't want you to think I didn't want you up and around on your feet." Frank laughed, a sort of hissing chuckle.

"Then what? Is there room for my kid?"

"Sure. There's two bedrooms and—well, I'll show it to you if you're interested. What do you say?"

"And what's this going to cost me?"

"Didn't I tell you? That's the best part. Nothing, absolutely nothing. Besides, you continue working."

Sherry shook her head. "I don't know, Frank. There's gotta be a catch there someplace. You're just going to let me use it and that's it?"

"I didn't say that. Every once in a while, when you're lonely for the touch of a man or the feel of a cock inside you, I'll come around. You know what I mean?" He tipped his head to one side and waited for her answer.

Sherry slowly nodded. "Let me think on it. Leaving Rob after thirteen years is a big decision. Let me think on it. All right?"

"Sure, Sherry. You think on it." He pulled out the 50 from his pants pocket and handed it to her. "Here. For services rendered."

She put the money in her purse and sat down, while Frank put on his shoes. When he was dressed they left the motel unit and headed for his Lincoln.

CHAPTER FIVE

April, 1951

Emil stared at the man sitting on his couch. He claimed to be John Remard of the county tax assessor's office, but Emil had not understood anything Remard was trying to explain to him. Emil had asked for identification when he encountered the well-dressed stranger confronting him. The card he presented with the state seal on it seemed to be genuine, and Emil had reluctantly allowed him to enter.

Just as he had closed the door, Emil caught sight of the bloodlike splotch on the table and stepped around his guest to quickly cover the spot with an old newspaper. When Remard showed no interest, Emil breathed easier. Why did he feel guilty and uneasy? Because of the blood? Because of the book? Because he had just discovered he owned a book worth at least $5,000?

Emil squirmed on his straight-backed chair and leaned forward. "I don't know what you're talking about, Mr. Remard. Could you maybe tell me again?"

John Remard smiled, but his eyes reflected none of his humor. "Very well, Mr. LaMotte, for the fourth time. When you seemed to purchase the five acres west of Nowaupeton, from Mrs. Henrietta Newton, the agreement she and you drew up was quite garbled. Our attorneys have looked at the copy in the assessor's office and have determined that, from the way it is worded, Mrs. Newton actually sold you the bulk of her property and house, leaving her only the five acres and cottage the two of you thought you had purchased."

Emil squinted and tried to swallow. Slowly, the information was sinking in, taking root in his brain. "Does that mean what I think it means?"

"Yes. In essence, you own the house and all of the property, including the five acres and cottage."

"The house burned down."

"The Newton house?"

"No. The little one. The cottage as you called it."

"I see."

"I don't see how any of this can be, though."
Emil shook his head.

"I know it's unusual, but I'm certain it would
stand up in a court of law."

"But don't she have any family? People who
could claim her property?"

Remard shook his head. "No, she had no one.
The property has been without tenancy for the
last few years since her death, and the taxes
haven't been paid. When we investigated, the
bill of sale was found, and since you are the
owner, you owe the taxes."

Emil slaped his thigh and whooped. "I knew
there was a catch. There had to be."

Remard looked at him aghast. "You mean
you think there's something wrong or illegal
with the situation?"

Emil nodded. "You want tax money, don't
you? Well, I ain't got no money for taxes. You
come in here waltzing around, getting my
hopes up, and then tell me I gotta pay a bunch
of money if I want to really own that big house.
Ain't that right?"

"The truth of the matter is, Mr. LaMotte, you
do own the property but you won't in another
month."

"Why's that?"

"Mrs. Newton paid the taxes while she was
living, believing, right along with the assessor's
office, that she owned the land and house. Now
that she's dead, the taxes haven't been paid for
four years. They're due and must be paid and
paid soon if you're to retain ownership."

Emil felt his head spinning. For once in his life he could have something he'd always wanted, something Magdalene and he once had coveted. Why wasn't she still living? She'd be so happy to suddenly realize a dream she'd had since she'd first seen the Newton mansion. But what had Emil provided for her? Nothing—just a little house where they'd been happy before it burned down. Their next home was a dump he'd lived in ever since her death.

He shook his head in an effort to clear his thinking. He had found the book and was, as far as he could determine, wealthy. The book! Of course. He *did* have money, but what if the value of it wasn't enough to pay the back taxes? Then what would he do?

"Ah, Mr. Remard?"

"Yes?"

"How much are these back taxes?" Emil held his breath, waiting for what he anticipated to be an exorbitant figure.

Remard fumbled through his briefcase for a moment and pulled out a folder. He seemed to move in slow motion, and when he pulled out the folded yellow sheet of paper, his efforts to open it appeared almost lethargic.

Emil waited while Remard scanned the form.

He cleared his throat and said, "The total back taxes, including interest, comes to $931.63." He looked up at Emil.

Emil said nothing. He could afford that if he sold the book for the value of the gold. But what if the book was worth much more than that? It might take a lot of time—months or maybe even years—to determine its value. In the meantime, he'd lose the chance to own the Newton mansion. He shook his head. The LaMotte mansion. That sounded better. What should he say to this man now? He didn't have the money? Could you wait a while? Might he be able to borrow the money? He doubted that since he had no credit rating at any bank and no form of steady employment.

"Well, sir," Emil said quietly, "that't not too high a sum of money. I'm not sure if I could raise that much. When do you need it?"

"As soon as possible. To close the books on it, you know."

"Say, now, you ain't kidding me about any of this stuff, are you?"

"No, sir. It's exactly as I've said it is."

Emil stood up. He felt tired. What could he tell this man? A thought suddenly struck at him. "You say, if I remember right, that when Mrs. Newton and I done business we messed it up. Am I right?"

Remard nodded, a look of exasperated resignation on his face.

"You said that she owned the five acres that I thought I bought. Is that right?"

Again, Remard nodded.

"Then what the Sam Hill happened when I sold it to Dan O'Malley, the Mayor of Nowaupeton?"

Remard sat up, a puzzled look on his face. Without speaking, he turned and opened his attaché case and fumbled through it. "Yes, here it is," he said more to himself than to Emil. He studied the papers for several long minutes, then looked up.

Emil waited and sat down again, facing Remard.

"According to this, since the first bill of sale made Mrs. Newton the owner of the five acres and you the owner of the bulk of the land, you couldn't very well have sold the five acres since you didn't own them. It would revert to the previous owner, Mrs. Newton."

Emil grinned crookedly. Of course. Now he had a chance to get even with O'Malley, the son-ofabitch, but he needed money to do that. He needed money to pay his own back taxes on property he didn't know that he owned until just a few minutes ago. Maybe O'Malley would drop dead of surprise or a heart attack or something. Emil would almost enjoy seeing that. If Emil could have his way, Dan O'Malley would be dead right now, and he wouldn't have to even think about dealing with him ever again.

"You said, Mr. Remard, that you needed the money as soon as possible. Is that right?"

Remard nodded.

"Put that in terms of time."

"Within the next few days. No later than next week."

Emil swallowed, the reflexive action catching on the lump in his throat. Could he get so much money together that quickly? He had no idea. He'd never had to deal much with banks, other than to borrow the few hundred dollars it had taken to buy the house he lived in and the one that burned down. But in that case the bankers had had equity to hold in case he forfeited the payments.

"You need all of it at one time?"

"All of it, Mr. LaMotte," Remard said slowly in a controlled voice.

Something fell from the table next to the couch, making a splatting noise when it struck the floor. Emil jumped. What had fallen? He looked at the table and saw the pictures of Magdalene and Edgar where they always were. There was nothing else on the table. He felt Remard studying him and turned to him.

"What's wrong, Mr. LaMotte?"

Emil stammered for a moment. "I . . . I thought I heard something fall. Did you?"

"Yes, I did. What was it?"

Emil shrugged. "I don't know." He leaned to one side and looked past the couch. A small book lay on the floor next to the old davenport. Emil got up and moved toward the small book.

"I don't think I can get that much together in a few days, Mr. Remard," he said, leaning over. His face drained of color when he stood up and saw what it was he had picked up.

"What's wrong, Mr. LaMotte? What is that?"

Emil opened the book and saw his name on the top line of the bank book. He'd never had a savings account in his life. Where had this come from? His eyes ran down the line of figures and widened when he saw the last entry. He couldn't believe it. $1,334.65. Over a thousand dollars in a savings account he knew nothing about. He checked the dates of entry but found them to be marked by only days and months, not years. There were at least 50 or so entries, but over how long a time, he had no idea.

He eyed Remard who still sat on the lumpy torn couch. Did this man have something to do with the bank book? That was crazy. A tax man didn't run around, offering people land for the payment of back taxes and then give them the money to pay the taxes as well. He coughed and looked at the book again. The figures ran together as Emil's vision blurred. He shook his head and rubbed his eyes.

"What is it, Mr. LaMotte? What's wrong?" Remard asked.

Emil tried to speak but found his voice choked. Instead he handed the book to Remard and waited.

Remard looked at the small bank book and nodded. "Well then, you do have the money after all, don't you?"

Emil sat down heavily in the straight-back chair. He shook his head and said, "I . . . I've never seen that book before in my life."

"But it has your name on it. I'm sure it's yours. Whose could it be if it isn't yours?"

Emil shrugged. What was happening? He knew nothing about the book or the money. Out of thin air, he found he owned land. He learned he owed back taxes but didn't have the means to pay for them. Now, all of a sudden, he did. What indeed was happening? "I don't know what to say," Emil said slowly. "I'm mixed up. I really am."

"I think you probably just forgot about the bank account when I told you about the land and all. Of course, you don't have to pay the taxes."

Emil brightened. "I don't? What happens if I don't?"

"The county will hold an auction and sell the land and the house. As long as the county gets its taxes it'll be happy. But, I promise you, the taxes will be paid one way or the other—by you or by someone else."

Emil relaxed. All he had to do was use the money in the bank account to pay the taxes and the mansion and the land would be his. He sensed it was illegal, but the tax man, who represented the county and was sitting in Emil's house, said it was all honest and above board.

It couldn't be better, Emil decided. First, he got the mansion and the land. He paid the back taxes which would make the property his, free and clear, with money that just materialized out of thin air. And best of all, he was going to get one up on Mayor Dan O'Malley. If nothing else, the last part was the best. He wanted to see O'Malley's face when he heard the news.

"Does O'Malley get his money back for the property he bought from me?"

Remard frowned for a moment and then slowly nodded. "Yes. Even though he paid you, the property actually belonged to Mrs. Newton. Since you now own the Newton property in total, you'd have to buy back or pay back, I should say, the money to Mr. O'Malley. Of course, you could give him title to the land and let him keep it."

Emil frowned. "No! But giving him money don't seem fair either, seeing as to how much I hate that bastard."

Remard smiled. "It's the legal thing to do. How much did he pay you for the land? Do you remember?"

"It wasn't that much. I think it was around fifty bucks an acre. I made the sonofabitch pay for the survey and the legal fees, though."

"Well, whatever the total was, you'd have to reimburse him or sign over the deed to that particular five acre tract of land. Which ever you decide will be fine with the county." Renard stood. "I'll be back in a few days. You will have the money for me then, won't you?" He handed the bank book to Emil.

Emil smiled. "Sure. I'll get to the bank and get the money for you."

"If you want to get a cashier's check, that'd be the smart thing to do. Just have the bank make it out to the county. That way no one can steal it, or if you should lose it, it would be worthless to whoever found it unless they turned it in for a reward."

He watched Remard walk out the door

toward the black Chevy. Those '51s sure had nice lines. Emil thought that maybe he might get one once the business with the golden book was finished.

Closing the door, he turned back into the living room and froze. There on the table the book with the gold pages lay on top of the paper he'd used to cover the spot of blood. How had it gotten there?

He felt his heart racing and took several deep breaths. He couldn't worry about it right now. He had to hunt up the sales papers he'd kept over the years since selling the land to O'Malley. He went to the bedroom and rummaged through the drawers until he found the manila folder that held his legal papers and other documents. When he found the envelope containing the bill of sale, he returned to the living room and sat down at the table. Once he had spread the papers out, he read them over, mumbling under his breath every nasty thought he could muster about Dan O'Malley.

When he found the total, he winced. $403.02. Now where would he get that much money to give back to that thief? How much would be left in the mysterious bank account once he'd paid the taxes? If there wasn't enough, he didn't know what he'd do. The thought of taking the land away from O'Malley had a pleasureable ring of revenge, and revenge was what he wanted.

Picking up the bank book, he opened it and wrote down the total on the old newspaper and subtracted the taxes that were due. $931.63. The remainder brought a gasp to Emil's lips. $403.02. The exact amount. A chill ran down his spine. It was as if providence or some higher power was mysteriously looking after him and his welfare. Whatever the situation, he had enough money to own the Newton property outright and pay back Dan O'Malley for the five acres of land he and Magdalene had thought they owned at one time.

Emil frowned. He'd have to find a way to get to Elksburg and go to the bank. He hoped he wouldn't have any trouble there. He wanted to empty the account and get the business completed. Then he could move his few possessions into the mansion. The best thing he could do was go up to the grocery store and see if he could hitch a ride into the county seat where the bank was located.

After hiding the heavy book in the cupboard once more, he stared at it for a long moment before closing the door. He'd placed the canned foodstuffs back on the shelf and paused to wonder about the book. He'd have to think on it later. He had to get to the store and make arrangements to go to town.

Fifteen minutes later, he walked into Ferguson's Grocery Store. Dot Ferguson looked up, staring at Emil over the glasses she precariously balanced on the tip of her bulbous nose. When she recognized him, she went back to reading *The Des Moines Register*.

"Hello, Mrs. Ferguson."

"G'day," she said sharply. "Something I can help you with?"

"I need a ride in to Elksburg to go the bank and the court house. You know anybody going in?"

"My husband goes in to work there everyday, as if you didn't know. When you want to go? You realize you'd have to spend the whole day there to ride home with him after he's done work, don't you?"

Emil nodded. "That'd be fine. I ain't been to Elksburg for a while. I need the change of scenery. You seen Dan O'Malley around?" Emil wanted to tell him what was going to happen, just to see him squirm a little. For once in his life, Emil was going to be top dog where the mayor was concerned.

"Ain't you heard?"

"Heard? Heard what?"

"Mayor O'Malley dropped dead of a heart attack about an hour or so ago. I thought everybody in town knew it by now."

Emil grabbed the edge of the counter and hung on.

CHAPTER SIX

September, 1989

The five o'clock rush hour traffic had long since cleared up, and Frank took his time driving the Lincoln along Brady Street. His night waitresses were competent, and he didn't have to worry about the restaurant operating without him. He glanced at Sherry sitting next to him. Every once in a while, she reached out and ran her hand over the padded dashboard.

"You like the car?" he asked, braking to a stop for a traffic light.

"Yeah, I sure do. It's nothing like that beat-up Subaru Rob drives." She turned to Frank and smiled broadly.

"You kind of like the good things in life, don't

you?"

"I don't know. I've never had much."

"That's a shame. You're a good-looking woman. You should have had better breaks."

"Tell that to my husband." She fell silent and stared at the traffic coursing by. When the light changed, Frank pulled away from the intersection.

"You aren't going to chicken out on your decision, are you?"

She turned to him. "How do you mean?"

"Your decision to leave him."

"Oh. I thought you meant about accepting the apartment."

"That, too. One goes with the other. I'm not trying to break up your marraige, but you've said enough for me to know that you don't need him in your life anymore. What the hell for? What good is he?"

"I suppose you don't want to keep me in your apartment for a little fun whenever you want it either."

"That's secondary. I'm just interested in your welfare, that's all."

Sherry nodded and said nothing.

"You know, you said you'd think on this tonight. What the hell are you going to be thinking?"

"What do you mean?"

"Well, you said you'd think about taking the apartment, right?"

She nodded and turned to him.

"How can you make an intelligent decision

without knowing what it is you're supposed to be deciding. You haven't seen the apartment. How can you compare it to the one you're living in now with him?"

Sherry grinned. "Good point."

Frank braked the car and turned the corner onto a side street.

"Hey, I don't live this way."

"I know," he said. "I'm going to show you the apartment, then you'll have something to think about. All right?"

"I guess. Actually, anything would be better than the hole we've been living in."

"Then you've made up your mind already?" Frank slowed the car.

Sherry sighed. "You might say that. I'd still like to see your place, though. Is it far?"

"Just a few blocks."

Neither spoke until Frank pulled up to the curb and stopped. When they got out, Sherry looked around. It was almost like an alley. Garages opened onto the street on both sides, and she couldn't see any houses. She looked at Frank, a quizzical expression on her face.

"What's wrong?"

She swept an arm to one side. "There's nothing but garages."

"Right. That's all you see here. The businesses are on the other streets. A few of the buildings have been converted to apartments on the upper floors. Most of them are used for storage."

"Which one is yours?"

He pointed across the street. "Come on."

Once they'd crossed over, Frank pulled out a key ring. He unlocked the door and held it for Sherry.

"Go on up," he said. "I'll lock the door."

She started up the steps, reached the top and waited for Frank.

In seconds, he stood next to her. After unlocking the door to the apartment, he stepped inside and turned on the light.

Sherry followed and admired the small entryway which was painted in soft pastels of brown and tan. She held her breath when she entered the living room. It was almost 30 feet long and had a small kitchenette at one end with a dining area. The rest of the dark oak paneled room was luxuriously appointed with modern furniture. Round glass tables had been placed at strategic points to hold lamps or pieces of sculpture. One light fixture was suspended by a long, gracefully bent rod that extended from behind a corner arrangement of couches.

"It's beautiful, Frank," she whispered.

"You haven't seen anything yet," he said, motioning for her to follow him.

He opened a door onto a full size bathroom. The sunken tub held Sherry's attention longer than the black marble sinks. Opposite a linen closet, a shower cubicle stood to one side, cleverly blended into the wall. A door opened to either side of the bathroom.

"There's only one bathroom but it has private

entrances from the two bedrooms. This one," he said, opening the door to the right, "will be your kid's." The room was neat, well lighted and decorated with a multicolor stripe of pastel colors that traveled the full perimeter of the room, broken only by the doors and windows.

"Jeremy would love this," she said quietly, forcing herself to stop imagining the two of them living in the apartment. This had to be a dream. She wasn't that lucky to have something given to her like this for nothing. Of course, there was a price to pay. Frank had already stated that in a roundabout way. She'd have to sleep with him from time to time to pay the rent. Wouldn't that make her a whore just like she said she would never be? What about her pride? She wasn't certain if she had any anymore, not after living with Rob all those years which had gone from bad to worse.

"It's beautiful, Frank. I guess you've got yourself a deal." She dropped her attention to the floor, afraid her face would show her embarrassment.

"I can't accept that. Not yet, at least."

Sherry looked up, startled. What was he doing? Playing a game? Was he pretending he'd help her and let her live here and then withdraw the offer at the very moment she elected to accept? "I don't understand, Frank. Have you changed your mind?"

"Come on, Sherry, you know me better than that. You haven't seen the other bedroom yet. Once you've seen it, then you can make your decision. I swear most people make choices in a half-baked way and then regret their decision after they've moved on it too quickly. That's why I wanted you to see the apartment before you started deciding."

He stepped around her and went to the opposite door in the bathroom. Opening it and turning on the lights, he said, "I hope you like mirrors."

"Mirrors?" she said, stepping through the doorway and sucking in her breath when she saw the room. Mirrors lined the ceiling and the walls. She looked at herself in endless reflection as she moved into the center of the room. A king-size bed dominated the bedroom and was balanced by two chairs and night-stands on either side. A huge, low dresser stood at the foot of the bed.

"Like it?" he asked.

"I'm . . . I'm speechless. Why mirrors?"

"Didn't I tell you? I'm a voyeur. I like to watch." He grinned.

"You're kidding."

"Yeah. Actually, the mirrors were here when I leased the place. The rest I had redecorated. But I do like mirrors. So, now that you've seen the whole place, what do you think? Want to move in?"

Sherry was puzzled over Frank's generosity. If he maintained a love nest like this, why didn't he have some 19- or 20-year-old sex kitten living here? She asked him.

"Good question. Actually, young broads want

too much. They might get to liking the good life and decide they want it all the time. You know how I feel about my wife. I don't want or need any problems that would upset my married life. If I bring a young one here, it's just for a roll in the hay. Nothing of a permanent or even semipermanent nature.''

"What are you saying, Frank? An old broad like me will be grateful for a good fuck in a nice setting every once in a while?''

"Naw, nothing like that. I happen to like you as a person, Sherry. You're attractive, and I can relate to you better than I can to some young pussy.''

"You sure you're not doing this for any reason other than what you've told me?''

"You got it.''

"All right, then. We've got a deal, but I want to be able to walk away anytime I choose. Is that all right?''

"Sure. As long as I can throw you out anytime I choose. Of course, I'll give you plenty of notice so you can find another place.''

"That sounds fair.'' She whirled around, watching the thousands of Sherrys doing the same thing.

"Want to consummate the deal?''

Sherry stopped. "You sure your wife doesn't know about this place?''

"What she doesn't know won't hurt her.''

"That's what they all say. What time is it?''

"Going on seven. You got enough time?''

"Just a quickie.'' She moved toward him and

slipped her arms around his neck. She reveled in the hardness of his shoulders and arms, while kissing him lightly on the lips. Her tongue jabbed into his mouth, and she felt his cock leap to life. Slowly lowering herself to her knees she unbuckled his pants and, after they dropped, pulled down his shorts. His erection bounced to attention, and she lightly kissed the tip before taking it in her mouth.

Rob twirled the pick in his martini. Damn, he felt good. He'd had two martinis already and was working on his third. One for each of the sales he'd made that day. He grinned. It was a good thing he hadn't sold a dozen policies and tried drinking a dozen martinis. He would have been so drunk he'd probably never have sobered up.

Once he was finished with the third one, he'd go home and wave the money he'd made up front in Sherry's face and remind her that she'd have to work at least ten days to make as much as he had in one. The $275 he'd made in front money would carry them well into the next week, and he'd be able to pay the rent. Now that he was back on track, he might even consider moving his family to a better place. Surely they could find something better than the apartment in which they'd been living for the last six months or so.

He could hardly wait to see the expression on Sherry's face. Maybe he should buy her some flowers and maybe a bottle of wine to celebrate. That was a good idea.

"Hi."

The sultry voice came from Rob's right, and he turned uncertainly to see who was speaking to him. A young woman, no more than 25 years old, had perched on the bar stool next to him. He grinned foolishly.

"Hi, yourself," he said. "What's a nice place like you doing in a girl like this?"

She smiled. "You're funny, you know that? What are you celebrating?"

"How'd you know I was celebrating?"

"Because you look so happy and content. Are you?"

"You might say that."

"Would you like to be happier and even more content?"

Rob looked at her closely. Her short black hair contrasted sharply with her milk white skin and trembled whenever she moved her head or spoke. He liked that. It made her seem very alive. Sherry's blonde hair on the other hand just sort of hung from her head even though she spent hours working on it. Maybe her hair was too long.

"What do you mean?"

"Want to buy me a drink and I'll tell you?"

"Sure, sure. Hey, bartender, give the little lady here anything she wants."

The bartender moved down to them and put a napkin in front of the girl. "What'll it be?"

"Oh, some Rhine wine would be good."

The bartender left to get the wine and the girl

turned her attention back to Rob. "I'm Lily. What's your name?"

"Rob."

"Do they call you Robbie?" she asked, moving closer and reaching out with one hand to play with his ear.

"Some people do."

"Tell me, Robbie, wouldn't you like to be even happier and more content than you are right now?"

Rob shrugged. "Whatcha got in mind?"

"Well, I thought we might be able to go someplace, you know, like your place or mine or maybe a motel. That would be fun, wouldn't it, Robbie?"

He shrugged again. "What would we do if we did?"

"Well, first, I'd take off all your clothes and then you could—"

The bartender placed the wine in front of her and looked at Rob who shook his head, pointing to the half-full glass in front of him. Taking a five dollar bill from the stack in front of Rob, the bartender moved away, rang up the sale and returned with a dollar bill.

Rob turned his full attention back to Lily who was sipping her wine. "Now, what were you saying?"

"Well," she said, moving closer to him, "after I got your clothes off, you could undress me. Would you like that, Robbie?"

He shrugged. "What would happen then?"

"Well, I'd see that you got real comfortable

on the bed and then I'd start running my tongue all over your body. I'd lick you every place you can think of. What do you think of that?"

"Sounds interesting," he said noncomittally.

"Just interesting? I'll tell you this much. I've got a very educated tongue, and you've never had your nipples sucked or teased the way I can do it. And as far as your cock is concerned, I'll probably spoil sex for you for the rest of your life."

"You wouldn't kid a guy, would you, Lily?" Rob asked, lifting his glass and taking half of the remaining martini in one gulp. After returning the glass to the bar, he took the pick and was ready to get the olive when Lily reached over and took his hand, guiding it to her mouth. She slipped the olive between her lips and held it in her teeth before pulling her head back, freeing it from the pick. She slowly bit it in two and chewed, smiling the whole time at him.

"Well, that's what you get to do. What do I get to do?"

"I was just getting to that part. After I suck you off, I'll make your pecker hard again and then you can do whatever you want to me."

"What do you like?"

"Anything. I like French, Greek, Arabic, Scottish, German, Ital—"

"Whoa! Wait a minute. Are we going to be speaking in foreign languages or do you know a lot more than me?" Rob turned to face her, waiting for her answer.

"Well, maybe I know a lot more than you and maybe you just know the same tricks I do under different names."

"Oh. Well, go on."

"Well, once I have your pride and pleasure all nice and firm again, you can ram it into my pussy or up my ass or anyplace you want. Doesn't that sound like a lot of fun?"

Rob smiled sardonically. "And what's all of this going to cost me?"

"I don't think we should discuss things like that here, do you?"

"We aren't going to discuss it anyplace else other than here," he said softly. "What's it going to cost?"

"You might be a cop, Robbie," Lily said, puffing out her lower lip. She looked down as if she were ready to cry. "If you're a cop, then, you'd arrest me if I said it would cost you $150. Wouldn't you?"

"Well, I'm not a cop, and if I were, I guess I couldn't arrest you for saying 'if I said it would cost $150,' now could I?"

She shook her head and grinned wickedly. "What do you say?"

"There's only one thing wrong with your whole plan."

"What's that?"

"We didn't talk about my fee."

"Your fee? What the hell are you talking about?"

"See, I'm so good, women usually pay me $200 for stud services. You got that much dough, Lily?"

She glared at him. "You smart cocksucker. Kiss off. Who needs an asshole like yours to make money?"

"Gee," Rob said, "if there wasn't so much talk about AIDS around, I'd consider using mine to make a buck or two." He stood and swilled the rest of the martini down, before scooping up his money except for a tip. "Take care, Lily. Don't take any wooden peckers." He laughed and walked from the bar.

Once outside, the early evening cool air sobered him to the point of being clearheaded. If a woman like Lily had approached him the day before, he would have just said no and let it go at that. But he felt good and had enjoyed teasing the prostitute.

He didn't notice the two men hesitate in the entrance of the bar behind him. After he crossed the street, they watched him stop at his rusty car.

When he reached the Subaru, he got in and started the engine. He'd be home in a short time, and then he and Sherry would have a good talk. First, he had to stop and get flowers and then a botle of wine at the supermarket.

Frank stopped the car several lengths from the corner. Sherry moved to get out.

"I'll be back in an hour to pick you and the kid up. Can you be packed by then?"

She nodded. "I'll meet you here. Don't pull up in front of the apartment door or Rob might see you."

"I won't. I wouldn't want him to think I was helping you." Frank chuckled and reached over to close the door after Sherry got out.

"Remember," she said, leaning down before he closed it, "no funny stuff in front of Jeremy. Understand?"

"Don't worry. I got kids of my own. I'll just be a friend who's helping you. All right?"

When she nodded, he closed the door.

Frank pulled away from the curb, and she stood for a long minute watching the Lincoln after it crossed the intersection.

When she reached her apartment, she found Jeremy doing his homework.

"Stop that right now," she said, swinging into the bedroom.

"Why?" Jeremy asked.

"We're moving. That's why."

"Moving? I don't understand. Where's Dad?"

"I don't know, and I couldn't care less. I'm leaving him and you're going with me."

"Ma!" His voice echoed with surprise.

"You heard me. Get a couple of grocery bags and put all of your clothes in them. Get moving."

"No." He glared at her from the doorway. She spun around. "What?"

"I said no. You're making a big mistake. I know. Dad and I talked this morning."

"And what did you talk about?" she asked, without realizing he had left for school before she had gone to work.

"I came back home after you left. I don't like you and Dad yelling at each other all the time."

"Then you'll get what you want, won't you? He won't be around for me to yell at. Get going, Jeremy."

"But he loves you. He said so. He said he loves me."

"Well, I don't love him. I'm sure that in his own dumb way he loves you, but we can't go on like this. He's no good when it comes to making money, and I've got to think of your welfare. I've got a real nice place for us to go to. You'll love it. Why, you'll even have your very own bedroom. You won't have to sleep on a couch anymore, not if I have anything to say about it."

Jeremy ran to her, throwing his arms around her waist. "Will I ever see Dad again?"

"If he wants to see you, I won't stand in the way. All right?"

"All right." Wiping tears from his eyes, he turned to get the bags and in a few minutes had gathered together his clothing and toys. Jeremy bit his lip to keep from crying. He felt confused. His father was so nice this morning after his mother had gone to work, and his mother was always nice whenever his father wasn't around. When they were together, they yelled and said bad things to each other.

"Are you finished?" Sherry called from the bedroom.

"Yes."

"Then come in here and help me."

Ten minutes later, they made their way down the steps and around the corner to wait for Frank Yearnall. Sherry hugged the wall and held her breath when she saw Rob's Subaru cruise through the intersection, angling toward the curb to park.

Jeremy took a step in the general direction of the corner, but Sherry grabbed him.

"Don't. I don't want a fight here in the streets. Thank God! Here's Frank," she said when she heard the Lincoln quietly pull up to the curb.

Another car pulled through the intersection and slowed down as it pulled into the curb around the corner.

Sherry quickly opened the back door and threw her things in. After pushing Jeremy into the back seat, she closed the door and got into the front. Frank pulled away as she put on her seat belt.

Rob got out of the car and reached back for the flowers and the wine. At first he didn't notice the two men getting out of the car that had pulled in behind him. He almost dropped the bottle of wine when they confronted him.

"Your name LaMotte?"

Rob nodded. He felt perfectly fine. The drinks hadn't affected him, and besides, if these guys were cops, they wouldn't know his name. But since they did know his name, he wondered who they were and why they wanted him.

"Do you know of an Emil LaMotte?"

Rob turned to face the speaker and saw a black Lincoln rush through the intersection. Emil LaMotte? He'd never heard the name before. Shaking his head he said, "No, I've never heard of an Emil LaMotte. Should I have?"

"We don't know. What was your father's name?"

Again Rob looked from one to the other. They both seemed like nice enough men, well-dressed and probably in their thirties. It was strange but he had always felt if anyone ever walked up to him like this and began questioning him, he'd feel panic and fear. Instead, he felt completely at ease and not the least bit afraid to answer their questions.

He coughed and said, "Edgar. Why?"

When one of the men reached into his inside coat pocket, Rob winced, but before he could be shaken, he saw a card in the man's hand.

"Here," he said, handing the card to Rob. "Contact this man as soon as possible. We'll tell him you'll be calling, and he'll expect you to do so."

Rob nodded dumbly and looked at the engraved card, which read:

Joseph Zwotney, Esquire
Attorney-at-Law
21400 East Highway Six
Davenport, IA 52808

Before he read the telephone number at the bottom of the card, he looked up and saw the two men already in their car. He ran to the automobile but it already was pulling away. "Hey, what's this all about?"

The car continued on, and Rob thrust the card into his pocket. He'd call tomorrow when he got to the office. Right now, he and Sherry had some celebrating to do.

Opening the door, he took two steps at a time, hurrying to the second floor apartment.

CHAPTER SEVEN

Fall, 1963

Emil ran a fingertip along his chin line and smiled. Where had they gone? The lines that had marked his face since he was in his late forties had slowly disappeared along with the gray in his hair. His hair had reverted to coal black, just like it had been when he'd been in his forties. Why was he rejuvenating, not that he minded? Instead, he felt everyone in the area who had known him over the years probably was envious of his appearance. After all, he was 74 and looked like he was in his early fifties or even late forties. The changes had been very subtle, so it had been quite some time before anyone even had mentioned anything about his appearance, and when they did, he passed it off as being an overactive imagination at work.

The best part about the whole thing was Emil's physical condition. He felt as if he really were a young man. His stamina was such that he could do almost anything he wanted. And his sexual drive, which had been dormant for a while, had sprung back to life, vigorous and lively.

The whole thing had begun after he had claimed the Newton mansion, and at first Emil had not noticed anything different. It had been that rainy afternoon when Margaret Woodless, the middle-aged widow whom he'd hired to help maintain the mansion once it had been redecorated, said how uncommonly handsome he had become.

At first he had felt flattered, and after he caught her admiring him several different times, he had said, "What are you looking at, Mrs. Woodless?"

"Why . . . why nothing," she said, looking away for an instant. "That's a lie. I was looking at you, Mr. LaMotte."

"Why, for crying out loud? Ain't you got enough to keep you busy around here without staring at me all the time?"

She dropped her eyes and stared at the floor. "I'm sorry. I really am. It was rude of me and I ask that you forgive me. It was most un—" She stopped when she realized that he was standing directly in front of her.

Emil reached out, grabbing her by the

shoulders, and said, "Look at me. How old do you think I am?" He'd fix her right now. She was only in her forties as far as he knew, and he was at least 20 years older than she, old enough to be her father. Emil smiled grimly when she raised her eyes to his.

"I'd say no more than 55, maybe. If I'm wrong and guessed you too old, forgive me. I'm not much good at this sort of thing."

"Fifty-five?" Emil hooted the words. "Why, I'm—" He stopped and glanced at the mirror behind Mrs. Woodless. Why hadn't he noticed before now? Releasing her, he stepped around the woman and went to the mirror. He *did* appear to be in his fifties. What had happened? Why hadn't he noticed before whenever he shaved or combed his hair in front of a mirror? He felt his penis jerk. That hadn't happened in a long time either. Could it have been caused by his closeness to the Woodless woman? Maybe, being a widow, she was as hungry for something as he suddenly discovered he was.

He turned back to face her, aware that his penis was hardening just because he was looking at her. She was an attractive woman. Sandy-colored hair, which fringed out from beneath the bandana she'd tied around her head to do her morning cleaning, matched her healthy complexion. Her dark brown eyes fairly snapped at times with humor and vigor and a lusty love of life.

"Mrs. Wood—? Margaret? May I call you Margaret?"

She took a tentative step toward him and stopped, fixing her eyes on him. "I wish you would."

For a split second, he wondered if she were going to call him Emil, but when she didn't, he forgot it for the time being. Instead, he ran his eyes up and down her figure. Her breasts weren't that large but they appeared firm and stood out, creating a nice curve to her flat stomach, belying the fact that she had a ten-year-old daughter.

"I'm sorry I scolded you for looking at me, Margaret." He stepped closer to her until they were mere inches apart. Without realizing it was happening, he suddenly scooped her into his arms and kissed her. Her tongue shot into his mouth, caressing his tongue, his teeth, the roof of his mouth, exploring every nook and cranny. When she withdrew, his own followed hers in pursuit to acquaint itself with the hidden secrets of her mouth.

His hands rubbed her back while he kissed her, and he felt her hand on him, dropping toward his crotch. This couldn't go on, not there in the front hallway. Picking her up, he carried her effortlessly up the wide staircase to the master bedroom and laid her on the bed. While he pulled off his pants and shirt, she sat up and unbuttoned the housedress she wore. In seconds they were both naked, and he lay down on the bed, next to her.

They kissed, and he ran a hand over the front of her body, touching, caressing, loving every inch of flesh he encountered. When he reached her breasts, her nipples stood hard, taut, expectant. Lowering his mouth from hers, he encased one hard mound between his teeth, chewing lightly, teasing it, daring it, driving it mad with an anticipation that seemed more provocative than anything he'd ever experienced in the past.

He felt her hand run down his front, making its way through the thick tangle of hair that covered his body. When she reached his penis, she found it throbbing, standing erect. Emil thrilled to her touch. How long had it been since a woman had done that sort of thing to him? He felt magnificent and ready. He couldn't understand the source of his energy. All he knew was he felt alive and vital since moving into the mansion four years before when it had suddenly become his.

He lay back when she pushed him flat onto the mattress. He felt her kisses on his belly, her tongue jabbing into his navel. Somewhere deep inside him, he felt a primordial scream being born and fought to keep it in check. Instead of giving vent to his passionate cry, he bit his lip when she enveloped his erect penis with her mouth. It felt so warm, so good, so right. A tear formed in one eye and ran down the side of his face.

Then she was lying next to him, and he rolled over, throwing one leg across her body. She helped him enter her wet vagina, and when they were locked together, they began the primitive rhythm of lust and animalistic urge.

Emil snapped back to the present and found himself smiling broadly at his mirrored image. That had happened eight years before, and Margaret Woodless had played an important part in Emil LaMotte's regeneration, not that he had confined his amorous attentions only to Margaret. There had been other women, and it seemed that he could have just about any woman he wanted as the years passed. And as the years did pass, Emil had grown younger in both appearance and vitality.

It had been a day or so after the first encounter with Margaret that Emil had sat in the large library of the mansion, staring off into space. When she had left for her own home an hour earlier, Emil had begun to contemplate the strange and peculiar situation in which he found himself. Why had he suddenly become so lucky? First he'd acquired the property of the Newton estate with a peculiar stroke of luck. It seemed whenever he required money, something would happen and he would have whatever it was he wanted and needed.

He'd been sitting in the library trying to put some handle on the run of good luck when he heard a smack of something falling to the floor behind him. Turning in his seat, he saw the leather-bound, golden plates he'd found in the strange tunnel that day when—

Emil leaped to his feet. The book! Of course. That was the connecting link that he'd been overlooking all this time. It had to have been the book. What else could it have been? He'd found it that same day the man from the county tax office arrived with the news that he owned the Newton property and that all he had to do was pay the back taxes and it was his. Out of thin air the bank book had appeared with enough money to pay the taxes and buy back the land he had foolishly sold to Dan O'Malley. When he went to arrange for transportation to the county seat to pay the taxes, he'd learned of O'Malley's death, which had fulfilled his heart's desire.

He picked up the book and caressed it gently and lovingly. "Are you the reason I've become so lucky?"

The book seemed to leap to life in his hand, jerking in such a way that Emil thought it actually was alive and answering his question. If such were the case, that the book was somehow responsible, he owed it to himself to care for it as if it were the most precious jewel in the world or the key to every mystery unknown to man. He grinned wickedly. With such a means, he could have just about anything he wanted.

"Is that true? Can I have anything I want?" he muttered aloud, and the book moved in his hands again. Clutching it to his chest, he knew he had to provide a safe place for it, to guard it, to keep it from ever falling into anyone else's hands.

He put the book on the library table and walked around the room, searching for a suitable place. When he turned back to the table, he gasped.

The book was gone!

But who— How? When? He frantically ran about the room, when he passed the wall of bookshelves wherein he had so carelessly thrust the book when he first took possession of the house.

He stopped in his tracks. The book was in its customary place. Who had put it there? He hadn't touched it since he laid it on the table. But if that were the case and he was the only one in the house, how had it gotten back onto the shelf? As he stared at the book, it wiggled in place.

One of his hands flew involuntarily to his mouth, and he bit a knuckle to keep from screaming out. The goddamned book was communicating with him. That wasn't possible. But it was happening nevertheless.

Little by little, Emil realized the power of the golden plates and found if he wanted something all he had to do was want it and it became his. If someone stood in his way of acquiring something or accomplishing something, that person soon found themselves in dire straits or, worse yet, dead. There had been more than one untimely death in Nowaupeton over the last dozen years, and Emil had been in a position to buy and sell whatever he wanted. The one thing he had done that had proven a boon to Nowaupeton was his directing the small community toward becoming a resort area. Trailer parks and motels, a second grocery store and three more taverns along with two small supper clubs had sprung up in Nowaupeton, most of which were owned by Emil LaMotte. He had also bought some of the land surrounding the small community. At the end of the twelfth year after finding the book, Emil was the wealthiest man in Blayton County.

When he learned he had no control over anything that didn't directly affect him, Emil set out building his fortune. He smiled grimly when he recalled the few times he had tried to do something for the world, something that wouldn't have profited him in any way other than peripherally. He demanded world peace —but nothing happened. He'd wished for the end of the Viet Nam war with the United States victorious—but nothing happened. When one or two other tries ended in failure, Emil concluded he could do nothing for anyone other than himself.

Often he wondered why it had been his good luck to find the book. Why hadn't someone else found it? Had he just happened onto it, or was there a bigger plan afoot, one he couldn't realize? Was he being used the way he used the townspeople to gain his ends? If that were the case, by whom was he being manipulated? Whenver he thought about things like that, he usually wound up with nothing more than a tremendous headache, so he soon learned not

to be overly concerned with that aspect of the
situation. If he were being used, so be it. He
enjoyed his life, and he enjoyed his power and
money and prestige.

The last time he had wondered about the circumstances surrounding his discovery of the
book five years after the fact, he decided that
he should relocate the tunnel and its unique
door. He walked to the valley and searched the
better part of a day without finding any trace
of the door or the tunnel. The place where he
thought it might be located had no signs of
recent or past mud slides or anything remotely
resembling a change in the topography. He had
found an old oil can, but he wasn't cetain if it
was the same can he'd brought to the tunnel
that day.

He grinned when he thought of Margaret
Woodless. She had stopped aging as well. After
eight years she appeared the same as she did
that day when she complimented Emil on his
presence. Her daughter, Tricia, whom Emil had
never met, passed her eighteenth birthday.
Emil had avoided meeting Tricia for fear the
girl might suspect something about her mother
and him. Margaret, on the other hand, did
nothing to promote a meeting for fear of upset-
ting her employer and lover.

Emil settled into a routine of wanting things
and acquiring them, making love with
Margaret and having anything his heart
desired.

When he approached the town council, the same town council he had helped elect, for approval of a new ordinance governing the parking along one side of the main thorough-fare through Nowaupeton, he was voted down. The opposition was led by Mayor Jim Bradley, Sr. Emil had taken the defeat in as dignified a way as possible, without telling the mayor or his puppets just how he felt.

As he left the town hall, he vowed to himself that Bradley and those who had voted with him would pay for their stupidity. The parking problem was out of control during the heavy tourist season and, because of the town's position along the hillside, there was no place left on the narrow ledge for another street. Emil had proposed off-street parking be provided in those places where it was possible. He fumed when he thought of Bradley's answer to that.

Bradley had stroked his chin and stared directly at Emil. "I cannot expect those poor people to park someplace other than where they're parking now. These people represent our life's blood in this town. We can't insult them and demand they do something just because we're enpowered to do so. I don't know how the rest of the council feels, but I'm dead set against this."

"Mr. Mayor," Emil said, mustering up as much respect as he could for Bradley, "the rise in the street as it goes along the hillside causes a blind spot, and someday there'll be an accident—head-on—in that very spot."

"I don't think so, Mr. LaMotte," the mayor said. "It's not nearly as bad as you make it out to be. It's never happened before, so why should it happen now?"

Before Emil could speak, Councilman Peter Simmonson raised his hand. "I'm disinclined to support this petition for a change in the parking ordinance as well. I agree fully with the mayor. It's never happened before, and it won't happen now. I can see no reason to run the risk of hurting the feelings of our out-of-town guests who happen to be the life's blood of our community. They're like our patrons, if you will."

Emil fumed at the word "patrons." He felt himself to be the only true patron of Nowaupeton. Though whatever he did he did for himself, the community prospered because of it, and now they were offending him with their stupidity. He glanced at Dot Ferguson who had supported the petition by signing it and offering land behind her store for a public parking lot to the city for a reasonable sum. She smiled in a resigned way, and Emil wished Bradley and his puppet, Simmonson, would meet head-on in a fiery crash on Main Street when one couldn't pass the other.

Two days later, during the afternoon of the fourth of July, when the town's population was almost ten times its normal size of 297, Jim Bradley drove eastward toward the Mississippi River. He was in a hurry to reach the park on the other side of the Milwaukee Road tracks where he would deliver his annual speech.

Peter Simmonson had had the good sense to go to the park early that morning and set up his picnic area for his family, but when he found they had forgotten the main basket of food, he told his wife that he'd hurry home and get it.

The two men drove toward each other, and when they were approaching the only blind spot on a steep rise, Mayor Bradley's auto's accelerator suddenly floored of its own volition and the Oldsmobile roared ahead.

Simmonson had followed an old truck which had finally turned off the main street and, realizing he was late, sped up. The two cars met at the crest and instantly burst into flames upon impact. Both were killed instantly.

A pall of gloom settled over the resort town for a few weeks until a new mayor and council member were elected. Then the more normal air of relaxation returned to the community once more, and the double tragedy was soon nothing more than an unpleasant memory.

At the first town council meeting, Emil raised his hand and approached the podium. He bypassed the usual opening remarks and said instead, "If you people don't know who I am now, you won't care what it is I have to say anyway. Concerning this problem of parking along both sides of Main Street, I feel that if the former mayor and former councilman were here with us and knew now what they should have known several weeks back when this issue first came up, they'd be a hundred percent for taking it off one side and encouraging off-street parking as I suggested in the past."

The town council members stared at Emil but said nothing, knowing full well that the eccentric man was correct.

"It was mentioned at the time and pooh-poohed by them as being inconsequential and insignificant that the rise in the hill was the danger spot in this town. They had to find out the hard way. Let's not let anything like that happen again. It's in your hands, ladies and gentlemen of the council." Emil turned and sat down without saying another word.

The ordinance was adopted by a vote of three to zero.

Shortly after Emil's 74th birthday, which he didn't celebrate for fear people would start wondering why he was growing younger instead of older, Father John Francis, pastor of St. Philomena's Catholic Church, came to his front door.

After letting the clergyman in, Emil showed him to the library where they took seats facing each other. Emil knew full well what the priest wanted.

"What can I do for you, Reverend?" he asked, staring intently at the young man until the priest had to turn away.

"Well, as you know, St. Philomena's annual church picnic is coming up soon. We at the parish meeting last night wondered if you would care to donate to our cause again, as you did last year."

Emil frowned. He'd given, yes, but not because he believed in anything the young whippersnapper of a priest or his convictions conveyed. He'd given various amounts over the years. One year he'd given $100. Another, he'd donated $500. Once he even gave $1000, but mostly the gifts had been in the range of $100 to $500.

"What did I give last year?"

"Ah," Father Francis said, laboriously pulling out a card which had a single figure written on it. "One hundred dollars. That was most generous of you, Mr. LaMotte."

"Hah!" Emil snorted. "You know I don't go to your damned church. Why do you come around and bother me every year?"

"Well . . . I . . . That is, we . . ." The priest appeared flustered as if he wished he'd never come and had never heard of Emil LaMotte.

"I see," Emil said. "I don't go along with all that mumbo-jumbo you people go through all the time. Give me one reason why I should give you any money?"

The priest's mind finally swung into gear, and he said, sitting up straight, "By helping St. Philomena's you help your neighbor. If they don't have to worry about supporting the church more than they do now and can count on outsiders' help with a picnic and donations, they can be better citizens and help you with your many enterprises, Mr. LaMotte."

Emil stood and walked toward the hallway door. He went upstairs to his office and sat down at the roll-top desk. After opening it, he pulled open one of the small drawers and pulled out a wrapped stack of bills. Slipping a 100 dollar bill partway out, he stopped, a wide grin forming on his handsome face. Slamming shut the drawer, he pulled down the top of the desk and returned to the library. He threw the stack of bills onto the priest's lap and sat down.

Francis's eyes widened when he saw the amount of money in his lap. The band around the bills carried the number 10,000. He looked up to find Emil staring off into space.

"Mr. LaMotte, are you serious? Are you really giving the church ten thousand dollars?"

Emil slowly turned his head until he fixed his baleful stare on the priest. "Get out of here."

The priest stared. "But what should I do with this?" he asked, holding the money.

"If you don't know, you'd better leave it here. Otherwise, take it and get out." Emil stood, drawing himself up to his full height of six feet.

The shorter man clambered to his feet. "Thank you, Mr. LaMotte. I don't know what to say."

"Try 'good-bye.'"

The priest fled from the library and hurried through the front entrance. As he ran down the steps, he could hear Emil's laughter echo through the large house.

Inside, Emil doubled over, an evil, maniacal look twisting his face as he roared with laughter. Then he stopped and hurried to the steps that led to the second floor. Margaret would arrive soon, and he wanted to be ready.

CHAPTER EIGHT

January, 1975

A wintery gale whipped the mansion, moaning not unlike a beast, toying with its prey. Inside, a bright fire blazed in the library's huge fireplace, casting shadows on the walls in the premature early afternoon gloom. Emil sat, slouched over in a leather easy chair, staring deeply into the flames. He had to do something. Margaret was getting too close to him. He felt trapped. Of course, he was fond of the woman and realized that she had many fine qualities, qualities that made her an attractive personality as well as a good companion. The fact that she didn't live at the mansion was a blessing since Emil coveted his privacy. He enjoyed being alone in the large house. He enjoyed being alone to relish the power he had developed over the years.

His eyes strayed from the fire to the bookshelves and stopped on the leather-bound golden plates. He often wondered what the contents might mean and had wrestled with different theories. Long ago, he had discarded the idea of pirates or Indians or Vikings being responsible for concealing the book in the tunnel. He had dwelled for a while on the theory that it was a book of spells, but who would have taken the time to set onto golden plates spells that worked miracles? To Emil, that didn't make sense. He thought it might be a work of the devil, but since he had never been much involved with any sort of religion, he knew little of the Prince of Darkness and his capabilities. Had it come from outer space? He shook his head. Why would someone with the ability to travel in space take the time to coneal a book made of precious metal? It seemed that any idea he conceived concerning the book was soon discarded, and his own thoughts became convoluted and turned in on themselves, neither solving his mystery nor giving him the solace of some type of conclusion.

All he knew was that the book had come into his possession, and for the first time in his life, his luck and fortune had taken a turn for the better—much better. He could have whatever he wanted, and the thing he wanted now was more distance between Margaret and himself, not that she was becoming possessive or head-strong where he was concerned. But he felt suffocated for some reason unknown to himself and at times thought his breath would be cut off and he would perish. The only thing he could think of was that Margaret, in some strange, almost incomprehensible way, was responsible. The situation had to be remedied.

Since he enjoyed their sexual encounters and she did her work quickly and efficiently, why then would he want to get rid of her? He looked up, repeating the words, "Get rid of her," in a hoarse whisper.

A dark look clouded his handsome features. Was that the solution? Wish for her to be out of his life? Wasn't that what he had done where Dan O'Malley was concerned? And Jim Bradley? And Peter Simmonson? And any of the others who had blocked the way of Emil LaMotte in one way or another? Did he want to see Margaret annihilated in some awful way?

He turned away from the shelves and the fire, staring out the window at the swirling snow. An involuntary shiver ran down his spine. The weather was gruesome in its furious assault, and he was relieved that he didn't have to venture out.

He refocused his thoughts. Maybe he should simply fire Margaret. What would the consequences be if he did? She might tell people of his habits and ways, but what of them? He did nothing out of the ordinary around Margaret. He never had. At best, he made every effort to keep from doing anything that would seem eccentric or strange. The only thing she might be able to talk of was his appearance, but everyone in Nowaupeton knew what he looked like. Those who remembered his frail stature and gray hair from the late forties and early fifties were either dead or had forgotten about it. Everyone else simply knew him as Emil LaMotte, the handsome rich man who lived in the biggest house in the county and had single-handedly built Nowaupeton into a fine resort area.

Still, the idea of dismissing Margaret bothered him. He couldn't be certain she wouldn't talk about him and perhaps make up lies and stories that, while they wouldn't be true, would nevertheless do him no good.

He jumped when she entered the library. He turned to face her and found himself admiring the handsome woman standing in the doorway. She hadn't changed an iota in the last 12 years.

"I was wondering if you'd have any objections if I left now. I have all my work finished. There's plenty of food prepared, and I—"

"Do you have plans of some sort?" Emil asked, a frown crossing his face.

"No. I just would like to get home before this storm really breaks on us the way the weather man said it would. This is nothing," she said, gesturing toward the window.

"It's to get worse?" Emil frowned deeply.

"Much worse, according to the forecast."

"Do you think it wise to go out into it then?"

"I have to if I want to get home."

Emil nodded and continued studying the woman.

When he said nothing, Margaret waited for a moment and said, "It's my daughter. She wasn't feeling well when I left this morning. I should be with her."

"She's not infantile, is she?" Emil growled the words.

"No, but she is ill. May I leave?"

Emil waved a hand at her. "Go."

Margaret bowed her head in a slight, jerky way and left the library.

Emil sat back in the chair, refocusing his attention on the fire. Margaret had to be taken care of—and soon.

Margaret pulled her scarf tighter around her neck. The wind cut through her like a knife. Icy needles stung her cheeks, and she sucked in her breath as a strong gust wrapped itself around her and tried to knock her to the ground. In some ways she was glad she hadn't driven to the mansion that morning. After all, she didn't live that far away. Yet, if she had driven, she'd at least be warm inside the Chevy.

But she had convinced Tricia to keep the car to go to Ferguson's Mighty Mart in the event she might need something for her upset stomach and headache. As a result, Margaret had to walk the three-quarters of a mile to her small home.

How long had she been walking? Not over ten minutes, that was for certain. She took the time to turn around and gasped. The mansion seemed to have disappeared in the swirling, thick snow. She should have been able to see it from this distance, but it was completely obliterated by the storm. Resuming her way, she breathed a quick, silent prayer that she wouldn't get lost between the mansion and her own home. That could be dangerous, and it could happen. They were just far enough removed from Nowaupeton proper that she might wander around for hours in the storm, never seeing anyplace for shelter.

Lowering her head, Margaret pushed ahead into the seething, white maelstrom.

Emil smiled evilly. If Margaret were out of the picture, he'd feel so much more relaxed than he had recently. The cause of his unrest had to be the woman. Everything else was normal. They went to bed, satisfying each other's needs whenever Emil desired. A whore could be had for money when he needed that sort of release in the future. At best, Margaret was a convenience who had fulfilled her purpose as far as Emil was concerned.

It would be much better if she didn't come back. In fact, it would be more convenient if she didn't make it home today. It would be the best solution for Emil LaMotte if Margaret Woodless simply died today.

Margaret's head spun, confused. Was she walking in circles? She couldn't remember spotting one recognizable landmark since she had walked away from the mansion. How long ago had that been? It seemed like hours. She was chilled, her arms and legs quickly growing numb from the bitter cold of the storm. And her face had no feeling in it at all.

She continued walking, automatically pushing one foot after the other, through the deepening snow. Her breath puffed in short gasps.

Then the stabbing pain struck, not unlike a hot, searing poker being plunged into her chest. Margaret managed a short high-pitched scream. What was wrong? What was happening to her? Her left arm felt even more numb than before, and her head spun crazily. The storm intensified, and she felt cut off from everything in the world. The agony shot even deeper into her chest, and her breath refused to leave her body. She gasped for air and saw her dead husband's face smiling at her from a boiling white nimbus. She desperately reached out to him for solace, for comfort, for succor, but he merely smiled at her as if waiting for something to happen.

Her daughter's face came into view, rapidly passing through her years from childhood to the rather plain young woman of 22 that she was at the time.

Margaret heard a growl come from someplace then suddenly realized it was she who was growling when Emil LaMotte had formed in her mind's eye. He was laughing at her. Why would he do something like that? She envisioned the two of them, naked, making love, writhing together, sweat glistening on their bodies. She had always enjoyed his passionate ardor but now for some inexplicable reason, she felt hatred toward Emil. It grew in its intensity until every ounce of remaining energy she possessed was focused in a loathing revulsion toward him.

Her head spun, and her chest burned as if on fire. The numbness in her arms spread to the rest of her body and legs, and she stood perfectly still for a long moment before collapsing in a snow drift.

The wind howled through the trees, and for an instant the snow cleared, revealing the small Woodless house not more than 20 feet from where Margaret lay.

The gale increased, and for a long moment the voice of the raging storm sounded like a sinister laugh winding through the hills and trees.

March 20, 1975

Tricia Woodless looked around at the splendor of the LaMotte mansion. Her mother had often told her how beautiful the house was, but Margaret had never done justice to it with her descriptions. Tricia had found it strange that Emil LaMotte, her mother's employer, had not come to his housekeeper's funeral last January. That strange bit of behavior hadn't stopped him from paying all the final expenses, and during all of February and now into March, he had continued sending her mother's pay to Tricia. With the last check, he had written a note:

Miss Woodless,
Please come to my home on the 20th of March. I would like to speak to you about several things.
Emil LaMotte

Tricia had seen Emil LaMotte but a few times while her mother was in his employ and had always felt in awe of the man. The last time had been almost five years before.

When she had rung the doorbell, he had answered, shown her to the library and promptly excused himself.

Now she sat, waiting for his return. She wondered what he wanted. Perhaps to extend his condolences? But this was well after the fact. She wondered why he hadn't been present for the wake or the funeral service.

A tiny sound behind her brought her upright from her chair.

"Stay seated, Miss Woodless," Emil said.

Easing herself back into the overstuffed chair, she looked up at him. He was even more handsome than she remembered, and he looked as if he hadn't aged a second during the intervening time. She followed him with her eyes, as he crossed the room to sit in the leather chair that was almost opposite her.

"You have no idea how very much the death of your mother has affected me," he said quietly, studying her face.

She nodded. She wanted to ask why he hadn't been present at her burial, if that were true. Instead, she bit her tongue. It would be impertinent of her to ask such things. After all, he had continued sending her mother's pay, and Tricia had needed every cent of it to continue running their small household. While Emil had been generous, the pay itself was not that large an amount.

Tricia looked up to find an air of compassion about the man and she relaxed. "It was most unexpected," she managed weakly. It sounded so stilted, so unreal. She wanted to cry out but elected to continue speaking to him instead. The priest hadn't been all that much comfort to her, and she had no one else with whom she could talk about the untimely death of her mother. Untimely? Wasn't death always untimely? Certainly it was seldom welcomed even by those who were ready to die. The human animal was tough and would survive if at all possible, but her mother hadn't had the chance to fight for her life. She had died of a massive heart attack within a few feet of her own front door in a blinding snowstorm.

When she waited for a moment and he didn't

speak, she continued. "I had no idea she had a bad heart, but if she had to die, I'm sure it was the way she'd have wanted to go. She wouldn't have wanted to be a burden to anyone."

"Did she ever say anything to you about her job here with me?" Emil sat back in the chair, bringing his fingers together to form a tent-like shape.

"Not really. She often said how happy she was working for you, Mr. LaMotte."

"I'm glad to hear that she liked her job and was happy at it. I always thought she was even though the subject never came up for discussion between us. Then, too, I couldn't always tell what mood she was in."

Tricia smiled. "I know. I remember how sad and depressed she was when my father died. I was quite young, yet I recognized how unhappy she was."

"Did she love your father very much?"

"I guess she did. She never really talked much about him—once she started her job here." Tricia felt at ease and thought it remarkable that she was able to carry on this conversation with such a wealthy and powerful man and not be the least bit uncomfortable.

"What are your plans now, Miss Woodless?"

Tricia felt taken aback. Why was he suddenly interested in her? She didn't have a job and had always taken care of their home while her mother worked at the mansion. Job opportunities in Nowaupeton were not that plentiful, and most businesses were family owned and operated, not creating much of a job market.

As far as her social life was concerned, it didn't exist. She'd stopped dating since her traumatic date with a schoolteacher from nearby Epburg. He'd been an awful man, all hands, and he had almost raped her. She knew her limitations as far as her own appearance was concerned. She also was realistic enough to understand that she would probably never marry. There weren't that many eligible young men in the vicinity, and even though a lot of college people showed up during the summer months, they seldom paid her any attention when seeing her on the street.

"My . . . my plans? I don't know. I haven't given them much thought."

"How old are you, my dear?"

Startled by his direct manner, Tricia swallowed. "Twenty-two."

"Do you have a boy friend or are you engaged?"

Feeling her face flush, Tricia shook her head and looked away.

"Well," Emil said, laughing a bit, "you won't stay single long."

Tricia turned back to him. He sounded serious when he said that. "But," she said in a voice she thought might be too loud. "I . . . I'm plain. No one will ever want me. I'll probably be an old maid."

Emil laughed heartily. "I doubt that very much. You're quite attractive in a very natural way. I like that in a woman. Perhaps that was why I liked your mother so much. She was pleasant to be around and refreshing to look at, if I may say so."

Tricia nodded. She would never think of contradicting the man. It was not in her nature to argue, especially with an older person. But Emil LaMotte didn't look that much older than she did. She wondered how old he actually was.

"Tell me something, Tricia. May I call you Tricia?"

She nodded demurely.

"Since your mother has passed away, I'm in need of a full-time housekeeper. Would you be interested in taking the job?"

Tricia brightened. "That would be wonderful, Mr. LaMotte. I had no idea what to do. I'm not trained for any sort of office work or anything outside the home. It really would be wonderful if I could have the job."

"Then consider it yours. I never broached the subject to your mother since I knew she wanted to be at home with you at night, but there's no reason for you stay in that house now—by yourself, that is. You can sell it and move in here. There's a lovely room upstairs that I'm sure you would enjoy. You could have the run of the house, so to speak, and treat it as your home, assuming you work out well and we like each other."

Tricia felt like shouting for joy.

The next day she moved in, after listing her property with a realtor. She never stepped back inside the small house again.

June, 1975

Tricia stood in front of the full-length mirror at the end of the upstairs hallway. She couldn't understand it. Since she had moved into the mansion in March, she felt her appearance was changing—and for the better. She felt most pleased with the way she looked. Her cheeks seemed a bit more drawn, and with the shadowed effect the hollow gave to her face, she looked most exotic. When she piled her hair up on top of her head, she smiled. It was a stunning way for her to fix it. She'd work on it.

"I like that very much," Emil said, stepping from the master bedroom.

Tricia instantly blushed and stuttered, "I . . . I'm very sorry, sir. I shouldn't be fooling with my hair when I'm supposed to be working. It won't happen again."

"I'm sorry to hear that, Tricia. I rather enjoyed seeing you fool with your hair like that." He stepped closer. "Don't change because you think I'm angry. I'm not."

He turned and walked away. Tricia breathed a sigh of relief and, after sneaking one more peek at her reflection, hurried into the master bedroom to ready it for Mr. LaMotte's retirement that night.

August, 1975

Tricia held the sponge up, slowly squeezing

it and letting the water run down her breasts. The rivulets cascaded downward, plunging from her nipples to the water below. The day had been hot and muggy and the cool bath was her reward for the hard work she'd done.

When the door suddenly opened, she sat, unable to move or tear her eyes from those of Emile LaMotte who stood equally still.

"I'm sorry," she said. "I didn't know you wanted to bathe as well."

"Forgive *me*, Tricia," he said pulling his robe about himself. "I'm the one who should beg you for forgiveness. I should have knocked."

Tricia had caught sight of his penis before he closed his robe. The mere glimpse had fascinated her. Still a virgin, she had found herself wondering more and more each day what it would be like to be with a gentle man, especially a man like her employer. A shudder ran through her for an instant when she thought of that schoolteacher. Thank God, her mother had arrived home when she did. She'd never been close to a man since, but now she found nothing wrong with her thoughts since she was no longer a child. And she was single, as was her employer. She wondered if he'd ever been married.

She struggled to stand in the long tub.

Emil remained in the doorway, a smile quivering on his full lips.

She wished he'd at least turn away.

"You know, Tricia, you're a most attractive woman."

Standing upright in the tub, she reached for

her towel and wrapped it around herself. "I . . . I am?" She couldn't believe her ears. He was so handsome that she felt he could have any woman he wanted, and here he was, telling her how nice she looked. And she was naked.

He stepped farther into the room.

Tricia remained standing in the tub and didn't resist when he reached out, lifting her by the armpits from the water. Gently lowering her to the floor, he pulled her close and his robe fell open as her towel slipped away.

She thrilled to his embrace and lifted her head when he touched her chin with one finger. When they kissed, Tricia felt jolts of electricity flow through her body as his tongue probed and searched her mouth. When his penis bobbed to life and touched her lower belly above the line of pubic hair, she wrapped her arms around his neck, offering herself to him.

Lifting her up, he spun her about and positioned her against the small commode. He gently probed her throbbing vagina with the tip of his erect throbbing penis. A soft moan escaped her lips, and he drove it into her body, ripping her hymen. A soft squeal of pain punctuated her moan, and he began his rhythmic assault. When he came, she writhed with the pleasure she felt from the warm intrusion of his semen gushing into her body. Her own sense of fulfullment spiraled, searching for the center of her physical being but failing to locate it.

When he finished, he held her tightly, and

once he withered and died within her, he pulled back. "Are you all right?" he asked quietly.

She nodded. "Yes."

Picking her up, he carried her to the room next to the master bedroom and opened the door. After they entered, he lay her on the bed and sat down next to her.

"Remember what I'm going to say. What we just did was fine. We can do it again and again. We can satisfy each other's needs in this way, but do not think you own me. You don't. No one does. No one ever will. If you become possessive or try to control me, you will pay and pay dearly. Do you remember?"

Tricia nodded, her eyes wide. What was he talking about? Control him? Possess him? Own him? She had no such intentions. Besides, what could he do to her even if she did try something like that? The worst would be to fire her. She'd enjoyed the sex they'd just had despite the initial pain she'd experienced. She wanted more. She didn't want speeches or threats or promises. She wanted more of his rock-hard penis in her body.

Reaching up she pulled him down to her. She kissed him deeply, exploring his mouth in detail. Her hand ran down the full length of his body to find his penis jerking to life once more.

She smiled.

October, 1980

Emil finished shaving and examined his face

in the mirror. He still couldn't fathom what had happened to him over the years. Yes, he knew the book was responsible, but how and why had it affected him in the way it had? He looked 50, if that. He knew how old he actually was. 90. He was 90 years old and as virile as a man of 25 or so. He could fuck Tricia anytime he wanted and satisfy her. She was only 27. If she had any idea that her occasional bed partner had been on earth for almost a full century, she'd die of heart failure like her mother had, and it wouldn't have to be induced as it had been with Margaret.

But today he had to do something he'd thought about for a long time. He had called an attorney, whom he had never met, and talked with him at length yesterday about his holdings, his money, his property and the fact that he had no known heirs. Though the lawyer had almost begged him to come to his office, Emil had steadfastly refused, suggesting instead that he write out his wishes for dispersing his property and wealth and have someone witness his signature. The last part had been the attorney's idea since the letter with the information contained therein would act as a will until a formal instrument could be drawn up. Emil had agreed and spent most of the night making notes about different details he wanted to include.

Once he finished breakfast, he would set about the task.

Emil looked up from his writing. He was

almost finished. It was the only aspect of this whole situation he didn't like. Had he gone to the lawyer's office, the lawyer would have asked him his age and where his birth certificate could be found. Then he'd have to tell him how old he actually was and the attorney would probably throw him out of the office for not being truthful. At least he could trust Tricia to witness his signature and have the will drawn up without meeting the attorney.

Emil closed his eyes for a moment to rest them.

Money held in trust. Property held in trust. Make all efforts to find any living heirs to enable them to partake in the fruits of his good fortune. Spare no expense in locating his son, Edgar William LaMotte, or his heirs in the event of Edgar's demise. If after a suitable length of time, not to be less than 10 years, and no evidence of living heirs to the estate of Emil LaMotte is found, all property is to be sold and converted into cash with the exception of the LaMotte mansion. All monies appropriated from said sale of properties will be placed in trust for Patricia Woodless, who will receive the mansion and all its contents, including the books in the library.

Emil rubbed his forehead. It hurt again. Ever since yesterday, after talking with the lawyer on the phone for hours, his head had hurt and he felt sick. Feeling sick was almost a new experience for Emil since he had enjoyed nothing but excellent health since finding the

137

book. He smiled ruefully. The book had done it all, and now, for some reason he could not understand, he felt almost compelled to write a will.

No matter. He was finished with it and it had to be signed and witnessed.

"Tricia?" He called out loudly.

In seconds, she walked into the library, her sandy blonde hair flowing around her shoulders. "Yes sir?" she said quietly.

"I want you to witness my signature on this letter. Will you do that?"

She watched as Emil wrote his name at the bottom of the legal-sized paper on which he'd written his will. He had written in a phrase identifying the witness and left a line for the witnessing signature as well.

He handed her the pen, and she leaned over the desk. After writing her name, acknowledging the fact that Emil LaMotte had indeed signed the paper, she stood and returned his pen.

"Will that be all, Mr. LaMotte?"

"That's all for right now. Go to the room next to the master bedroom and wait for me, if you would. You may as well undress. I'll be back in a few minutes."

Tricia turned and left the library, hurrying to the second floor.

Emil picked up the paper after she'd left and folded it, placing it in the envelope along with the letter he'd already written. After sealing it and affixing postage to it, he stood and left the room.

He walked in a slow, almost lethargic gait toward the road where the mailbox stood like a silent sentry guarding the driveway.

His head still hurt and his stomach seemed upset as well. He hoped a romp with Tricia in bed would take his mind off his ills.

After placing the envelope inside and standing the metal flag up to alert the mailman that there was outgoing mail in the box, he turned and hurried back toward the mansion, a smile twisting his lips as he anticipated the pleasure he'd receive from Tricia. Behind him he could hear the postman driving up to the box and stopping. He'd get the mail later, once he and Tricia finished.

Starting up the steps, he stopped, rubbed his forehead and sighed. That felt somewhat better.

Then Emil LaMotte slowly evaporated and disappeared.

CHAPTER NINE

September, 1989

Rob squirmed on the couch in the waiting room of Joseph Zwotney's law offices. He wondered what the attorney might want of him. As far as he knew lawyers didn't seek business in this manner. Could it be that someone was going to sue him? But for what reason?

Suddenly, Sherry's face crashed into his mind's eye. Of course. She had to be responsible. It had to be Sherry's first step at seeking a divorce. There couldn't be any other reason.

His forehead puckered. But, if that were the case, then why did the men who approached

JOHN TIGGES

him outside the apartment ask if he'd ever heard of a man called Emil LaMotte? Maybe he had misunderstood them. Maybe they had asked if he were Emil LaMotte and they had the name wrong at first. His frown deepened. That wasn't the way it happened at all. They had asked, without finding out his name, if he knew an Emil LaMotte. Then they had asked him what his father's name was. Rob shook his head. They hadn't even asked what his first name was.

Rob slumped in his seat. None of it made sense, especially last night. When he finally got home, after his encounter with the two strangers in the street, he had found the apartment empty. At first, he hadn't been upset. Jeremy could have been at the nearby playground. As for Sherry not being there, it wasn't unusual. Sometimes she had to work late, and sometimes she would stop and buy the makings for dinner at the supermarket a few blocks away.

He had waited and waited. By seven o'clock, he was concerned and worried. Where were they? Why weren't they home? He paced around the small apartment, cursing under his breath one minute and the next fervently muttering a prayer to a God with whom he was all too unfamiliar.

His path through the apartment became the same. Around the living room once before going to the bedroom where he walked to the far side of the bed before retracing his steps

142

back to the living room. Then he walked to the kitchen where he passed the sink and the counter with its single cupboard hanging from the wall above it. When he returned to the living room, he would go to the double window, which overlooked the street below, just to see if perhaps his wife and son were crossing the street.

When he didn't see them, he'd begin another turn around the apartment. It was dark by the time he felt his sense of panic growing. Where were they? At eight o'clock, he sat down heavily at the small kitchen table, his hands shaking. Had something happened to them? But how could that be? They hadn't been together—at least, not that he knew. Maybe Sherry had come home early and taken Jeremy shopping. Then, if that was what had happened, something most certainly could have happened to both of them.

He got up and began his route once more and stopped automatically at the front window. The street below was deserted. Where were they? Turning, he went to the bedroom after passing the couch. He stopped short just before entering. For the first time, he noticed something missing. Jeremy's clothing was always piled up at the end of the couch where he slept. He turned and stared. The clothes were gone.

He turned once more and ran to the bedroom and threw open the closet. Transfixed, he stood staring at the empty hangers. His own clothes hung to one side, but Sherry's clothing was gone as well. She'd left. She'd left and taken Jeremy with her. He didn't mind so much if she went, but Jeremy was his, too. She had no right simply to take off like that. Not a word. No note. Nothing that Rob could see. She'd just left. Where were they staying for the night? Had she thought about leaving for a long time? Sherry wasn't a stupid woman. She had to have planned it for sometime.

Rob ground his teeth, his anger seething. She'd planned it all along, and here he was working his ass off, trying to click with some sales and feeling worthless when he didn't. Just when things seemed to be turning around for him, she takes off without as much as saying goodbye or you can reach us here or there if you want. Well, he wanted to reach them. He wanted to punch Sherry in the face and hug Jeremy. Maybe he'd find out where they lived and take his son away from Sherry, just the way she'd taken him away from his father.

His sense of despair mounting, Rob went to the kitchen and sat down. Cradling his head in his arms, he tried to focus on the pattern in the Formica tabletop but he was too close. Instead, he closed his eyes and pictured Jeremy's face. His rumpled hair, the lonely look that generally governed his face. Rob wondered what his son was lonely for. Companionship? Boys his own age who lived nearby? There were none, and those who usually did live in the neighborhoods where Rob would take his family to live were scum. The kids were into gangs and dope and running to all hours of the night and dropping out of school at the first chance. Rob didn't want that for his son, but he couldn't do better for him with the situation the way it was most of the time. Sherry didn't want that for their son, either. Rob knew that, but he also knew that Sherry blamed him for their lack of success and money and poor living conditions.

When he thought of Sherry again, he clenched his fist and pounded the table. Jeremy suddenly crowded out the anger Rob felt for his wife, when the talk he and his son had had that morning came back. What had he said? After Jeremy had asked with whom he'd live if his parents got divorced, Rob had reassured his son that he had nothing to worry about. Rob felt the lump in his throat grow until he choked back the sob that had been building. Giving vent to his emotions, tears poured from his eyes. For a long time he sat, head on his forearms, leaning across the table while his agony poured out.

Spent, he stood up and fumbled for a handkerchief. Reaching in his coat pocket, he felt something and pulled it out. It was the card the men downstairs had given him. He looked at it through his tears, the printing slithering about, refusing to stay in focus long enough to read. When he found his handkerchief, he wiped the tears away and blew his nose. *Joseph Zwotney, Attorney-at-Law* leaped off the card at him.

A smile had crossed Rob's lips. Maybe this

attorney could devise a plan to get Jeremy back from Sherry.

"Mr. LaMotte?"

Rob's thoughts snapped back to the waiting room. "Yes?"

"Mr. Zwotney can see you now. This way, please." The shapely young woman turned, leading Rob down a short hallway and stopped at an open door.

"Mr. Zwotney? This is Robert LaMotte."

Zwotney stood, coming around the desk and thrusting a hand out in front of him. "Mr. LaMotte? Come in. You have no idea how happy I am to see you."

Rob took the proffered hand and sat down in the chair the lawyer indicated. Why would this man, whom he didn't know, be happy to meet him?

"I suppose you're wondering what I want to talk over with you. Am I right?"

"The question did pass through my mind a couple of times," Rob said, keeping a defensive tone in his voice.

"Well, sir, I've been more or less working on a case for another attorney up in Guttenberg. He's been trying to settle an estate for the past nine years and as a last resort contacted attorneys within a thousand miles of his place to help locate the heirs to an Emil LaMotte. Have you ever heard of him?"

Rob shook his head. "No sir. The men who talked to me asked the same question. Who is he?"

"We don't know yet, at least where you're concerned. How about the name Edgar LaMotte? Do you know him?"

Rob nodded. "My father's name was Edgar. Is that important?"

"You bet it is. Can you locate your birth certificate and other proof of your identity?"

"Such as?"

"Social security records. Marriage certificate. Army discharge papers if you were in the service. Driver's license. Any other sort of license that will verify your name."

"I know who I am. Why do I suddenly have to prove it?"

"Most of the time," Zwotney said, "people can get away with one or two pieces of proof, but in a case like this, I'm afraid the court is going to insist upon a lot of it."

Rob stared at the man. "The court? What's this all about?"

"There's a considerable amount of money and property at stake. They aren't about to take someone's word about identification. Do you follow me?"

Rob slowly nodded. Was this actually happening? Could this be real? Was he having a dream of some sort, or was someone playing a nasty trick on him? He cleared his throat. "How much money are you talking about?"

"You have to understand. I'm not the attorney in this case. I'm only helping to locate the heirs. I don't know specifics of the case, but I do know that there are millions involved."

Rob's tongue stuck to the roof of his mouth.

147

After a herculean effort he managed, "Mi-millions?"

Zwotney nodded. "Do you know of any other people by the name of LaMotte? People who might be related to this Emil LaMotte? Do you know the whereabouts of Edgar LaMotte?"

Rob told him of his father's mental illness and that they hadn't heard from him in over 35 years. "My mother, I believe, had him declared legally dead shortly before she died herself. As to other LaMottes, there's my wife and son. Beyond that I don't know of any."

"It seems that Emil LaMotte would have been your grandfather. From what the other attorney told me, I gather that he had but one son—Edgar. His will stipulated that all effort be made to locate his son, Edgar, and any of his heirs or other relatives."

"When did my grandfather die?" Rob asked. It seemed peculiar for him to use the term "grandfather." He'd never known one in his life. In fact, he'd found it strange when others talked about relatives, since he considered he had none himself.

"Quite some time back. I believe the lawyer in Guttenberg said that he was about ready to throw in the towel and go the alternate route as outlined in the will."

"Alternate route?" Rob asked, narrowing his eyes.

"While no time period was specified, the attorney, Allan Weipert, told me that he was going to execute the will on the tenth anniversary of Emil LaMotte's death. I think that would have been next year."

Rob still felt weak. Millions? His? Was the money all his? He fought to keep from smiling. He wanted to shout from sheer elation in the worst way, but he knew he should remain as calm and passive as possible. He wanted to yell and dance just to release some of the pent-up feelings he knew were inside him. If he were going to be a millionaire, he'd best start acting like one.

"Tell me, Mr. Zwotney, what's my next step?"

"I'll call Mr. Weipert and tell him that I've located you. I'm sure he'll want you to come to Guttenberg."

"Is that where my grandfather lived?"

"No. He lived in a small town called Nowaupeton."

"And that's where my grandfather made his millions?"

"I guess so."

"May I ask you a question?"

Zwotney smiled. "I'm sure you'll have quite a few in time."

"How did you locate me?"

"A private detective from Dubuque who was working for Weipert was visiting his elderly aunt and uncle here in Davenport. He spotted a brochure or something with your name on it. What line of work are you in? Insurance or something, isn't it?"

Rob nodded. Usually he or any of the other salesmen didn't leave their names behind. The operation called for a one-step sales presentation with a lot of pressure exerted on the prospective buyer. If they didn't buy, that was it. Twice recently, when his luck had turned sour, Rob had left his name with prospective buyers, hoping they would call the office and say they'd changed their minds. Now, because he'd broken a rule of the company, he was going to become a millionaire.

"While I'm contacting Mr. Weipert, I'd like you to get together evidence of who you are. Is it all right if I make an appointment for you?"

"For when?" Rob asked.

"Since it's at your convenience, tell me when you'd be able to go to Guttenberg."

"Anytime. Tomorrow? Yes, tomorrow will be fine."

"Can you get your birth certificate and other proof by then?"

"I'll get what I can, and if he needs more, I'll get it."

"That sounds good to me," Zwotney said, leaning forward to pick up his telephone. He told his secretary to contact Weipert and hung the receiver back in its cradle. Standing, he came around the desk and offered his hand to Rob again. "Mr. LaMotte, I'd like to congratulate you on your good fortune. It isn't every day that a person can become a millionaire as you just have."

Rob stood, taking the attorney's hand in his.

He thought his palm was damp with sweat. So what if it was? Goddamnit, he was a million-aire, a fucking millionaire, and he didn't care if he had sweaty palms or not.

"Thank you, Mr. Zwotney."

"Give my girl your home address and where you can be reached. She'll give you Weipert's office address in Guttenberg. Good luck to you."

Rob turned to leave the office and paused at the door. "Thank you, Mr. Zwotney. Thank you very, very much."

After stopping by the insurance office to tell them he was not feeling well, Rob drove to Frank's Place where he hoped he'd find Sherry. If he knew anything, she'd be willing to let bygones by bygones and come back to him.

He parked the old Subaru across the street from the restaurant and hurried over. Since it was almost noon, he wanted to tell Sherry what had happened before the place became too crowded. His spirits fell when he entered, since half the tables and booths were already occupied.

Spotting Sherry near the service station, he walked back to her, passing the cash register where Frank Yearnall sat, waiting for customers to pay their bill.

"Hi. I gotta talk to you," Rob said amiably.

Sherry looked up, startled to see him there. "I haven't got time. I've got orders coming up. Don't make a scene. I'll have my attorney contact you. All right?"

"What? Your attorney? You really want a divorce? You can't be serious."

Sherry picked up a menu and went to greet a woman who had just walked into the restaurant, hurrying away from Rob and leaving him at the service window.

Rather than follow her and make a scene, he waited, knowing she had to come back to the window.

When she came back she said, "I'm as serious about this as you are about being a failure in life."

"Order up," the cook said from the kitchen through the service window.

Sherry looked at the ticket and picked up the tray and moved away.

"That's just it. I'm not a goddamn failure anymore. I'm going to be—" He stopped. Why tell the whole world? He'd wait until she came back.

"You're going to be a what? A bigger joke?" she asked when she came back. "I wish you'd get out of here. Frank is staring at us. I don't want to get fired. I can't afford it. Maybe you can manage without working, but I can't."

Rob grabbed her by the shoulders, turning her to face him. "Listen to me, goddamnit! I'm inheriting some money. We can make it now. Better than you could ever imagine."

Sherry stared at him for a long moment before speaking. "No, it won't work, Rob. You're making it up, just to get me back. It won't work, damnit. Some people are meant to be successful and some are supposed to be failures. No matter how you cut it, you're a failure. Even if what you're saying is true, you'll only piss the money away in no time and be right back where you are now."

Rob glowered at her. "That's what you know. I'm going to—"

"What's going on here?" Frank asked, walking up. "Tell him to get the hell out of here, Sherry. I assume this is your husband?"

Sherry nodded and turned to Rob. "Please leave. Now. You're only going to get me in trouble and cost me my job. I said I'll have my attorney call you at the office. All right?"

"No! It's not all right. Quit your job. Right now. Quit it."

"You are crazy, aren't you?" She grinned broadly, a look of contempt on her face.

Rob turned to glare at Frank and then turned back to Sherry. "I'll be able to buy this guy out of my pocket change when I get my inheritance," he whispered hoarsely.

"Rob, please," Sherry said quietly.

"Couldn't you hear me?" he asked, raising his voice. "I'm sorry," he yelled, "I said I'll be able to buy this jerk—"

"That's it," Frank said, grabbing Rob by the shoulder and pushing Sherry back out of the way. He whirled him about and pushed him toward the door.

"Where's Jeremy?" Rob yelled at Sherry, turning to face Frank who blocked him from going to his wife.

"He's in school where he belongs. I'll see to it that he makes something of himself and not be a bum like his old man." Sherry turned away, breaking into tears.

"Come on, scum," Frank said, pushing Rob toward the door.

"Don't push me, Yearnell. Don't push me."

Frank pushed him by the shoulders again. "Get out of here and don't ever come back."

"Don't touch me," Rob shouted and threw a punch at Frank. It went wild but Frank reacted instinctively and counterpunched with a right to Rob's cheek.

The blow caught him off guard, and he staggered backward toward the door. Catching himself at the door frame, he shook his fist at Frank.

"You bastard! I'll get you for this. Sherry?" he shouted. "You haven't heard the end of this. My attorney will get ahold of you—bitch!"

When Rob turned to leave, Frank helped him, shoving him through the entranceway once the door was opened.

Rob caught his foot on the threshold and fell forward, sprawling onto the sidewalk. In the background he could hear the relieved laughter of the customers, all of whom had witnessed the scene. They were laughing at him. Him! A millionaire! What right did they have? None! None, goddamnit! He'd show that cunt he'd married who was boss, and that asshole boss of hers wouldn't have a nickel left once Rob

LaMotte got finished with him.

Slowly getting to his feet, Rob brushed himself off and crossed the street to the Subaru. After getting in, he thought for a moment, tapping his fingers on the steering wheel.

First things first. He had to get to Guttenberg and claim his inheritance. Once he had the money, he'd show Sherry who the hell was successful and important. He'd teach her a lesson or two about respect and how to treat a millionaire.

He smiled at the thought and started the engine. He was a goddamned, fucking millionaire.

CHAPTER TEN

October, 1989

Rob's Subaru wound through the hills of northwest Iowa along county highway C30 toward Nowaupeton and the Mississippi River. A silly, half-grin held his face in a frozen, clownlike expression. He was truly a millionaire. He owned over 1000 acres of land, most of the businesses in Nowaupeton and what was more than likely the largest house in Blayton County. He pictured the mansion resting on its hilltop perch, overlooking the river and valley wherein Nowaupeton nestled. The house itself was a magnificent example of Queen Anne style architecture, and he'd been quite startled to learn that a housekeeper went with it. He had yet to meet Tricia Woodless, who had been on her first vacation since being employed by his grandfather. Allan Weipert, the attorney, had insisted she take one before the new owner moved in.

Rob smiled broadly. New owner! It had such a nice ring to it. When he considered what it was he owned, his smile widened even more. Weipert had shown him through the mansion, and Rob had to admit he remembered little of what he had seen. The first time in the lawyer's office, everything seemed to have been mixed up. Weipert talked so long, listing the properties he owned, that within a few minutes Rob had been totally confused.

"I realize all of this is brand new to you, Mr. LaMotte," Weipert had said, adjusting his glasses and staring at Rob over the rims.

"It's just that I've never had much in life," Rob said, his voice cracking uncharacteristically.

"I appreciate that, sir. In time, you'll become acquainted with the businesses and other holdings."

"How much is there to running these businesses?" Rob was concerned about that sort of thing. All he knew was selling. He knew nothing about buying stock for a store or keeping books or managing a business.

"You're in luck there, Mr. LaMotte. The way your grandfather had everything set up was quite unique. He did nothing where the businesses were involved. He acquired them by buying up concerns and then hiring the former owners to run the establishments. If he opened a new business he hired experienced people to run it for him. I'm not too certain if your grandfather had the expertise to run a business as such. Ah, no offense meant by that."

Rob nodded. "None taken. I'm just happy to hear that I won't have to be making any sort of business decisions." He relaxed. If that were the case, then all he had to do was take in the money and live a life of leisure.

He looked up to find Weipert studying him. There was one thing he had to bring himself to ask. Coughing to clear his throat, he said, "How . . . how much money is there? In cash, that is."

Weipert stood up and walked to one of the windows overlooking Riverfront Drive and the Mississippi River beyond. "That's something that's bothered me ever since I received your grandfather's will and letter. Once it became apparent that something had happened to him, I became involved. I've searched in every conceivable place—banks, credit unions, savings and loans—and I've gone through the house with the housekeeper, but I found nothing, not a single bank book or check book of any sort. There's not a safe in the house or any sort of secret hiding place, at least that I could find."

"You mean there isn't any money?"

"There's income from the businesses, of course. Apparently your grandfather didn't believe too much in banks. Of course, you'll have money coming in every month but there isn't a lump sum of any sort of which I'm aware."

Rob's face darkened. "How much comes in each month?"

"That varies according to the season. During the summer months, the income shoots up to an astronomical figure, considering the location of Nowaupeton. I believe it exceeds well over one hundred thousand dollars per month then. When the crops are sold, a considerable amount comes in at that time. You see, your grandfather always made the agreements to benefit him first. He got his cut or percentage off the top, without expenses."

"About how much per year?"

"Depending on the variables, I would say that there's at least four to eight hundred thousand per year."

"What's been done with the money since my grandfather's disappearance?"

"That money is available, naturally. I've invested it in certificates of deposit and Treasury notes and bills. It's all quite safe."

"How much?" Rob had to know. There must be a large amount if around a half million a year came in.

"The total is," Weipert said, picking up a sheet of paper, "$4,752,568. That's the principle, and the amount will be higher when the interest is calculated. Does that satisfy you?"

Rob nodded, his mouth dry. "Will I have

money now, you know, for expenses and what have you?"

"If you're short of funds, I can arrange a letter of credit at the bank, if you'd like. Say, fifty thousand. Would that be satisfactory?"

Rob looked up. "That . . . that'll be fine, Mr. Weipert." He bit his lower lip to keep from laughing like an idiot. He'd never had more than a few hundred dollars at any one time in his entire life. And when he did, he usually spent it foolishly. Now, he had thousands—no millions at his command.

He looked up and said, "Can you handle a divorce case?"

"Of course. Yours?"

Rob nodded and launched into a recitation of the incidents that had led up to Sherry's moving out with their son the night before talking with Zwotney. He related the scene as it had unfolded in the restaurant and how the owner had thrown him out.

"Has she begun any action yet?"

Rob shook his head. "Not that I know of."

"Well, it was a bad move on her part, wasn't it?"

Rob agreed but looked closely at the attorney, a puzzled expression contorting his face.

Weipert smiled. "Let me explain to you why that's the case. I'm sure you'd like to beat her to the punch, so to speak, and file first. Am I right?"

Rob nodded. "Isn't that the right thing to

do?"

"Not necessarily. You see, if she files first and sues you, the judge should be more sympathetic to your situation, in light of the fact that you went to her and told her of your inheritance. On the other hand, if you were to sue her for divorce, it would appear that you'd be trying to dump her because of the fact that you now have money. Do you follow me?"

"I understand what you're saying." Rob threw his head back and laughed for a moment and then just as quickly stopped. "I'd like to fight for my son, however, no matter who sues who."

"Of course. That would seem to make sense, since you'll have the means to do more for him. It might be a case of joint custody but I'm certain you won't be shut out of his life."

Rob nodded and fell silent.

Picking up on his sudden change of mood, Weipert said, "Is something else bothering you?"

"It's nothing really. I was just wondering about my grandfather. What was he like? How did he die? I never knew him and all of a sudden, because of him, I'm rich."

Weipert returned to his chair. "I never met him. As a result, I can't tell you anything about him. As to how he died, no one knows. There were many stories that I heard about him but none of them seem to make sense. For instance, most people who knew him claimed he looked to be about fifty years old or so about the time he disappeared. But records seem to indicate he was around ninety at the time."

"I know he disappeared, but what do you mean by it?"

"Just that. He walked out to mail something. I happen to believe it was the letter to me with the witnessed provisions for his will. He started back to the house but never went inside. The housekeeper became concerned after a while, and in time a wide scale search was made. No trace of him was ever found."

"What about the housekeeper? Was she investigated?"

"Completely. Her mother worked in the same position until her untimely death. Then Miss Woodless went to work for your grandfather."

"I suppose she's trustworthy?"

"Considering that she was to inherit the entire estate from your grandfather if there were no heirs, I'd say Emil thought quite highly of her. She's maintained the mansion and has been responsible for it and the upkeep of the grounds since he . . . well, died. I had him declared legally dead after seven years."

Rob narrowed his eyes. "And no one suspects her of anything, even though she was to inherit the estate?"

"I'm certain she doesn't know anything about the contents of the will your grandfather drew up and sent to me. He said as much in his letter that accompanied it. She's never seen it, other than to witness Emil's signature at which time the paper was covered, except for the bottom.

You're the third person, other than Emil and myself, to know about that provision of the will."

"I see," Rob said, slowly nodding his head. "Would you recommend I keep her on as housekeeper?"

"Definitely. At least until you get to know the house."

Following that first meeting in the office, Weipert had taken Rob to the bank and set up a letter of credit in the amount of $50,000, with a direct order to Rob not to use it for any expenditure without Weipert's approval. The attorney explained that he didn't want Rob to be able to display any sudden show of wealth to his wife. After they left the bank, the attorney had taken Rob to Nowaupeton and showed him his holdings before going to the mansion.

Weipert's last instruction had stayed with Rob all the way back to Davenport when he drove home. "By no means go anywhere near your wife. You might accidentally or even purposely tell her just how much you stand to gain from your grandfather's estate."

The whole scene that had taken place in Yearnall's restaurant, which ended with Rob's being thrown out, had scarred his memory. Sherry would pay dearly for being responsible for Rob's embarrassment and humiliation. Still, he had eventually agreed with the lawyer's advice and managed to stay away from Frank's Place, which was the only place he knew where he might run into Sherry.

Five days after returning to Davenport, he

finished his job and checked out without so much as a backward glance. He'd called Weipert and found out that Tricia Woodless had returned. He had decided to be the final judge on retaining the woman's services and was anxious to begin the life of ease and plenty he envisioned for himself.

Rob braked the old Subaru and turned into the lane that wound up the hill toward the mansion. When the car was pointed directly at the building, he stopped. From his vantage point, he could see the entire front of the house. A wide porch stretched across the front, and he envisioned himself sitting there, sipping a drink before dinner. If he remembered correctly, the house had appeared to be in an excellent state of repair. Since he and Weipert hadn't spent much time examining the house, he wanted to do that as soon as possible. Better yet, he'd hire someone to make a thorough examination and report back. That's the way a moneyed person would handle it.

Easing out the clutch, he drove ahead slowly. The car jerked but continued climbing the ascending drive. That was something else that needed to be remedied soon. He'd get a new car but keep the Subaru to drive to Davenport, just in case Sherry might see him. If he did that, she'd never suspect anything of his new wealth. She'd had her chance to share in it, but she elected to allow Frank Yearnall the opportunity to protect her instead.

He pulled into the horseshoe-shaped driveway and got out. A chill wrapped itself about him when he mounted the steps. Was this the place where his grandfather had disappeared? Had he actually disappeared, or had he merely gone away and left a mystery behind? Rob frowned. Maybe something more devious had happened to Emil LaMotte.

He reached out to ring the bell but stepped back when the door opened.

Tricia Woodless stood in the entrance, dwarfed by the large oak door. "Mr. LaMotte?"

Rob nodded. "Yes, I'm Robert LaMotte."

"Welcome home."

Rob couldn't control the smile spreading across his face. He felt as if he were watching himself in a movie wherein he played the role of a rich man returning home. Wasn't that exactly what he was?

"You're Miss Woodless?"

"Yes," she said, bowing her head slightly to the right. "You may call me Tricia if you'd like." She stepped aside to allow him to enter.

Rob caught a delicate scent of perfume when he brushed past her and entered the front hallway.

After she closed the door, they stood looking at each other for several minutes, and then they both laughed at their embarrassment.

"Did you have a nice vacation, Tricia?"

"Yes sir, very nice. It wasn't long enough. Mr. Weipert had said I should take a longer one, but since it was my first ever, I thought it best to start with just a short one."

Rob mentally frowned. He'd never had a

vacation in his life either. Well, that was another thing that would be remedied soon.

"Where did you go?" Rob turned to study the paintings hanging in the hallway. He wondered if they might be worth a lot of money. An elaborate, obviously old, hall mirror with hangers for hats and coats caught his attention. Antiques. He vaguely recalled seeing a lot of antiques when he and Weipert had toured the house. Such artifacts along with the paintings would be worth thousands. He stopped himself. He didn't have to worry any longer about money. Thousands indeed. He had millions! According to Weipert, he'd have more money coming in than he could ever spend. Was he questioning the attorney? Why should he doubt him?

"It was my very first ride in a plane. I went to Florida and sailed on a cruise ship for three days. It was just heavenly. Just like the *Love Boat*." She closed her eyes, reliving the romantic interlude she'd enjoyed, even though she'd been too shy to speak to any of the men for more than a few minutes at a time.

"Would you show me the house, Tricia?"

She nodded. "Certainly, sir. Follow me." She turned and led him down the hallway toward a set of double doors that stood open.

They entered a huge dining room that was furnished with a large oval table lined with six chairs along each side plus an armed chair at each end. A built-in breakfront lined one wall, which also had a service window of frosted glass that Rob assumed opened into the kitchen for the convenient serving of food. More paintings lined the walls and complemented the buffet opposite the breakfront. A conservatory at the far end of the room held one plant, a gigantic fern, which balanced on an oak pedestal.

The kitchen was plain, and Tricia explained that as far as she knew the room had been planned for a hired cook. As a result, it held few refinements as such. After inspecting the butler's pantry, they returned to the entrance hallway and went to the parlor. Overstuffed chairs and wood-trimmed sofas were placed about the room. A large fireplace covered with dark cherry wood dominated the drawing room at the far end.

After Rob had perused the parlor and its furnishings for a while, Tricia led him to the library across the hall.

While walking about, admiring the books and wall hangings, he said, "What was my grandfather like? I never knew him."

"He was a most remarkable man," she said, her eyes brightening. "He was very rich—and very generous. Why, he even continued sending my mother's pay for several months after she passed away. Then he offered me the job and had me move in to run the house."

She continued talking in glowing terms about Emil LaMotte, and Rob turned to look at her several times, only to find her staring into space with a wistful expression on her pretty face while she extolled the dead man's virtues. He wondered if the woman had been in love with his grandfather. He studied her for several seconds while she continued her praise. She was attractive enough but surely not over 35 years of age or so. Hadn't Weipert said something about his grandfather looking youthful but being close to 90 years of age when he disappeared? That thought still bothered him. How could his grandfather have looked like he was 50 if he actually was around 90? That made no sense at all.

"Tricia?" he said when she finally stopped.

"Yes?"

"How old would you say my grandfather was at the time he disappeared?"

"I'm not the best judge when it comes to determining a person's age, but I would say he was somewhere in his early fifties or so."

"Did you know that records showed him to have been around ninety at the time?"

She shook her head. "I've heard stories like that, but I don't believe them for a minute. He could do things no man that age could do."

Rob intensified his pursuit. "Such as?"

"I'd rather not say. Well," she said, hesitating for an instant, "all right, if you insist. He could go up and down steps every bit as good as me. He was never short of breath from doing anything that was strenuous. He just couldn't have been that old, sir."

"How old do you think I am, Tricia?"

She looked at him closely, as if seeing him

for the first time. A smile came and went for a second time before she said, "I have no idea, sir."

"I'm forty years old. I have no reason to lie. That would mean my father would have to have been born when my grandfather was . . . let's say ten years old, and my dad would have to have been about ten years old or so when I was born. Does that make any sense to you?"

"I know what Mr. LaMotte looked like. He was not ninety years of age. Far from it, sir."

"How long did you know him?"

"I came to work for him when I was twenty-two. He disappeared five years later when I was twenty-seven. Five years, I guess. I never once met him when Mom worked for him."

Rob did some quick addition and determined that Tricia Woodless was around 36 years old. She looked nice, possessing a natural beauty that made cosmetics unnecessary. He thought of his grandfather. What if he actually had been 90 and looked as if he were 50? Why hadn't Rob inherited those genes? He glanced in an oval mirror hanging opposite the library's fireplace. He looked every bit his 40 years.

Turning back to face Tricia, he said, "Let's forget his age for right now, all right? Tell me about the day he disappeared."

She told him the same story that Weipert had related to him when he had first met the lawyer. An ominous silence fell over the room for several minutes when she finished.

Rob coughed to break the quiet. "You liked my grandfather very much, didn't you?"

Tricia dropped her eyes to the oriental rug and nodded. "Very much."

"Would you like to stay on and take care of the household duties for me?"

She looked up. "Aren't you married? Won't your wife want to take care of the house?"

"I'm married right now, but I won't be soon."

"If you think it'd work out, I'd be happy to stay on. This is the only home I've known for the last fourteen years."

"Good. Then it's settled."

Tricia smiled shyly. "I thought you might dismiss me."

"Why?"

"I thought you'd be married, and there wouldn't be a need for me."

"Not so. Of course, you'd have to know my wife to appreciate the situation I'll be getting out of soon."

"Could I be excused, sir?"

"When will I see the rest of the house?"

"I'd like to get the evening's meal under way. I won't be too long, then I can show you the upstairs, if you'd like."

"I'd like that. Go on. I'll stay here in the library and browse among the books while you're busy."

Tricia turned and left. Rob walked over to one of the built-in bookcases. He felt wonderful. He felt like a million bucks. He laughed.

He was a million bucks. He didn't bother
reading the titles on the spines but turned
again, taking in the whole room with a glance.
A leather easy chair caught his eye, and he
walked over to it. Plopping into it, he chuckled.
The sensations running through him quickly
led him from one thought to the next. God bless
grandfather Emil LaMotte. No matter how he
had made his money, Rob was grateful. He
wondered for a split second how the eldest
LaMotte had struck it so rich. Had he done
something wrong or illegal to gain his ends?
Rob doubted that, since the attorney was open
and honest in anything he said about Emil. If
there had been any doubt about the man's
honesty, Rob felt certain the lawyer would have
said something, but nothing had been said.

He jumped when something fell with a loud
smack onto the floor from one of the bookshelves. For an instant he sat, unable to move,
from the sudden shock of noise. Then he slowly
stood.

"Tricia?"

No answer. He was alone.

He walked toward the bookcase, and when
he rounded the library table in the center of
the room, he saw it—a leather-bound book.
Bending down, he picked up the object and
examined it. It was much too heavy to be a
book.

For an instant, he thought it had moved of
its own accord and grasped it in a tighter hold.

Rob turned and went back to the leather chair. Once he was seated, he opened the strange looking object and gasped when he saw what appeared to be golden pages within.

CHAPTER ELEVEN

Rob turned the book over in his hands. He'd never seen anything like it. His expertise when it came to books was virtually nonexistent since the most experience he'd had with books had been only while at school, and he'd dropped out before completing high school. Still, he felt he held something completely different, something totally out of the norm. He'd never heard of a book with golden pages. Who would have made such a thing? The cover appeared to be very old. If he were correct about the age, had it belonged to his grandfather? Possibly forebears, of whom he knew nothing, from the distant past might have owned it at one time.

He leaned back in the easy chair. One by one,

he turned the thick pages. Each one, with the exception of the first or what would have been the title page, had small, raised markings. Leaning forward, he looked closer. Could it be writing? Why not? It was a book, and books had writing in them, didn't they? But it certainly wasn't English. Rob was certain of that. But if it wasn't English, what language could it be? He looked closer. Few of the tiny characters seemed to be repeated. If they were, Rob didn't recognize them immediately.

Once he'd gone through the pages, he turned back to the front, where the single blank page of gold had been. When he looked at it carefully, he saw a scratch in one corner. What he needed was a magnifying glass. With something like that, he could see the markings much better. Perhaps there was one somewhere in the library.

Standing, he crossed over to the library table. He stopped, clutching the book in one hand, almost afraid to breathe. In the center of the table there lay a large magnifying glass. Had it been there all along? He couldn't recall. Still, for some reason, he felt the table had been completely bare, with the exception of the antique, paisley scarf that lay the length of it. He was being foolish. The damned glass had been there all the time. He'd merely overlooked it in his excitement of moving into the mansion.

Laying the book on the table, he picked up the large glass and reopened the cover of the book. Focusing on the first page, he found the scratch to be that and nothing more. Someone might have tested to see if it were actually gold. What else could it be if not gold?

Rob frowned. Maybe it was brass, or copper, or something that only looked like gold. But the weight of the book seemed to say it had to be valuable, and brass or copper wouldn't be that valuable, not the way gold would be.

Moving the glass back and forth to better see the irregular mark, he noted the indentation was of the same color as the surface. Perhaps he should scratch it himself, just to see if the underlying metal would be bright and shiny, like gold. A letter opener that had escaped his notice as well caught his attention, and he picked it up. Digging the point into the surface of the first page, he smiled when he saw the glittering of the bright metal. It had to be gold.

He turned the page and examined the next one. There he found the writing to be raised, as if molten gold had been used to record whatever message the book contained.

He adjusted the glass to better see the writing and suddenly realized there were many repetitions of markings, something that had escaped his unaided eye. Each page held well over 50 lines of the irregular figures. Looking up, Rob frowned. What language could it be, if it actually was a language? Such things usually didn't interest him, but he had seen examples of oriental writings and this didn't resemble anything like that. If he had to put a tag on it, he'd have to say it looked like the meanderings, although orderly and in straight lines, of a drunken worm.

A smile broadened his face at the thought of a drunken worm.

He returned to his chair, taking the glass with him. He wondered if the book were actually gold. It would be worth a handsome price if it were. He shook his head again. There he was, calculating the value of something when the idea shouldn't even enter his mind. So what if it were worth a lot of money? A month ago that would have been important to him. Now it didn't make a whit of difference. He hefted the book in his hand and roughly estimated it to weigh about ten pounds. At the current rate of gold on the market, he was holding a small fortune, but he didn't care. He laughed. It was just one more piece of valuable property he owned.

"Mr. LaMotte? Sir? Dinner will be ready in a few minutes. Would you like a drink or something before you eat?"

Tricia stood shyly in the doorway, looking at Rob but not fixing her eyes on him.

Rob looked up and turned partway around to face her. "What do you have?"

"I'm afraid the supply isn't too large but there is some bourbon and Scotch as well as wine."

"Bring me a little Scotch on ice, Tricia. Thank you for thinking of it. I'm afraid I'm still too excited about moving here and all."

"When will your things be arriving, sir?"

Rob laughed shortly. "I've got everything

with me in the car."

Tricia fixed her full attention on him. "Everything?"

Why should Rob admit to her, his housekeeper, that he'd been a failure all his life? If she thought everything he owned could be loaded into a small, rusty Subaru, she might not respect him the way he wanted. He smiled and stood up to return the magnifying glass to the library table.

"Everything that I wanted to bring along, that is. I . . . ah . . . disposed of the rest."

"I see," she said, dropping her eyes and turning to leave the room. "I'll be right back with your drink."

By the time she returned with the Scotch, Rob had returned the book to the shelf. She left without saying anything and Rob tested the whiskey. It burned at first, and he decided to stock vodka and gin as well. Scotch wasn't his drink and neither, for that matter, was bourbon.

After he finished the drink, Tricia appeared in the doorway once more. "Dinner is served, sir," she said.

Rob carried the empty glass with him, handing it to her as he passed her and went to the dining room. He imagined what Sherry would think if she could see him now and he almost roared with laughter. Here he was, sitting down to a meal in a room three times bigger than their second floor apartment had been, ready to be served by an attractive housekeeper in his own home. His thoughts quickly sobered when he thought of Jeremy. He wished his son were with him to share the experience. Rob silently swore he would make certain that his son would soon be with him.

A huge pendulum clock in the hallway sounded and Rob looked at the cheap watch on his wrist. Five forty-five. It was still light outside but it seemed to be getting darker by the minute.

Tricia entered the room, carrying a serving platter. "Why is it getting dark so quickly?" he asked her.

"There are clouds building up. I'm afraid it's going to storm. At least the weatherman on the radio said as much."

"I thought perhaps maybe night fell more quickly here than in Davenport." He laughed but realized it sounded foolish.

"When we set the time back to standard at the end of the month, the evening will be on us much sooner." She busied herself, cutting several slices of roast, and then stepped back. "If there's anything you need, sir, I'll be in the kitchen. Just ring the bell." After indicating the small, crystal bell next to his place setting, she bowed and left the room.

Rob inhaled deeply. The meat smelled delicious and spicy. Ah, if Sherry could only see him now. He frowned. That was wrong. He didn't want to share any of this with her. The bitch had seen fit to have him embarrassed and humiliated by that asshole, Frank Yearnall. She deserved from life whatever she got, and Rob hoped it wouldn't be too nice.

While he ate and the premature dusk settled outside, the library fell dark. On the shelf, the book sat where Rob had put it, but a small puddle of blood oozed from beneath it, building until it spread along the edge of the shelf for a moment and then, drop by drop, fell to the oriental rug below. The sanguine droplets built until a puddle rested on top of the tightly woven wool. Instead of soaking in, it lay there for several minutes and then disappeared.

Rob sat back in the leather easy chair. Tricia was an excellent cook, and if the first meal and the manner in which it had been served and the way the woman conducted herself was any indication as to how his life was to go, he was more than happy that he'd listened to Allan Weipert's recommendation to keep her on for awhile. Awhile, hell! He'd keep her forever.

A low rumble of thunder announced the arrival of the storm Tricia had mentioned. Rob wondered if the wind and storm would be very loud in the house. For some reason, which he couldn't quite fathom, he felt secure and safe, as if nothing on earth could harm him. Certainly neither his wife nor any sort of financial problem could faze him. Sherry would have her price which he'd happily pay to be rid of her. How strange things had worked out. Only a week ago he'd have sold his soul for a sale or two to recoup his feelings of self-respect. When he'd accomplished that, he'd been deliriously happy and rushed home after a few celebratory drinks to share his renewed sales ability with his wife. Would he have stopped to let the two men talk to him if they'd arrived a few seconds later? Would she still have been in the apartment, waiting for him, if he'd been able to go right up? He doubted it. She was already gone by then. She'd made her decision. When he'd told her of his inheritance, she'd thrown it right back at him, insulting and humiliating him.

Rob yawned. He felt tired. Possibly the excitement over his legacy had taken its toll, and now he was relaxing enough to allow his body to recuperate.

"Tricia?" he called loudly.

After a short wait, she answered from the doorway, "Yes, sir?"

"I'm feeling sleepy, Tricia. Could you show me to a room upstairs?"

She stepped back to allow him to leave the library, and when he entered the hallway, she moved around him to take the lead up the wide staircase. When they stood on the second floor, she headed toward the master bedroom and opened the door.

Rob stepped through and sucked in his breath. The room was gigantic and held a canopied bed that dominated one side of the room. A large fireplace balanced the bed, and various pieces of furniture were arranged here and there.

Coughing, he stepped back. "I . . . I can't sleep here. It's . . . it's too big. I . . ."

"But this is the master bedroom, sir. It's yours. It was your grandfather's."

Rob glanced at her in a quick, nervous way. "I'm sorry. I've got to get used to this house first. You say my grandfather slept in here?" He looked around again.

"Yes sir."

"Well, I can't. Show me another room." He backed out of the room into the hall, shaking his head.

Tricia followed him, a look of confusion on her face. She looked to her left and then to her right, as if unable to decide which way to go. When her eyes landed on the door opposite the master bedroom, she stepped across the hallway and opened the door.

"If you can give me enough time, sir, I can prepare this room for the night." She stepped aside to allow him to enter.

The furniture was covered, and a certain staleness filled the air. Rob stepped in and looked around. "I don't think so. I'm tired and want to go to bed now. Find me one that's ready."

As he turned and left the room, he caught sight of the door next to the master bedroom. "What's wrong with this one?" he asked, striding toward it.

When she saw where he was going, Tricia quickly turned off the lights and closed the door behind her. "But, sir, that room is . . . I can't . . . it isn't . . ."

Rob opened the door and turned on the light. The room was in perfect order. It would be ideal. Then he had a thought. "Is this your room, Tricia? If it is, I'm sorry. I should have asked first."

"No sir, it's not mine. My room is down the hall and toward the back of the house."

"Then why is this room in such good order? Were you expecting I'd have people with me?"

The woman's face flushed. "That room is where . . . Yes. Yes, I thought you'd have your wife and family with you, sir." A sudden look of relief passed over her face. "I didn't get all of the rooms prepared, you see."

"Is there any reason I shouldn't stay in this one, then. I'll move into the master bedroom in time but not right away."

She bowed her head and said, "It's your home, sir. I'm sure I have nothing to say as to where you sleep."

Rob stepped into the bedroom. A clap of thunder sounded, and he felt more tired than he had in the last few weeks. The bed would feel good, and he wanted nothing more than a good night's sleep.

"Is there anything I can do for you tonight, sir?" she asked. "I still have some work to do in the kitchen."

"No, that'll be fine. You go ahead, Tricia. I'll see you in the morning. Is there a telephone here?"

"No sir. I had it taken out. Mr. Weipert said it was all right."

"That's good. Not that I'm expecting any calls, but it's good to know I can't be bothered by any either. Good night, Tricia."

"Good night, sir," she said softly, closing the door behind her as she left.

The first splattering raindrops smashed against the windows of the room, and the wind moaned as it wrapped itself about the mansion. Rob undressed and went to the adjoining bathroom. He smiled. Strange, no telephone but a bathroom off the bedroom. Though it had antique fixtures, they were clean and functional and he couldn't have asked for more. Who was he kidding? He'd slept in places that seemed like pigsties compared to this room. Well, why not? He didn't have to live like a loser anymore because he wasn't one anymore. He had millions.

After he finished in the bathroom, he went to the bed and turned down the covers. The bed looked so inviting. Slipping between the cool sheets, he settled in. Tomorrow he'd have to bring in his bag. Tonight he'd sleep in his underwear, but tomorrow he'd go to one of the stores, perhaps one that he owned, and buy or simply take whatever he needed. He wondered if that was the way it would work. Would he have to pay since he owned the place?

His thoughts grew fuzzy as he drifted into his first deep sleep, one in which he quickly became lost.

Outside, the storm continued building as the rain pelted the house. The thunder drew closer as it filled the evening with its booming resonance. One loud explosion almost directly overhead shook the mansion, and in the deafening silence that followed, broken only by the drumming staccato of the unceasing rain, Rob sat up in bed.

He shook his head, trying to associate himself with his surroundings. Where was he? The room wasn't at all familiar.

Another blast of thunder overhead brought him wide awake. The rain drenched the house while spasmodic flashes of lightning revealed the room in which he found himself.

Shaking his head again, he slowly drew the pieces together, fitting them into place. Of coure. He was at the mansion. In bed. In *his* mansion. In *his* bed.

A bright glow of lightning hung on for longer than normal and he could see the room in its entirety. Something was on the bed. He reached out for it, but the stygian blackness closed in on him once more. What was it? Stretching his arm for the nightstand light, he found it and fumbled for a moment, trying to find the switch. When he did, he turned on the lamp and blinked in the sudden, steady brightness.

Rubbing his eyes, he looked about, trying to focus them. Then he saw it.

The book!

The book lay on the bed next to where he had been lying. At least it looked like the book. He turned and reached out for it. The familiar heft told him it was the same book, or that possibly he had more than one. One in this room as well as one in the library?

When he opened the cover, he instantly recognized the first page, where he had scratched it before dinner. How had it gotten in this room? Had he brought it along? Had he been that tired, so tired that he'd carried a book weighing some ten pounds and wasn't aware of it at the time?

What time was it? What time had it been when he went to bed? If he remembered correctly, the hall clock downstairs was almost ready to strike eight o'clock when he and the housekeeper had come up to find his room. But what time was it at that precise moment? Had she already retired? Had she put the book here on the bed next to him? If she did, why had she done it?

The questions rambled about his head, gathering momentum as he tried to understand what was happening. Was it that important? Was it serious enough to awaken the woman if she were in bed and ask her what would sound like an insane question to her?

"Excuse me for awakening you at this hour, but did you place this book on my bed? And if you did, why?"

That would make her think she worked for a nut.

He lay back on the pillow. He'd wait and see how she acted in the morning. If he felt she might know about the book, he'd ask her for an explanation. If he decided she was acting perfectly normal, he wouldn't mention it but would keep an eye on her for future strange happenings.

Rob closed his eyes. The bed still felt good. Downstairs, the clock tolled the hour after playing the Whittington Chimes theme, but he lost track of the number of gongs. It seemed to have struck quite a few times. Perhaps he still had a whole night to sleep.

He rolled over, taking the book with him. It landed on the pillow, almost touching his head. In seconds he fell back asleep and the storm continued.

After a while, he turned and his cheek lay full on the cover of the book.

The last thing Rob heard was a crash of thunder before slipping back into the warm vise of sleep. His mind spiraled down until it rested.

Then he dreamed. The house billowed outward, leaving him until he stood in the middle of a large meadow, totally nude. He felt good, warm, relaxed and not the least bit inhibited when the naked women ran out of the surrounding woods and began dancing in a circle about him.

One by one they reached out, stroking his genitals as they passed. He felt himself being aroused and reacted the instant the women pointed to his erection, applauding with their hands but making no sound. One of them, a striking beauty whose long black cascading hair contrasted acutely with her alabaster skin, stepped closer. Her breasts jutted out in an almost haughty way as she smiled seductively at him. She was wiggling a finger for him to come to her; he tried to move but couldn't. She laughed without any sound coming from her mouth. Again she beckoned for him, and though he felt hands pushing him, he still couldn't move.

The woman ran a hand down her breasts, fingering the dark aureoles and playing with them, but never taking her eyes from Rob's. She ran her hands down from her breasts to her stomach, fingering her navel while lightly running her tongue over her lips.

Rob wanted her. He wanted her in any way he could get her, but he couldn't move. He thought he'd go mad with desire when her hands reached her pubic hair and she began rubbing her clitoris.

Reacting to her own self-induced stimulation, she silently pleaded with Rob to come to her. She inserted a finger into her vagina and pushed in and out, pointing to his erect penis with her other hand.

Finally, a push from behind broke his bond, and he moved toward her. What should he do first? Who was she? For some reason, she looked familiar. She was beautiful and she wanted him, but where had she come from and who were the women with her?

When he reached her, he embraced her and

could feel her body heat as their skin touched. She was burning with desire.

The woman threw her arms around his neck and kissed him, her tongue jabbing into his mouth. Falling backward, she wrestled Rob to his back and quickly mounted him.

Rob lay quietly, trying to fathom the situation. When he looked up at her, she smiled complacently. When he tried to move, she stopped him with a look. Then he felt it. She wasn't moving, yet he could feel his penis being massaged by a series of muscles moving in her vagina. He felt himself nearing a climax but reached only a certain plateau, one without satisfaction. Though she appeared to be satisfied, he felt no release, no pleasure.

Then a sudden warm deluge spilled over them, and he could hear laughter from all around. He looked up. The other women had poured something on them. When he realized what it was, he felt his stomach heave.

Blood! They had drenched the woman and him with blood. The strong, coppery smell filled his nostrils, and when he looked at the woman again, he felt a beastial, primeval scream building within him.

The woman had turned into someone else— some*thing* else. Her smooth complexion bore eruptions of pustules and open sores, from which pus oozed. Her teeth, broken in places, gleamed brightly through the sanguine coating, while her pendulous lips stretched back and over them. Her eyes burned with a fierce desire that he felt no human could ever satisfy. He sensed the scream rising ever closer to his throat, and when it did, he gave vent to it and opened his mouth.

The cry began as a moan—a frightened, almost gutteral groan—and quickly grew in volume until it reached a high-pitched screeching wail that fled from the bedroom, through the house to accompany the rain and thunder and lightning.

CHAPTER TWELVE

The sound of a key turning in the lock brought Sherry around to face the door of her new apartment. That was the only aspect of her arrangement with Frank Yearnall that displeased her. Frank could enter any time he wanted. That in turn meant she could never have any friends up for fear her boss would walk in on her, completely unannounced. At best it was only a temporary situation, and she and Jeremy could find another apartment soon and move out from under the umbrella of Frank's generous but conditional protection. Unfortunately, anyplace she could afford within the next six months would more than likely be nothing more than a small improvement over the place she had just left.

The door opened and Frank stepped in, a smile spread across his face. He grinned even wider when he saw Sherry standing in the doorway of the mirrored bedroom. "Hi. Getting ready for me?"

She wanted to say, "Don't flatter yourself," but decided to play the role she was supposed to where he was concerned. "I suppose you might say that. I didn't think I'd see you tonight."

"My wife had to go to a women's kitchenware party or something. I've got nothing to do for the next few hours. Got any ideas?"

Sherry shook her head. "It's too early. Jeremy's doing his homework in his room. We can't do anything until he's in bed, asleep."

Frank snapped his fingers and frowned. "Damn! Oh well, how about a cup of coffee or something to kill time until he does go to bed. What time does he usually go?" He crossed the room and went directly to Sherry who was stepping into the kitchenette.

"Around 8:30 or 9:00." She busied herself making coffee and stopped spooning the grounds into the basket when he slipped his arms around her waist. "Don't," she whispered.

Frank turned her around to face him, despite her weak protestation, and lifted her face to his. Leaning down, he kissed her on the mouth, ramming his tongue in through her teeth. Her mouth opened, welcoming the intruder.

Sherry slowly put her arms around Frank's neck and pulled him closer. She didn't love him and really didn't even like him that much, but he was doing her a grand favor by helping her get away from Rob. For that fact alone, she was grateful. Frank could have been the ugliest man in the world and she would still have favored him for such an act. After several minutes, she pushed him away, gasping for breath.

"Give a girl a chance to breathe, will you?"

Frank stepped back, chuckling. "Sorry about that."

"Why is it that every time you kiss me I get the impression you're measuring the inside of my mouth for your pecker. Is that true?" She turned back to finish making the coffee.

Frank laughed. "That could be. I don't know. It's just that you sort of bring out the animal in me. Do you know what I mean?"

Sherry shrugged. "I guess so. I sort of respond to you in the same way."

"Hey, who's better? Your loser husband or me?"

"Well, I've got to give Rob his due. He's pretty good in the sack. His only trouble was timing. It seems he always wanted to screw in the morning while I much prefer something like that at night." She sat down after turning on the coffee maker.

"Speaking of him," Frank said, taking the chair opposite Sherry, "have you heard from him since I threw him out of the restaurant?"

She shook her head. "No, I haven't, and that isn't like him. It's been five or six days since I walked out on him. The only time I saw him was the next day, when you gave him the heave-ho. I'll be indebted to you for a long time on that one, Frank."

"You're working the bill off right now, you know." He reached across the small table and took her hand in his. "I'm glad I threw the bum out. If I hadn't, you might feel you should take off pretty soon and I wouldn't like that."

"I hope I never see the sonofabitch again." Sherry stood, went to the cupboard and took out two coffee mugs.

Frank leaned back in his chair. "Me, too."

"You know," she said, setting a mug in front of Frank, "he even tried telling me that he's inherited some money to get me to come back."

Frank sat up. "No, I didn't know. When was this?"

"The day you threw him out. He was just going to say it real loud when you stepped in and threw him out."

Frank narrowed his eyes. "What was he going to say real loud?"

"He'd whispered it to me and then started to say it again, real loud."

"What, for Christ's sake?" Frank asked, impatient for her to tell him.

"He said he was inheriting enough money to buy you out with his pocket change or something dumb like that."

"Didn't you know he had rich relatives?"

"That's just it, he doesn't. Not as far as I know, he doesn't."

Frank drummed on the table with his

fingertips. "I wonder why he never told you about them."

"He's just bullshitting. He doesn't have any rich relatives. Believe me, I'd know if he did. If he had them, he'd have been trying to sponge off them somehow. That's just the way Rob is."

Frank focused his attention on Sherry. "No rich close friends or somebody like that who could have left him money?"

She shook her head again.

"I can't understand why a guy would make up a lie like that, knowing he'd be found out as soon as someone called his bluff."

"That's the way Rob is. He likes to talk, just to hear himself say something." She stood and brought the carafe over to the table. After filling the mugs, she returned it to the coffee maker and sat down. She found Frank staring off into space.

She reached out and snapped her fingers. "Hey, come out of it. It's only bullshit, I tell you."

"Yeah, I suppose so." He stood and walked around the corner of the table. Reaching down, he pulled her to her feet and kissed her again. Hugging her tightly against his body, he could feel her breasts pressing against his chest. "I want you. I want you now, goddamnit."

Breaking away, she stepped back and found herself against the table. "Don't make any noise. I don't want Jeremy walking out here and finding you doing something."

"Doing what? Kissing his old lady?"

Sherry nodded.

"Why don't you check on him? Maybe he went to bed already."

"Not likely, but I'll look in on him," she said, thankful for the respite to get away from him for the moment. Later, once her son was sound asleep, she wouldn't mind going to bed with Frank, but she'd do it on her terms where Jeremy was concerned.

Opening the door to the smaller bedroom, she found him buttoning up his pajamas.

"Hi," she said quietly, entering the room. "All finished with your homework?"

He nodded but said nothing.

"How come you didn't come out and tell me?"

"You've got company." The boy continued fidgeting with his pajama buttons.

Sherry looked away. She hated to feel guilty in her son's presence, especially over something like a man being with her when she was still technically married to Rob.

Jeremy looked up at her. "Frank's still here, isn't he?"

"*Uncle* Frank is still here." Her voice carried a hard edge.

"He's not my uncle. Where's Dad? When's he coming to get us?"

"Look, Jeremy," Sherry said, sitting down on the edge of the bed, "you've got to call Frank something. I don't think Mr. Yearnall would like you calling him by his first name. Will you call him 'uncle'—for me?" She reached out, lifting the boy's chin to better see his face.

Jeremy shrugged in a resigned way and said, "Is *Uncle* Frank still here?"

She nodded.

"When's he leaving? When's Dad coming back?"

"Get something straight, Jeremy. Frank is doing us a big favor by letting us stay here until I can find a better place for us to live."

"Better than this?" Jeremy asked, waving an arm through the air.

"Don't get smart. You know I mean better than what we've had in the past. This place is too expensive for you and me."

"How can you afford to live here then, if it's too expensive?"

Sherry bit her lip. Why did Jeremy have the ability to see through her deception? Her stomach heaved a bit. She wasn't fooling him for an instant. He was just being too kind to ask truly embarrasing questions, but she had to tell him something. "Ah, Jeremy, Mr. Yearnall is doing us a favor as I said. I work for him, and he understands that I can't afford an apartment right now. Because I'm a good employee, he's letting us stay here without it costing us any money. Do you understand?"

Jeremy turned away and nodded. "But when's Dad coming?"

"I don't know. I haven't heard from him in five or six days. I guess he's getting ready to divorce me. I don't know. I don't know anything anymore." She caught her breath when she felt a sob coming. Sure, she'd been rough on Rob but he wasn't living up to his potential. Why she had stayed with him all the years she had, she'd never understand. She'd never had much in her life, and at the time of their marriage, Rob seemed to be the answer to her prayers. But everything he tried had never worked out with any degree of success. He never stayed with a job that had potential long enough to build a career, and he claimed it was never his fault. On the other hand, a man like Frank Yearnall had opened his own business and expanded it twice in 15 years. Frank was money oriented and successful. Rob was a loser and a bum. She had to get away from her husband to salvage her own life and that of her son.

"You crying?" Jeremy asked.

"No. I . . . my breath just caught for a minute. You go to bed. Frank'll be leaving soon, and I'll look in on you before I go to bed. All right?"

"Uh-huh," he said, standing and turning down his bed covers.

After he crawled in, Sherry leaned down. "Don't I get a good night kiss?"

Her son looked up at her. "I guess." Reaching out, he pulled her down and kissed her on the cheek. "G'night, Mom."

"Good night, Jeremy." She went to the door and turned out the light. A night light went on automatically and feebly glowed, creating monstrous shadows on the walls. She smiled when Jeremy turned over and pulled the covers up around his neck and then quietly closed the door.

She found Frank sitting at the kitchen table.

"Is he asleep?" he asked, looking up.

"He will be in a few minutes."

"I want you. I need you, Sherry."

"What about your wife?"

"What about her?"

"Go home to her."

"Hey, you forgetting our arrangement?"

Sherry sat down. "Look, Frank, I told you no fooling around when Jeremy's home. I don't mind you being around when he isn't or if it's late at night after you close up, but for Christ's sake, the kid's still awake. What kind of guy are you?"

"I'll tell you what kind of guy I am. I've been thinking while you were in there, and I think you'd better look into your husband's so-called inheritance. You might be passing up one helluva deal."

"How do you mean? I told you, Rob's just blowing so much hot air."

"If that's what he's done in the past, he might want you to think that now. Maybe he really is inheriting a lot of money."

Sherry frowned. Could that be? Could she have jumped to a wrong conclusion? She turned to Frank. "What should I do?"

"I don't know yet. Let me think on it. Whatever you do, don't sign anything for anybody. Don't agree to see him or an attorney unless you've picked one yourself. Understand?"

Sherry nodded. "But what then?"

"I said I wanted to think on it. First thing we

got to do is locate him. Find out where he's staying. Probably at your old apartment, right?"

She shrugged. "More than likely."

"I really think you owe it to yourself to look into this. If I can help, I will."

"And what's all of your concern and worry going to cost me?"

Frank threw open the palms of his hands. "Hey, have I asked for anything? I don't want anything from you. Maybe a piece of ass once in a while but no money. I don't work that way," he said, his voice growing louder. "I've never taken a goddamned cent from a woman and I never will."

Sherry put a finger to her lips. "Shhh, you'll wake up Jeremy."

"Sorry. I got carried away there for a minute. You know it's supposed to rain tonight, don't you?"

Sherry cocked an eyebrow and looked at him in a quizzical way. "So? What are you doing? Giving weather forecasts on the side?"

"You forgot, didn't you? I get horny as hell when it rains. I like to lie in bed with a good woman and sort of diddle the wet weather away. Come on, Sherry, you've got to do me a favor."

"A favor? What?" She looked at him, not knowing what to expect.

"You've got to help me get it out of my system. I'd rather you got rid of my horniness than my wife."

"Why is that, Frank?"

"You're better than she is in the sack, that's all. Marge is a nice woman and lovely to look at and the perfect wife, but she doesn't fuck worth a shit. All she does is lay there on her back and check the ceiling for cracks and look to see if it needs paint."

"What'll happen if she ever catches you here in this apartment or someplace else with another woman?"

Frank fell silent. Finally he said, "I don't know. I never once thought of it happening. Still, I provide for her in a way that most women would kill for. I'd hope she'd overlook it."

"And you won't leave her?"

"Never. Not in a million years."

"Why, Frank? Suppose you found a woman who was everything your wife is and could fuck like a five hundred buck a night hooker. Wouldn't you leave your wife then?"

He shook his head. "She'd make me pay and pay and pay. That's why I tend to think she'd overlook it. She likes the good life, and I'm giving it to her. I can always get a hooker if I have to."

He stood and took her hand. "Come on. We can go into the bedroom and be real quiet. He won't hear us."

Sherry stood and followed him, more by reflex than by any desire on her part. If she hadn't been certain about looking for Rob and trying to find out if he were telling the truth about an inheritance before, she was now. In his own inimitable way, Frank had just told her she was being a hooker for him, and she didn't like that one bit. She'd let him fuck her now, but it would be all over pretty soon, as soon as she found her husband.

When they were in the bedroom, they undressed, Frank in a quick way and Sherry in a lethargic, uncharacteristically slow manner.

"Come on, Sherry. Get a move on, will you?"

She turned around and shushed him. "If you awaken Jeremy and he finds us like this, I'll kill you."

"Come on, baby, I'm a lover, not a fighter."

Sherry placed one knee on the bed and caught the sight of thousands of blonde Sherrys doing the same thing in the endless reflections of the mirrors. For an instant, she studied her images. Her breasts sagged a bit but were for the most part relatively firm. Her tummy had a slight mound but nothing that couldn't be considered a sexy little bulge. Her legs were shapely, and her face, although it didn't deny her age, still was pretty.

When she lay down next to Frank, he enveloped her in his arms. His hairy chest and stomach were firm, and although he was over-weight, his body was sound and solid. They kissed deeply and ran their hands over each other's body, his in an excited, exploratory search and hers in an automatic, perfunctory way.

Despite her attempts to be nothing more than a sex partner with her employer, Sherry found herself being aroused when he expertly manipulated her clitoris. She could feel the initial excitement turning to the hot, drilling sensation that began in her lower abdomen and spiraled outward, embracing her entire body. The feeling grew, spreading and encompassing her while Frank played with her.

She could stand no more and spread her legs. "Now. Frank. Now. Do it now, for Christ sake's. Fuck me!"

He propped himself up and rolled over. She helped his penis enter her body and thrilled at the man's size as he pushed into her. Frank pumped fiercely, massaging her clitoris and sending the burning perforating feeling to a fevered high pitch.

"Oh, God! Fuck me, Frank!" she cried and raised her hips to meet his.

She continued pumping against his cock and hips while his semen gushed inside her.

In the mirrors, the scene was duplicated myriad times, while overhead, when she opened her eyes, she could see the broad, hairy back of Frank's body slowing its gyrations until he lay full upon her. Despite the discomfort of his weight resting completely on her, she enjoyed the feeling of having surrendered completely to him.

Jeremy opened his eyes. Had he heard his mother cry out? Then he heard the rhythmic beat of the bed springs squeaking in the next room. The commotion was familiar to Jeremy. He'd lived in close proximity to his father and mother long enough to understand that a husband and wife did certain things that made them giggle and moan every once in a while. He'd heard it and noted the fact that both his parents were usually in a much better frame of mind once they stopped their silly laughing and groaning and making the bed squeak. Though the bed in the next room did not make that much noise, he could hear what was happening.

Could his father have come back? He threw the covers back and jumped from the bed. He was almost to the door when he heard his mother cry out, "Oh, God! Fuck me, Frank!"

Jeremy stood rooted to the spot. Was Frank Yearnall still in the apartment? If he were, what was he doing in the bedroom with his mother? It definitely had been his mother who had cried out and called Frank by name.

He felt the sob rising before it had become a thought. He knew what the word "fuck" meant. It had to do with making babies and sticking a guy's dick into a girl's pussy. He knew. And he knew what his mother was doing with her boss. An unfamiliar feeling of revulsion and loathing filled him.

Turning, Jeremy went back to the bed and sat down heavily. Where was his dad? He wanted him. He wanted him in the worst way. He couldn't be happy with his mother anymore.

He wondered if he even loved his mother now. He wanted his dad. But how would a kid his age go about hunting down his father? His mother had said she had no idea as to where he was. Had she told him the truth? Suddenly Jeremy found himself doubting everything about his mother.

He lay back on the bed and turned on one side, jamming his face into the pillow. When he allowed the sob to be born, the crying instantly followed and he muffled the sound in the pillow.

CHAPTER THIRTEEN

The scream seemed to hang in the air, reverberating in Rob's head for a long time. Who had screamed? He opened his eyes and stared into the half-gloom of the night. Someone had put a light on but it didn't seem to completely illuminate the room.

Who had screamed? He shuddered when he replayed in his mind that terrifying wail. The memory of blood flowing over him—him and—there had been someone else. Who? A woman. A beautiful woman. No. She had changed into something else. A beast. A monster. An ugly countenance of loose skin, huge eyes, weeping pustules and broken teeth crashed back into his memory. Who had screamed? It had been he.

But why? Why such a horrible dream? Weren't dreams supposed to mean something other than the content seemed to indicate? What could such a terrible nightmare mean? He sat up and screamed again. Someone was sitting on the bed. The shadowy figure, outlined by the small lamp on the dresser behind it, moved forward toward Rob. He shrank back, pressing against the oak headboard of the large bed.

"Don't. Stop. Get away," he managed in a choking sob.

"Mr. LaMotte, it's all right. It's me. Tricia. Remember? Remember me? I'm your house-keeper. You screamed, and I came in to see what was wrong. Are you all right?"

Tricia? Who was— Housekeeper? Where was he? When the previous day and his arrival at the mansion fell into place in his mind, he relaxed a bit. Shaking his head, he propped himself up more.

"I . . . I'm sorry. Really I am. I seldom do things like this. Did you say I screamed? What happened? Do you know?"

Shaking her head, Tricia stood, suddenly aware that she was sitting on her employer's bed in a most familiar way. She pulled her robe around her body, accentuating the line of her breasts, and stepped back. "All I know is I awoke when you screamed."

"Are you sure it was me?"

"I didn't scream, and there's no one else around who could have. You must have been

210

having an awful nightmare or something. Are you all right now?"

He nodded spastically. "I guess so. Just now, when I sat up, I recalled the dream, or at least part of it. It was terrible. Awful."

Tricia took a tentative step toward the bed and stopped. "Would it help if you talked about it? Do you want to tell me?"

Rob looked up at her. She sounded like a mother talking to her child who had awakened in the middle of the night. A rueful smile crossed his face. The woman seemed totally embarrassed by the situation. Why shouldn't she? He felt a bit the same way. They had barely met and here they were, employer and employee in the middle of the night in the employer's bedroom because of a stupid nightmare.

"No. That is," Rob said, "I don't think it's necessary that I talk about it. I'm not the type to dream that vividly. More than likely, it was caused by a combination of things. The new bed. The new room. The idea of living in this mansion. My inheritance. Everything must have ganged up on me and made me dream. I'm sure that's all it was."

Tricia lowered her eyes. "I hope so, sir. You were thrashing about like a . . . like I don't know what, when I opened the door and came in."

Rob looked up at her. "You just walked right in?"

"No sir. I knocked several times—very hard. Then I just walked in. I had no idea if you were being attacked by someone like a prowler or burglar. Forgive me, Mr. LaMotte, it won't happen again."

She turned to leave, walking toward the door.

Rob called after her. "Wait a minute, Tricia."

She stopped and turned to face him, her embarrassment fully evident by the blush on her face. "Yes sir?"

"Don't apologize for having walked in. Suppose it had been one of the things you'd suspected. You might very well have saved my life in that case. As it is, no harm's been done. I won't accept your apology since there's no need for it."

Tricia stared at him, barely nodding her head.

At that moment Rob enjoyed looking at the woman. She wore a dark robe and no slippers. The top of her nightgown edged the opening of the robe at her throat. She had pulled the sash quite tight, and her slender waist seemed to call attention to her breasts and full hips. Tricia had brushed her hair before retiring, and it hung in brown waves across her shoulders. Tricia Woodless was a most attractive woman as far as Rob was concerned. For a split second, he pictured her without clothing and marveled at the dark brown aureoles of her breasts, which he imagined to be perfect. Her arms, folded as they were, did not cover her navel which was nothing more than a slight dimple in the middle of her flat, smooth abdomen. His eyes dropped momentarily to her vagina, and he smiled. He wanted to make love to her, right then and there, without any sort of hesitation or debate. Should he take her? Would she refuse? Fight? Be insulted? Want to quit her job?

Pulling himself together, he looked into her eyes. "I suppose you can go back to your room now, Tricia. Thank you for coming in. I really do appreciate it."

"Thank you, Mr. LaMotte. Good night."

"Good night, Tricia."

She went to the door and opened it, standing with her back to him but looking over her shoulder nevertheless. Their eyes locked for a second, and then she was gone.

He could hear her going down the hall toward her room. In seconds, the door closed and a heavy silence pressed in on him.

Rob reached out, turning on the nightstand lamp, and got out of bed to turn off the light on the dresser. The image of Tricia Woodless standing in his doorway, looking back over her shoulder, stayed with him. Had she wanted to stay? Had she used his screaming as an excuse to come into his room? Easing back into bed, he smiled. She must have been having the same sort of thoughts as he'd had right before she left.

Lying back, he adjusted his pillow and reached out for the lamp. Once the room was black, he felt wide awake. He'd have trouble getting back to sleep now that he'd been awake for a while.

He wondered what had caused the dream. His evening meal? He doubted that very much.

The food had been prepared expertly, and he'd had no aftertaste in his mouth once he had returned to the library. If he thought about it long enough, he felt confident he'd accept his earlier explanation, the one he'd given Tricia, about his new surroundings and new status in life.

What had the dream been about? He recalled the monster the beautiful woman had become. But who had the woman been? In a strange way, she had seemed very familiar. There had been many women and they'd all been naked, but the one in particular had stood out—the striking woman with the black hair and white skin. She'd almost appeared, now that Rob thought about it, like a geisha girl with her face whitened and black hair piled high on her head, though she hadn't been oriental, nor had her hair been coiffed.

The other women had stroked his penis, and when the black-haired woman had beckoned to him, the others had pushed him toward her. Finally they had gotten together, and he was making love to her when she began changing into an awful beast of some sort. And he remembered the hot blood. That must have been when he screamed. Yes, it clearly came back to him. He remembered the scream building from deep within him and erupting into an almost primitive wail of terror.

Rob sat up in the dark and fumbled for the light. He was sweating profusely. What was wrong with him?

Once the lights were on, he relaxed some. Who *was* the woman? Someone from his past? He couldn't recall ever having seen anyone like her before in his life. She didn't resemble Tricia or Sherry in the least. Then who could it have been? There were no other women in his life. Could she be someone he would meet?

A frown crossed his face, and he dropped his legs over the edge of the bed, sitting up. What could possibly have prompted that dream? What had he been thinking about before he went to sleep?

Suddenly he froze. He'd been thinking about Tricia and going to her room and asking her if she'd put the book with the golden pages on his bed.

The book! He'd found it on his bed when the storm had awakened him earlier. He'd seen it lying near his side when a lightning blast lit up the room for an inordinately long period of time. Of course. That was it. His sleep had already been disturbed earlier, and he'd gone back to sleep and suffered the awful nightmare.

He stood and pulled up the covers over the pillows. Where was the book? What had happened to it? It should have been right there on the bed. Rob remembered picking it up and looking at it, and then, when he lay down to go back to sleep, he'd still been holding the book.

When he awoke, Tricia was sitting on the bed and the book had been nowhere in sight. If it had fallen to the floor, he felt certain he'd have heard it. Had Tricia taken the book with her?

He pictured her standing near the bed as she had been doing when he mentally undressed her. She had nothing in her hands and the pocket of her robe was flat and not sagging as it would have under the weight of the book. Maybe she had taken it away before he awoke. That was a possibility. But why would she have done that? He had thought of going to her room to ask her if she had placed it there when he had awakened the first time. Instead of doing that, he had decided to observe her to see if she acted strangely when he didn't mention finding the book. She had to have put it there. He hadn't, and there was no one else in the house. He grinned when he remembered why he hadn't gone to her room in the first place. He hadn't wanted to appear eccentric in front of his housekeeper. That was a laugh. Here she was playing with his mind by slipping into his room and putting a book on his bed and then taking it out without giving any sort of explanation.

Still, he wouldn't condemn her until he was abolutely certain. If nothing else came of the situation, he'd been made aware of her sensuality. In time—and not too much time if he didn't notice anything peculiar about the woman—he'd try to find out if she might be inclined to consider a more intimate arrangement than they presently had.

The book was still the mystery. How had it come to be on his bed in the first place and where was it now if Tricia had had nothing to do with it? Rob distinctly remembered picking it up and looking at it. He'd leaned against the headboard and opened it, admiring the golden leaves.

"It's got to be here," he said, standing up and patting the top of the bed. There was nothing in the bed.

He knew it just couldn't have gone away by itself. Someone had to have carried it in, put it on the bed and then taken it away. But if Tricia didn't and he hadn't, who had? He threw the covers back in the hope that he'd simply overlooked it in some way, but the book wasn't there. Maybe Tricia had seen the book, realized its worth and took it, stole it for herself.

A sense of panic rose in him. A cold sweat formed on his forehead. He'd been robbed. Was this the way it would be from now on? He'd have something and someone else would want it and simply take it from him? If that were the case, he didn't want to be rich or have property or have money.

As quickly as the sense of fear and panic had flooded him, it vanished, and in its place, Rob felt a peace and calm he'd never before known. He felt assured of himself, confident that he could properly handle any given situation that might come along. What could have made him feel like that all of a sudden? The house? The idea that he had millions of dollars? Probably. It seemed to Rob that all things could be possible to anyone if one simply had money— and he had money, more than most people would have even in half a dozen lifetimes.

The thought of Sherry suddenly pushed everything else aside. He'd show her a thing or two about faithfulness in a marriage partner. If she wanted a divorce, she'd get one. She'd pay by not having the chance to partake in his inheritance. His money and property were his and his alone. In time, he'd see to it that Jeremy received it when he himself was dead, but Sherry would never receive one penny. She'd always wanted the good life, or at least she had said, "Enough to be comfortable and not have any worries." Well, she'd had the chance, and she completely blew it.

And Frank Yearnall? He'd get his, too. If anything, Rob would see to it that Frank did. It would be legal and it would be final, whatever it might be.

Rob shook his head. Why was he thinking like that? He wasn't a vindictive person, certainly not the way in which he'd just been thinking. But if he had the money and the power to inflict a little hurt on Yearnall, he'd do so just to get even for the way in which Yearnall had thrown him out of the restaurant. Rob would never forget or forgive that.

But what had happened to the book with the golden pages? It was valuable, of that Rob was most certain. Maybe he should awaken Tricia. If he did that, she couldn't help but think of him as an eccentric who wanted to search for a book in the middle of the night.

He had to get to sleep. He was overwrought

and exhausted. Maybe a glass of milk would help him relax. After slipping into his robe, he went to the door and hurried downstairs, doing his best to remain quiet and not disturb Tricia. He remembered how, just a few days ago, there hadn't been any milk in the house for their coffee once Jeremy had finished the carton. Those sort of days were gone forever from his life. If Sherry wanted to drink her coffee black, that was her choice, but he'd see to it that Jeremy had anything he wanted, no matter what it might be.

Rob reached the downstairs and started back along the staircase toward the kitchen. Once he poured a glass of milk for himself, he wandered through the dining room and into the library.

Then the sensation of being watched crashed into his consciousness. He spun about, almost spilling the milk on the oriental rug. He'd had that feeling in the past, shortly before he found out he was rich. Had someone actually been watching him then? He didn't know. This time it had to be his imagination. There was no one who could be watching him now.

Or was there? Tricia? She had to be up. He sensed it. He could almost feel her presence. Why was she doing this to him? If she were doing this now, she had probably put the book on his bed and taken it back. But why?

The feeling of being watched intensified until he felt he could almost touch it. It came from all around him, from the windows that showed nothing but the black night outside, from the hallway, the corners of the room, everywhere. He could feel eyes watching him from every direction.

"Who's there?" he called out in a desperate whisper.

No answer.

"Tricia?"

Nothing.

Rob walked slowly toward the double doorway that opened onto the hall. When he had tiptoed almost up to it, he leaped the remaining few feet and jumped into the hallway. Nothing. There was no one there. He looked up the stairs. No one. Where could they be? He knew they were there. He could feel them. Was Tricia one of them? Was he in danger? For that matter, was Tricia in danger if she weren't one of them? Who could they be? Why did they want to watch him? To harm him? Did they want his money? His property? What?

"What do you want?" he called out loudly again and jumped at the sound of his own voice.

The house fell silent once more.

His hands trembling, Rob brought the glass up to his lips and downed half the milk. It made him feel better. At least the milk was real; he could taste it and feel it coursing down his throat.

Still, the eerie feeling of being watched persisted.

He turned and went back into the library. A

chill wound its way down his back, and he shuddered. He felt threatened. Perhaps it was because he was in a house—his house, his home. When he'd experienced the feeling before, he'd always been outside or someplace other than where he lived. Here, the sanctity of his new home and life style was being threatened by someone or something he couldn't see.

He walked around the library several times, trying to shake off his anxiety and calm down. When he passed the shelves upon which the book with the golden pages had rested before falling to the floor, he stopped. His eyes widened. The book was in its place on the shelf.

"Now what in hell—?" He reached up for the book and brought it down. "What's going on? How did this get back down here?"

Tricia had to be the one behind these shenanigans. Perhaps there were secret passages throughout the house and she could go about without being seen. That was silly. What if she were demented in some way? Would it be silly then?

Rob replayed in his mind her leaving his bedroom. She hadn't had anything in her hands or pockets at that time. He'd heard her go directly to her room and heard the door close. That was all well and good, but if there were passages through the walls, she could have taken the book from his room before he awoke and then returned it to the library without having had to pass his room. Maybe she'd gone down the back stairway and through the kitchen.

He shook his head. What was happening? One moment, he felt on top of the world, wealthy and without a care, and the next he could almost touch the reality of someone watching him and playing games with a book made of gold.

Maybe he'd dreamt the whole thing about the book. That had to be it. Why hadn't he thought of that sooner? The book had never been in his room in the first place. How dumb could one person be?

He stretched, sliding the book back into place. How wonderfully imaginative his mind had been. He'd actually thought he'd seen the book on his bed, sat up, turned on the light, looked at it, and went back to sleep. That dream had become reality when he had awakened a while later, screaming his head off and probably scaring the daylights out of his housekeeper.

He pictured Tricia once more. She was very attractive, and he made up his mind that he could be a bit more than just interested in her. She seemed bright and naturally intelligent, but he doubted if she'd had much formal schooling beyond high school. So what? He'd dropped out of high school, and Sherry was anything but a mental giant. Tricia on the other hand seemed to have a natural, inherent grace. Perhaps his grandfather had had something to do with training her in the ways of being a housekeeper in a mansion like this.

Rob shook his head and started for the

double doors. He could stay up all night and sleep the entire next day if he wanted. He had nothing to do the next day that was pressing or urgent. Still, he felt tired. Yawning, he picked up the glass to return it to the kitchen. He'd go to bed, sleep the rest of the night and get up the next morning. Everything would be fine.

Reaching up for the light switch, he thought once more about having dreamt that the book had been on his bed and laughed aloud.

His laugh stopped short when the loud smack of the book falling from the shelf to the floor echoed through the house. Rob didn't have to look back. He knew what had fallen. But why? And how? He had put the book back on the shelf, and there was no way it could have fallen without help of some kind.

What was going on? He started toward the kitchen and stopped next to the mirrored hall tree. He peered at his image. Was he going mad?

CHAPTER FOURTEEN

Rob leaned back in the armed, wooden office chair and stared at the cluttered desk before him. Emil LaMotte must have been as poor a bookkeeper as he was. Rob could make no sense out of the papers he had found in the antique roll-top desk. Tricia had shown him the rest of the house, including the attic, and when they came to the small office on the second floor, Rob had made up his mind that he would go through it as soon as the tour was completed.

He'd found sheets of paper with notes, which Emil had apparently made to remind himself of certain things. Some of the papers had a single number written on it. Some had nothing but doodling. He found one ledger that contained rows of numbers but nothing to identify what the numbers might mean.

Another book, which was jammed into the back of the top drawer on the left side, contained three written pages. Both the original and the carbon were there, intact. Rob studied the first, a frown slowly crossing his face. There was no amount written into the appropriate places. The name on the top bill was that of Dan O'Malley. Emil had signed it and had written across the face of the page in a tight, pinched script, which matched the signature: "Paid In Full."

Rob looked up. What had been paid in full? There was no amount of money apparently involved with the transaction, since no dollar amount had been written down. He turned the white and then the yellow duplicate page. On the next white one, he found another, similar to the first. The only difference was in the name —Jim Bradley. Again, no dollar amount was included but "Paid In Full" was written across the face of the sheet. On the third set of bills, he found yet another, made out to a Peter Simmonson. No money was involved but the page was marked "Paid In Full."

It didn't make sense to Rob. Three men had been written bills, and they in turn had been cancelled by having "paid in full" written across them. Was that a normal business practice? He didn't know. All he knew was that in the insurance business, all he had to do when he accepted money from a customer was write out a receipt for the amount of the premium and give it to the person. As the salesman, he didn't keep the receipt. Why had his grandfather kept these bills? Or were they receipts? He had no idea. And there hadn't been any money involved. So why the need for a bill or a receipt in the first place?

Getting up from his seat, he went to the door and called, "Tricia?"

He waited for a long minute before calling out again, "Tricia, can you come up to the office for a moment?"

"Yes sir, I'm coming," she said from the stairs and hurried to answer his call.

When they were in the office, he said, "Do you know anything at all about any of these papers?"

Shaking her head, she took a defensive step back toward the door. "No sir. Your grandfather never confided in me when it came to matters of business."

"Did Allan Weipert go over these?"

She nodded. "Yes, he did. In fact, he asked me the same thing you just did."

Rob's frown deepened. Apparently his grandfather had been some sort of financial genius to accumulate the sort of wealth he'd possessed, but where were the records and the books? There had to be some. Did he have an accountant? He asked Tricia.

"I don't believe he had one. If Mr. LaMotte did, I never once heard him mentioned nor did he ever call for your grandfather when I answered the phone. And," she hastened to add, "I always answered the telephone."

Rob tapped his fingers on the desk top. "I see." A wave of uncertainty swept over him.

"Will that be all, sir?"

He looked up. "Yes. Yes, of course."

She slipped from the room, but Rob didn't notice her leave. He felt confused. During the night, when he had vacillated between mental highs and lows, he had felt confident and sure of himself to a degree he had never before known in his life before feeling completely inadequate. Now a sense of trepidation hammered at him. He couldn't understand why or which emotion he was supposed to feel. For some insane reason, he even felt impotent.

He thought back to the night before. He'd had exotic thoughts about Tricia when he had awakened to find the woman sitting on his bed. She had not made mention of it that morning when he first saw her, and after breakfast was over, he had come to the office following the tour of the upper floors. He shouldn't be feeling upset over any of that, since it had made no impression on her—at least one he could ascertain. But then, would she have said something? It would have been out of line for her to do so, as far as he could determine.

If it weren't Tricia making him feel anxious, what was? The idea of the millions of dollars again? He shook his head. The thought hadn't even formed, and he honestly was growing accustomed to the idea of having money. Was it the thought that perhaps his grandfather had been involved in less than honest business practices? That might be, but it didn't mean he had to do the same sort of thing.

The thought of Tricia surfaced again. Had she been acting that morning? Was she capable of acting that well? Certainly Rob could see nothing that indicated she was the least bit uncomfortable with him. Yet there seemed to be something in her eyes or maybe in her whole being that seemed to be crying out to Rob. Was that true or was he imagining things? Certainly she was an attractive woman and not the least bit intimidated by living in the same house with a man she just met. Of course, it was an employer/employee relationship, but even the most proper person would feel a bit of trepidation over such a new situation.

He suddenly found himself wanting to be with her, to see her. To touch her? Rob shook his head. He must be crazy. Still, he found it suddenly impossible to erase thoughts of her from his mind. He had to go to her, but he needed a reason. What could he say if he suddenly showed up in the kitchen or wherever she might be working?

The book wherein he found the three bills marked paid in full suddenly fell into his line of vision. That was it. He'd go to her and ask who these men were. Did she know them? If they were from Nowaupeton, she probably knew of them in some way. At least it would be a legitimate excuse to speak with her.

Scooping up the book, he hurried down the hall toward the steps and the first floor.

He found her in the kitchen, wiping off the stainless steel counter. She jumped when he spoke from the doorway.

"Tricia?"

"Yes sir?" she said, spinning about to see him.

Noting her startled expression, he said, "I'm sorry. I didn't mean to frighten you."

"It's not that, sir. It's just that I've lived here alone for some time now, and I'm just not used to you being here yet. That's all. What may I do for you?"

"It's nothing that important. It's just this book." He held the small, black book up. "Could you tell me if this is my grandfather's signature?"

He circled the round kitchen table and held out the book, opened to the first page.

Tricia wiped her hands on a towel and leaned forward to look without offering to take the book from Rob.

"Yes, that's his handwriting." She looked up, a smile on her face as if proud of the fact that she was able to help him with something.

"Do you know who Dan O'Malley is?" He thrust the book forward and she took it.

Tricia wrinkled her forehead, before slowly shaking her head. "No sir, I don't believe I know him. There are O'Malleys around

Nowaupeton but no Dan that I've heard about."

Rob turned the page and said, "What about this Jim Bradley? Do you know him?"

She brightened. "Jim Bradley's our mayor. No. Wait. Jim Bradley, Jr. is the mayor. I believe this Jim Bradley was his father. Jim Senior was also the mayor until he was killed."

"Killed? How was he killed?" Rob felt his throat go dry. Had his grandfather been involved in some way?

"He was killed in a head-on collision."

Rob relaxed. "And what about this man on the third page?" he asked.

She took the book and turned the page. "Peter Simmonson? Why, he was the man in the other car."

Rob looked up. "Are you sure?"

She nodded. "It was on the Fourth of July when they crashed right in town. Both men were killed instantly."

"Wasn't that a bit unusual? Or does it happen quite frequently?"

"You mean head-on accidents like that?"

He nodded.

She laughed softly. "No. It was the only time as far as I know."

"You're sure?"

She nodded again. "I remember it quite well, although I was only ten years old at the time. It ruined the holiday for everybody."

"How long ago was that?"

She paused for a second. "Twenty-six years ago."

"Do you know what this Simmonson did for a living?"

Tricia frowned. "I'm not real certain, but he was on the city council at the time of the accident."

Rob looked up. "Both men were on the city council?"

She nodded.

"Wasn't that a little strange?"

"That's why the holiday was ruined."

"Yeah. I guess it would have been."

She held out the book for Rob to take, and in so doing, his hand brushed hers. For an instant their eyes locked. Rob could see the hunger there and forced himself to look away. He'd felt no surge of desire at that moment while the thought of possibly being impotent rammed its way to the forefront. Even though he'd had erotic thoughts about her the previous night, he wanted nothing to do with a situation that might prove to be premature or disastrous because of his own sudden and unexpected inability to perform.

He bit his tongue and took the book from her without looking directly in her face. Why didn't he feel at ease with her? Was there something ominous or threatening about her that he sensed but couldn't identify? Had he been married too long to be able to look at an attractive woman without feeling some sort of guilt?

That bitch Sherry sure had done a number on him mentally as far as he could determine. He felt less than masculine whenever he thought of her and the incident at Frank's Place. One thing he had to work on was his own self-esteem. Last night in the library, he hadn't even thought of his masculinity and had felt confident enough to want to take on the world if necessary.

Now he felt less than able to hold his own in any sort of conflict.

He took the book, and looking up, he found her staring at him in a wistful way.

Rob turned to leave and stopped. "Tricia?" he asked without fully turning around.

"Yes?" Her voice was nothing more than a tiny whisper.

He turned enough to glimpse her without actually facing her. "Another time—perhaps?"

Tricia looked up, a startled expression on her face replacing the wistful one. Then a smile played at the corner of her mouth, and she nodded demurely.

"I . . . I need some time, I think," Rob said hesitantly.

Tricia nodded again.

"It'll be soon, all right?"

"I believe I understand, sir," she said quietly.

Rob started for the doorway that would lead to the hall. When he reached the door, he stopped and turned once more. Tricia stood, watching him, a hauntingly benign smile on her face. He felt she wanted to say something but decided he wouldn't push for any more conversation.

When he reached the front hall and stood

opposite the entrance to the library, he stopped and looked in the hall tree mirror. For some reason he felt he might look different after talking with Tricia in such a flirting yet intimate way. When he saw his image, he choked back a gasp. He'd changed somehow. He looked closely. His hair! His brown hair looked as if it were thicker, as if there were more hair than had been there yesterday.

Dropping his attention to his eyes, he noticed the tiny lines that had been forming there the last few years were gone—but that was impossible. He stepped back a way and continued studying his reflection. If he knew anything, it was the fact that somehow he looked better than he had the day before, better, in fact, than he had looked in several years. Before stepping out of the mirror's range, he ran a hand through his hair. It even felt thicker.

An involuntary smile brought a short puff of laughter with it when he realized he was trying to convince himself that he looked younger, and he walked into the library. The hands of the clock on the fireplace mantle pointed to 11:15. He had better than an hour before his lunch would be served. He wanted a little time during which he could relax.

The book with the golden pages caught his attention, and he crossed the room to get it. Why had he dreamt the book had been on his bed last night? Shaking his head at the thought, he took it to the couch and sat down. The relatively straight back of the Victorian piece brought him to a quick, fidgeting stage, and he brought his legs up and turned sideways to be more comfortable. He opened the book and ran his fingertips over the irregular surface. What did it say? What did it mean? Who had written the book? When had it been written and why? The questions zoomed through his mind and he stretched out even more. He wouldn't be able to rest any if he thought of the book and the mysteries surrounding it.

Turning onto one side, he closed his eyes for an instant then quickly opened them when the book slipped from his grasp and slid to the floor with a resounding slap. Realizing what had happened, he leaned over the edge and retrieved it. He clutched the leather volume to his chest and yawned. His disturbed sleep last night had robbed him of a good night's rest, and he closed his eyes once more.

The warm glow of rest and unexpected sleep washed over him, and he settled into an even deeper slumber. His body became heavy, but he wanted more comfort and brought his arms up, carrying the book with them until it nestled in the crook of his arm for a moment. Not completely comfortable, he wiggled around and lay his head on the hand holding the book.

Rob yawned again and fell into a deep sleep.

He found himself sitting in a different living room, opposite a man who appeared to be very interested in everything Rob said. Then he realized he was selling the man insurance.

When he asked the man a question about method of payment, he looked up. Narrowing his eyes, Rob studied the man. Two distinct, curved horns grew from the forehead, just below the hairline. His customer seemed normal in every other way, except for the tail that swished around on the floor next to the man's legs.

"Could I sell *you* something?" the man asked Rob.

"What might that be?"

"I'm in retirement property. You plan on retiring one day, don't you?"

"Why, I'm already retired. I have lots of money." Rob grinned foolishly and then wondered why he was trying to sell insurance if he had so much money. How much did he have? He couldn't remember.

"You'd like this," the man said. "Warm the year around. Nice people there, already settled in, enjoying themselves."

"I don't think so," Rob said quietly.

"Let me show you a couple of things." He waved a hand to one side and said, "Look!"

Rob turned and sucked in his breath. Sherry was with some man who was screwing her. He looked more closely and realized it was Frank Yearnall. Who else would it have been?

"That's not important, is it?" the man asked.

Rob found himself shaking his head. Of course, Sherry wasn't important anymore. He had tried to reconcile with her, but she wanted no more to do with him. As far as her boss was concerned, he could do whatever he wanted. It made no difference to Rob.

The couple disappeared, and the man said, "Look. Here's an example of the shoreline that would be near the property I have in mind for you."

A beach stretched for miles in either direction, and Rob looked closely. The sand appeared to be black. When he fixed his attention on the water, his eyes widened. Instead of water, a seething, raging fire burned out of control for as far as Rob could see. He didn't like the place at all. Turning away, he felt better once the conflagration was out of sight. He felt comfortable, warm, at ease. He wished he had power that would allow him to control everything about him, power that would give him confidence in anything he attempted.

A warmth from overhead brought his attention upward, and he looked directly above to find a light, brighter than anything he'd ever seen. But his eyes didn't hurt because of the brilliance. In the center, the figure he saw appeared to be warm and friendly. The figure held out its arms and then dropped them to its side, head dropping forward. Shoulders shook as the figure wept. Then the light and the silhouette diminished in size, retreating swiftly from Rob's view.

When the figure and the light disappeared in the distance, a blackness fell over him, and he groped about looking for some point of reference. His head spun.

Power!

The word crashed into his mind. He would have power. Somehow he knew that but he had no idea as to how or from where such power would come.

Blinding lights flashed on and off, leaving a kaleidoscope of color in Rob's mental vision. Where were they coming from? He looked about in the alternating gloom and brightness but could not make out the source. The brilliance hurt his eyes.

"You shall have power over your own fate and over the fate of others where your own destiny is concerned," a sultry voice murmured seductively.

"I . . . I don't understand," Rob said hesitantly. "Who are you? Where are you? I can't see you."

"I am who I am. I bring gifts to you. I am the gift bearer."

Rob looked around him. He could see no one. Who was the gift bearer? "Where are you? I don't see anyone."

"I am where I am. The gifts are for you."

"Why? Why bring me gifts?"

"I want you. Anything you want shall be yours, when you want it. If you desire something or someone to do your bidding, simply wait for it and it shall be."

Rob smiled crookedly. "There is no free lunch. What's all of this cost?"

"That is of no concern now. Use the gifts I

give. You will enjoy them."

"Don't lie to me. There has to be a price for such a wondrous gift."

"Do you want this power?"

Rob hesitated. Of course such ability would be something to have in one's control. Perhaps if he did have such power, he wouldn't be pushed around anymore. Things would definitely be different. "How much power and for how long?"

"As much as you want for as long as you want. I can do no better than that."

"And the price?" Rob asked.

"Don't worry about such things now. If you have the power, what will be yours will be yours. Whatever you want shall be yours for the asking. No earthly consequence shall be heaped on you as long as I am with you."

"But where are you?"

"With you."

"But where? I can't see you."

"I am with you now and for all your days on earth."

"Will I ever see you?"

"Perhaps."

"Where?"

"Perhaps in your dreams. Perhaps in your mind."

"Have I already seen you?"

There was no answer.

Rob waited.

Then the voice whispered in a sultry tone. *"Take and keep whatever you want! It shall be* yours. *You have the power. It is yours. Take! Keep!"*

"How is this possible?"

"The book! The book gives you the power and the right. Do it."

"My grandfather. How did he come by it?"

The voice laughed. *"The fool. He never learned how to use it. Quite by accident he gained some victories and some wealth. He found it after I conveniently led him to it and allowed him to find it in the tunnel I had randomly prepared for it."*

"And it is mine now? Mine to do with as I wish?"

"Yes."

"Where did it come from? Who wrote it?"

"No one wrote it. It was willed into existence, and it came from the one who willed it."

Rob swallowed. Was any of this real? Was he dreaming? He looked around. There was nothing that he could do. It was as if he were lost in some sort of black void.

Then the words began hammering at him once more, just disconnected phrases. *"Just wish for—"* *"Pay later—don't worry."* *"The Dead."* *"What is your desire?"* *"Power!"* *"How much?"* *"As much as you want."* *"The Dead!"* *"Die, you bastard!"* *"Power!"* *"Yours."* *"Mine."* *"Take."* *"The Dead."* *"Keep."* *"Yours."* *"The Dead."* *"All Yours."* *"All mine."* *"The Dead."*

Rob felt his heart race. What was The Dead? What did that mean? "What is the meaning of The Dead?" he screamed.

No answer. Instead, he felt himself spin about and found that he was back on the shore with the raging fire once more. He hated this place. Why didn't the figure in the bright light come back again? When he had seen that person and that light, Rob had felt totally at ease, warm and comfortable and—and something else he couldn't quite pinpoint. Had it been peace? Had it been a true feeling of love?

A movement to his right brought Rob around to face it. Something had moved. Had he thought he'd seen something move? Or had something been there but was gone now? The fiery ocean lay behind him, and he peered into the darkness.

Then he saw the motion again. It appeared to be a man, and the man was walking right toward Rob.

"Hello? Who are you?" Rob's voice sounded muffled and strange, unlike the way it should.

The figure kept walking toward him, apparently unmindful of Rob's calling.

When the shadowy figure was no more than ten feet away from him, Rob tried to reach out toward the shape but found he couldn't move his arms. "What's wrong? Who are you? Speak to me. Why don't you talk to me?"

The figure walked up to Rob and continued, passing through him. Rob felt cold, icy cold, as the figure slipped through him. It was an old, old man. He'd never seen such an old person before in his life. Who was it? Why hadn't he spoken? Hadn't he seen Rob? How could he walk right through a person like that?

Then Rob could see others just like the old man. They shuffled along, unmindful of him, ignoring his pleas for them to speak, walking right through him as if he stood in their way. What was happening? He couldn't stand it anymore. He had to touch one of them or hear one of them speak.

Power. The Dead. Desires fulfilled. Power. How much? Yours. Mine. The Dead. Die, you bastard. Take. Yours. Mine. Keep. The Dead. Steal. Keep. No earthly consequences. Yours. Mine. The Dead. Yours. Mine. All yours. All mine. The Dead. The Dead. The Dead.

Rob reached out, trying to stop one of the shadowy figures walking by him, but his hand passed through, leaving it feeling cold and clammy.

Rob sat up, startled, pushing the book, on which his head had rested, to the floor. The solidity of the noise awakened him immediately. Where was he now?

The walls of the library came into focus, and he smiled when he recognized them. He was in his own house, in his own library. He was all right. Reaching up, he ran a hand through his hair and brought it away wet. Sweat poured from his face and body.

Then the dream came back to him—the faceless shadows, the cold icy feeling he had experienced when they seemingly passed right through him. His eyes widened as the scenes replayed in his memory.

Suddenly it all became clear. He understood the dream, and he knew what the book meant. He understood it and knew how to use it.

The book lay at his feet, and he reached down to pick it up. When he held it, he looked at it more closely than he ever had.

A malevolent smile replaced the look of horror that had twisted his face. The book was his.

CHAPTER FIFTEEN

The sun had long since risen and Rob had sat up the whole night, contemplating the dream he'd had. Had it been a dream or some sort of revelation? He had no idea. All he knew was that the mystery of the book, for the most part, was solved. It gave incredible power to the owner—power over others, a power over life or death if the owner chose. Rob had the ability to wish for things, and his wishes would be granted. Now he understood how his grandfather had acquired his wealth. He'd merely wished for it. Rob understood the wishes his grandfather had made, had been granted in roundabout ways. He knew who Dan O'Malley had been and why his grandfather had wished him dead. Rob wondered if Emil ever knew directly of the power of the book. Or had Emil just considered himself lucky when it came to certain matters?

Rob yawned and stretched. The library swam in his tired vision. His body and mind ached from the all night session, and a crooked smile twisted his lips. He could wish for anything, and it would be granted. What power!

He wondered if he should perhaps nap for a while and refresh his body and mind to better cope with his new knowledge. Another yawn tore at him and he wished he'd gone to bed. At least he'd now be feeling brighter and more alert.

His mind cleared instantly, his body tingling with newfound energy. He'd wished for it, and he instantly felt better. If he could only market something like that. It would be the easiest sale in the world to make, and he could make millions with it. A sly grin crossed his face. He didn't have to think like that anymore. All he had to do was wish for whatever he wanted and it would be his.

Did it work on people as well as material things? He knew Dan O'Malley had died because Emil had wished for it, but did that mean the owner of the book could wish for anything where others were concerned and have them bow to such wishes? He had no idea. Still, if it were the case, all he had to do was wish Sherry out of his life and Tricia, or someone else like her, into it.

Rob basically did not have a vindictive

nature. He had learned long ago to roll with the low blows in the boxing match of life, and he didn't want to see Sherry hurt. He'd fight back only if she hurt him first, and she had done that when Frank had thrown him out of the restaurant. But he wouldn't wish anything harmful of a permanent nature on his wife. After all, they had been together for many years and had brought Jeremy into the world together. Jeremy was the only bright spot in their marriage, and now that marriage would die a legal death like so many others. Rob got out of the easy chair and crossed over to the shelf. He'd held the book or had it close to him all night while he tried sorting through his myriad, spiraling thoughts.

The one aspect of the dream that bothered him was the phrase "The Dead." What did it mean? That was the only thing he couldn't bring into focus. The Dead. The dead what?

Reaching up he slipped the book into its place on the shelf. It had been a while before he figured out why he suddenly knew all about the book. When he realized he had lain with his head on it and had somehow absorbed its information and knowledge, he'd wondered if Emil had ever done that. There were still many things about the book he didn't understand. Who had written it in the first place? How had it come into his grandfather's possession? How old was it? Were there any consequences in owning it and using it the way his grandfather had and the way he intended? Surely, it couldn't be a one-way arrangement. There had to be some sort of reciprocal payment in kind for all the luxuries and enjoyment such a book could give.

Crossing the library, he stepped into the hall and caught his reflection at an angle in the hall mirror. Stepping over to it, he looked at his image. He'd half expected that he'd look awful but he appeared as if he had had a good night's sleep and didn't have a worry in the world. Again the book had to be responsible. He felt in the few days he'd been at the mansion that his appearance had changed for the better. He looked less tired, and his hair seemed to have filled out considerably. No wonder his grandfather had looked like he was 50 when in reality he was close to 90. Again it was because of the book.

A wave of nausea swept over him and he felt his stomach lurch. What was wrong? Why did he suddenly feel ill? He hadn't eaten anything for quite a while. The sensation spiraled outward, racing through his entire body and sending his head spinning. Reaching out, he grabbed at a radiator and steadied himself. Then, as if someone were speaking to him, he heard a name. *James Bradley, Jr. James Bradley, Jr. James Bradley, Jr.*

Rob looked about the hallway. No one was there.

"Tricia? Are you there?"

She didn't answer.

His forehead puckered when he tried to

replay in his mind the sound of the voice. Had it been male or female? He wasn't certain. It had been more of an awareness rather than an actual sound, now that he thought of it.

But who was James Brad—? James Bradley had been the mayor who had been killed in the head-on collision in Nowaupeton. He remembered Tricia telling him of the incident when he found the name James Bradley on a page in the ledger, which had been marked "paid in full."

A sudden realization of the meaning crashed into Rob's mind. Emil, his grandfather, had wished for Bradley and the other council member, Peter Simmonson, to be killed because of some disagreement over parking, of all things. Rob felt a film of perspiration form on his upper lip. His grandfather had used the book in a vindictive vengeful way.

But why had the name James Bradley, Jr. suddenly exploded in his mind?

The bits and pieces came in a blur of words and phrases. *Plot. Get even. Prove he is a phony. The land and the mansion acquired in a mysterious way. Prove LaMotte is crook. Phony. Phony. Emil bad. Grandson just as bad. Prove it. Prove it. Prove it.*

Rob's head swam, and he steadied himself on the radiator once more. He had to get to the bottom of this and soon, otherwise he feared he might lose everything he had just inherited. What could Bradley know? Did he know that Emil had been responsible for the elder

Bradley's death? But Rob had nothing to do with that. Could the younger Bradley somehow demand he hand over the book? Did Bradley even know of the book's existence? Rob wondered. He'd have to take aggressive action and be on his guard until James Bradley, Jr. was taken care of and no longer posed a threat to him.

"You've been bothered all these years?" Edith Simmonson asked.

James Bradley, Jr. squirmed in the easy chair she had shown him to, when they entered her home. He nodded and smoothed his prematurely graying beard. "Haven't you ever once thought that somehow the thing was rigged?"

Edith shook her head. "How does one go about arranging a head-on collision? I think you're completely wrong about this, Jim."

Bradley exploded from the chair. "No, I'm not. Goddamnit, I'm not. I know that somehow that old bastard killed your brother and my old man."

Edith remained calm and studied the heavyset man angrily pacing about her living room. "I think that's highly unlikely. Why would he have done something like that, assuming he could arrange a wreck without being anywhere near it?"

"How do you know he wasn't anywhere near it?" Bradley asked, turning to glare at the thin gray-haired woman.

"I was as distraught when Peter died as you are right now. All my grief has been spent, and I no longer think about it. Still, at the time, I did wonder if perhaps there might have been something strange about the accident."

Bradley snorted. "You sure got a way of talking, Edith. What did you suspect then?"

"I had been at the town meeting the night Emil LaMotte proposed a change in the parking along Main Street."

"So?"

"So, when Peter and your father voted against it, the petition was naturally thrown out. I saw how Emil reacted."

"How was that?"

"He didn't."

"What?" Bradley narrowed his eyes until they were mere slits.

"I said, he didn't react."

"That don't tell me anything. What do you mean?"

"As much as he claimed to be interested in the project of creating off-street parking, Emil just turned around and left the meeting room. There wasn't a sign of emotion on his face. No disappointment. No anger. No frustration. Nothing."

Bradley rubbed his fleshy cheek. "That's interesting, but it don't tell me nothing."

"Do you know what he reminded me of?"

"What?"

Edith shuddered. "A snake. He looked like a snake about to gobble up its prey. No remorse or emotion of any kind."

"Now you're saying you think Emil might have done something to get even with my old man and your brother?"

"I'm not saying that at all. I'm just saying that he took the rejection of the proposed change rather strangely."

"You must think the old fart was nuts enough to kill them because they didn't agree with him." Bradley fiddled with his beard nervously, something he did when he became excited or agitated.

"I didn't say that, Jim. You did. And watch your language please. This isn't Tooger's Tavern, you know. It's my home."

"Yeah, yeah." Bradley sat down again. "That's something else that bothers the hell outta me." Reaching up he scratched his head and smoothed the thinning hair back into place on his balding pate.

"What's that?" Edith asked, leaning back in her recliner.

"How'd that old geezer get his dough?"

"Well, I . . . He must have . . ." Edith's face clouded. "Isn't that strange? I don't know. I never once thought about it. Isn't that strange, indeed?"

"How old are you, Edith?"

"Well, now, aren't you getting a little bit nosy?"

"No, I got a reason for asking. How old are you?"

Edith blushed and patted her graying hair.

"Well, I'm in my middle to late fifties."

"How old, for Christ's sake?" Bradley blurted.

"Watch your language, Jim." She coughed quietly and said, "I'm fifty-eight. Why?"

"Well, then, you should remember Emil LaMotte from before he had money, right?"

"I don't know. When did he become rich?"

"You've got me topped by ten years or so, and I think it was around the early fifties. Isn't that right?"

Edith's face puckered into a series of lines, all of which led to her pursed lips. "I guess so. Yes, I think you might be right. Why? Is that important?"

"You'd have been in your early twenties. Am I right?"

Edith nodded.

Bradley grunted. "I was just a snot-nosed kid then. I would've been around ten or twelve. Remember what he looked like?"

She shook her head.

"Well, I do," he said. "He was old and looked like hell. Real thin. Gray hair. Lost of lines on his face. Then, all of a sudden, he had money, and he started to look younger and younger. Remember what he looked like before he took off?"

"How long ago was that?"

"Almost ten years. He looked better'n me. He looked like a movie star who had all the creams and stuff and face lifts to take years and years off a person's appearance. You know what I mean, Edith?"

Edith nodded. "What brought all of this on? Why are you worked up like this all of a sudden?"

"I was over in the county seat a day or two ago. I got to nosing around in some old records, looking for a record of deed my old man was supposed to have had at one time. That's when I ran across it."

"Ran across what?"

"The damndest thing I ever saw. The payment of back taxes on the Newton mansion. It didn't make any sense, so I asked one of the county workers there about it."

"What do you mean it didn't make sense? What didn't make sense?"

"Emil LaMotte's name was nowhere on the tax records before he paid the back taxes of four years or so. From then on, his name was there regular as clock work."

"I don't understand."

"Neither did I until I asked one of the girls there what it meant."

"What did it mean?"

"It meant that he got the Newton place and all of the land that went with it for some $900 in back taxes. I asked why it went to him. Do you know what she said?"

"How could I, Jim? I wasn't there. Tell me." Edith leaned forward.

"She said there was some mix-up between old Emil and old lady Newton who owned the property and that because of wrong wording or something, Emil had been the owner all along and she had been paying taxes for him. Then, when she died and the taxes stopped coming in, they hunted him down and made him pay his own taxes. Ain't that something?"

"Well, for heaven's sake."

"What do you make of that?" He leaned forward.

"I don't rightly know what to make of it. Was it legal?"

"I asked the same thing, and the girl said it apparently was. The county set the whole thing up."

"Well, I never."

"While I was there, I did a little more checking. That's about the time that Emil started buying up businesses and having the former owners run them for him. Do you remember any of that?"

"I remember Papa and Peter talking about it, but I never paid much mind to it. Are you suggesting something is crooked in that situation?"

"I don't know, but it sure smells fishy to me. Don't it to you?"

Edith shrugged. "What are you going to do?"

"I'm going to do a little more snooping. As mayor of Nowaupeton, I believe it's my duty to do so. Don't you think?"

"I suppose so. Where are you going to start?"

"With his grandson. He's living up there now, and he's sure a peculiar one."

"Do you know him?"

"No. But the sonofab—. Sorry, Edith. He ain't got no right to come in here and take over like he's going to."

"You don't know that for a fact, do you, Jim?"

Bradley shook his head. "But he will. Those rich, fat cats are all the same."

"You really think there's something more there than meets the eye?"

"You bet your life I do."

"What do you think is going on?"

"I don't know but I'm going to do a lot more digging and get to the bottom of it."

"You be careful. You've been a good mayor, and I wouldn't want to see anything happen to you because you got carried away with this thing."

"Don't worry. I'll be real careful. Remember, I was the mayor when old Emil disappeared. I know what it was like trying to do things without getting him involved. It was damned near next to impossible. I've rather enjoyed leading Nowaupeton the last eight, nine years without a rich guy butting in all the time. If I can find something to get rid of this Robert LaMotte, I will. I think the whole community will be better off without him. What do you think?"

"I don't think anything right now. You're the mayor. You're supposed to take care of things like that. I think the whole town will support you a hundred percent, Jim, no matter what you do."

"I hope so. I don't think I'll have any trouble,

but if I run into any, I want everybody behind me. I've got enough right now to go to him and try to bluff him. I've called some TV stations, and they're supposed to come here. I'll get to the bottom of this, by God."

"You be careful, Jim."

Tricia lay back in the tub. She'd worked hard that day and the hot, sudsy water was soaking away her fatigue. Idly squeezing the washcloth over her breasts, she relaxed as the water ran down to rejoin the foamy suds. Her thoughts drifted back to the night before last, when she had been awakened by her employer's scream. At first, she'd been terrified and had run to find out what was wrong. After she left him and returned to her own room, she'd found herself fantasizing about him, not sexually but in a general way. What sort of person was he? He seemed nice enough but had said something about divorcing his wife soon. Did that make him a bad person, or had his wife been at fault? She didn't know much about things like that, only having lived in a small town like Nowaupeton all her life. No one ever got divorced there. Anything she knew about divorce she'd learned from watching soap operas and reading novels when she was younger. Hardly real life in the raw.

She liked Rob LaMotte. He seemed like a nice person, and if he was anything like his grand-father, she would feel lucky indeed that he had kept her as his housekeeper. Tricia didn't want much from life. She had enjoyed the physical relationship she'd had with Emil but had never once thought of bettering her own lot by pushing for marriage.

When the incident in the kitchen took place yesterday, she had found out that Rob liked her more than just as her employer. He had said something about the two of them doing something together soon. As far as his inability to handle a relationship now was concerned, she could understand. He'd been married, probably for a long time, and was not used to being with someone else. Whenever he was ready, she'd be ready.

She found it strange that she had never once thought of another man after Emil had disappeared, until Rob showed up to claim his inheritance. Over the last few days, she'd found herself daydreaming in a more direct, intimate way, and now that she dwelt on it, she concluded that she was infatuated with him.

Her face darkened when she thought of the fact that Emil was Rob's grandfather. That couldn't be possible. Still, he insisted it was so, and certainly no one could fool Mr. Weipert, the lawyer who had handled Emil's affairs for the last nine years. When Rob's face formed in her mind, she smiled. He looked better now that he had when he first arrived. Perhaps he had been tired and hadn't rested well the last two nights. No, that wasn't necessarily correct. The first night, he had screamed in his sleep and awakened her. The next morning he still

looked tired. As for last night, had he even
slept? She wasn't certain. She'd turned down
the bed in his room, but no one had lain
there when she checked that morning. She'd
gone to the master bedroom, but it hadn't been
used either. The fact that Rob was already up
and dressed when she first went downstairs
had bothered her, but at the time she hadn't
suspected that he hadn't slept. Had he? She
didn't know.

She wondered if he would move into the
master bedroom soon. When he took the room
next to it the first night, she'd been mildly
upset. That had been the room in which she and
Emil had always made love. But now that she
knew her new employer a bit, she had no objections at all.

Still, if he hadn't slept well since his arrival,
how could it be that he looked so much better
than he did? She sat up straight in the tub. As
far as she knew, she even looked better now
than when she had first come to work for Emil.
Then she'd been plain and even a bit over-
weight, but today she looked fine. Her body's
muscle tone was far better today than 14 years
before. Her hair was bright and shiny, and her
face had thinned just enough to give it a
haunting look with the slightly sunken cheeks.
Her eyes were brighter and more alert. All in
all, Tricia Woodless felt quite at ease with
herself and her appearance. Was it completely
natural that a person looked better as one got
older? Wasn't it supposed to be the other way

around? It made no difference to her. She was satisfied.

Her thoughts turned back to Rob once more. She enjoyed spying on him, watching him do whatever he was involved with at the moment. She'd watched him sleep on the couch the day before and left when he began moving around a bit, thinking he was ready to awaken. She didn't want him to catch her.

Tricia ran a finger down her full breasts. They tingled with excitement when she touched one nipple. She pinched it a little, then harder. Emil had always enjoyed chewing on them. She wondered if Rob would. Tracing a route to the underside of her breast, she continued moving her fingers to her navel, then to her wet, soapy pubic hair. A tiny gasp escaped her lips when she touched her clitoris. It had been too long since she'd had a lover. Hopefully, she and Rob would find a natural liking for each other and her needs would be fulfilled by a man instead of her own fingers.

She ran her forefingers into her vagina and slowly began masturbating while envisioning Rob. As she reached her climax, she increased her manipulations until they rapidly brought her to fulfillment.

Lying back in the water, she thought of Rob. Was she falling in love with him as she had with Emil? Strange how she hadn't thought of Emil at all except for the first day when Rob asked her about him. Then, the memories had come flooding back, and she had fought to restrain herself from telling Rob the truth. If she told him, Rob would probably not want anything to do with her. Now she had thought of Emil and Rob while she soaked in the tub. Emil was gone, but Rob was there, someplace in the mansion. Emil was past history. Rob was the present and maybe the future. Memories of Emil would not bother her anymore, not with Rob LaMotte there.

She leaned back once more and smiled. Tricia was in love.

CHAPTER SIXTEEN

Rob wiped the corners of his mouth. The late lunch had been excellent. After he drank a cup of coffee, he'd go for a walk around the grounds, something he'd promised himself last night before he fell asleep. He had no idea how far the property extended or what type of terrain it was. All he knew was the house sat on top of a hill and that the Mississippi River could be seen in the distance.

He felt good. He'd finally had an uninterrupted night of sleep, and it had completely rejuvenated him. He felt alert, wide awake, ready to take on the world, if need be. His relaxed state surprised him. At first, he thought he might be paranoid to some degree concerning his sudden wealth. Since he had become aware of the power of the book, he felt a steady flow of confidence building by the minute. He knew what he could do in any given circumstance, which was something he had never before experienced in his life. He wondered if many people had. No matter what might be said about him, he knew he enjoyed the new life style that had suddenly been thrust on him. He liked the good life, if that's what he was living.

Furrows slowly formed across his forehead. Several aspects of the dream still bothered him. He knew he had power and could have virtually anything he desired. The one thing he could not do was control events outside his life. If the thing he wanted did not affect him in a direct way, he could not attain its end. That really didn't bother him, but something like that was not merely given away. There had to be a price he would have to pay, but what was it?

A shudder ran down his back when he thought of the shadowy figure that had come toward him when he stood on the black beach near the fiery ocean. Who had the old man been? What did he represent. Why wasn't that part of the dream clear? The same questions hammered at him concerning the other figures who had shuffled past him and through him. He had been able to make out some of their faces, but like the first figure, they had been beyond comprehension, dried up, wizened and wrinkled until they looked more like caricatures of old people than living entities.

Living? Had they been alive? He didn't know. Perhaps. But when they passed through him, the cold, clammy feeling had frightened him. The sensation had been all too real.

What did it mean?

Snapping out of his funk, Rob found himself sweating, his hands shaking. Was that from the dream or because he was reliving it? He had to get a grip on himself. Pulling out a hand-kerchief, he wiped the sweat from his brow and fixed his attention on his empty plate. The lunch had been very good. He'd have to make certain he complimented Tricia.

Just then the door opened and she entered, carrying a carafe of coffee. After she filled his cup, she turned to leave.

"Tricia?"

She stopped, turning to face him. "Yes, sir?"

"The lunch was very good. I enjoyed it."

Tricia looked down, embarrassed by his kind words. "Thank you, sir."

He wondered why she persisted in calling him "sir." After all, he had all but asked her outright to go to bed. She hadn't acted shocked or insulted by his covert statement in the kitchen the day before. Perhaps she hadn't understood what he had meant. He reflected for an instant and pictured her, the demure smile on her mouth, the turned-down eyes and the way she had acknowledged his suggestion of another time. No, she had fully understood. Then the only reason she continued addressing him as "sir" had to be that she was keeping up

265

the appearance of an employee/employer relationship so that she would never slip if someone else were around.

When he said nothing more, Tricia bowed her head and turned, leaving the dining room. Just as she reached the door, the bell at the front entrance sounded harshly.

Rob made a token gesture to stand but was stopped when Tricia said, "I'll get it, sir." She left the room and went to the kitchen to rid herself of the carafe then hurried toward the front of the house.

Rob could hear her heels clicking on the tiles of the hall floor. Then the sound of the large front door being opened and muffled voices filtered back to him. Who could be calling on him? He hadn't really met anyone here, other than the few business associates that Allen Weipert had seen fit to introduce to him on that first day he perused his holdings.

After the front door had been closed, Rob could hear Tricia coming toward the dining room.

"The mayor is here to see you, sir," she said quietly. "He's waiting in the library."

Rob couldn't help smiling. Just a few days ago, no more than a week, he was struggling, trying to make an insurance sale to win back the respect of a wife he no longer wanted and to gain enough confidence to carry on with his life. Now the mayor of Nowaupeton was calling on him, not that Nowaupeton was any great shake when it came to towns, but the idea of the top-ranking town official calling on him without invitation made him chortle inside.

"Thank you, Tricia. Ah, what's his name?"

"James Bradley, sir."

Rob's face twisted as he tried to place the name. Mouthing the name several times, he suddenly looked up in surprise. "I thought he was killed in a car collision. That's what you said, wasn't it?"

Tricia controlled her desire to laugh, which was all too evident on her face. "Yes sir, he was. This is his son."

Rob shuddered. James Bradley, Jr.? He'd been warned. A warm confidence filled him. "Thank you, Tricia. If I need you, I'll call for you."

She nodded and went to the kitchen.

Rob stood and straightened his clothing. He'd best look presentable. He checked his appearance in the hall mirror and strode into the library.

Jim Bradley, Jr. stood with his back to the doorway, examining some of the book titles. He stood directly in front of the shelf where the book with the golden pages rested.

Just as Bradley reached up for the book, Rob said, "Good afternoon, Mayor Bradley. What can I do for you?"

Bradley turned, a cold, calculating expression glinting in his eyes. Stepping away from the bookcases he walked up to the table and stopped, resting one hand on the oak top. "How do you do, Mr. LaMotte. I'm not here on any sort of pleasant business so I'll get to it right away."

Rob stepped farther into the room and went to the leather easy chair. Indicating the mayor should sit down in another chair that sat at an angle to the easy chair, Rob eased himself down and waited.

"I prefer to stand," Bradley said shortly.

"Whatever," Rob said in a quiet voice. The man looked positively ferocious with the graying beard and balding head. His belly puffed out, overhanging his belt like an overly ripe melon.

"I've found out some rather disturbing news, Mr. LaMotte. Perhaps you can clear it up for me."

"What's that, Mr. Bradley?"

"I learned how your grandfather acquired this house and property. What do *you* know about it?"

Rob sat up, almost getting out of his chair but stopping himself. A wry smile crossed his face. "I know nothing at all about my grandfather or his affairs."

A startled expression crossed Bradley's round face. "Well, that's interesting. How is that?"

"How is it that I don't know about him? I didn't know I even had a grandfather until a couple of weeks ago."

"Ah, well then, maybe you'll be reasonable and help me set this thing straight."

"What thing? What are you talking about?"

"I have reason to believe that Emil LaMotte, your grandfather, acquired this property and probably most of his businesses in something of a less than honest way. I've—"

"Just a minute," Rob said, leaping from his chair. "Are you saying he was a crook of some sort?"

"Well, that is, let's not jump to any hasty conclusions, Mr. LaMotte."

"I assume you have proof of some sort?" Because he had been forewarned, Rob bore in confidently.

"The fact of the matter is, I don't have conclusive evidence but I'm working on it. There's some serious questions that need to be answered."

"I think you'd better leave, Mr. Bradley. You're way out of line."

"No sir! I want an explanation about all of those dealings, and I'm starting with you."

"Well, I don't happen to have one for you. Now please leave."

"You'd better get one ready. I'm holding a press conference later on this afternoon, and I might even notify the sheriff. If you can't explain, perhaps someone reading the papers or seeing the story on TV will have an answer or two. Someone's got to know the true story."

"You shouldn't have done that, Mr. Bradley," Rob said icily. "If you carry through with this, I'll have my attorney sue the daylights out of you and the town, since you're obviously acting in an official capicity. Now get the hell out of my home."

Bradley glowered at Rob before stepping around the library table. "Get your answers together, LaMotte. You're going to need them before I get through."

Rob watched him storm toward the front entrance, throwing open the huge door. He tried to slam it, after jamming his cap onto his head, but the weight of the door was too much for him.

Rob went to the window and watched him climb onto a Harley-Davidson motorcycle. Bradley revved up the motor, which alternately backfired and roared in a way that seemed to reflect the mayor's personality. After he sped away, leaving the horseshoe driveway and careening down the hill toward the county road, Rob turned away. It figured that such a mayor would look like some deviate from a motorcycle gang.

Jim Bradley watched the man with the TV logo pull up outside Tooger's Tavern. A sly look replaced the apprehensive one that had clung to his face since he had left the LaMotte mansion. He had called the different newspapers in the area, but none of them had shown up, nor had the radio people he'd contacted. Of the half dozen television stations he'd called, one unit had shown, and it was twenty minutes late. He had to be cool about this. He didn't want to turn the TV people off by blowing his stack at them for being late.

A young woman stepped out of the van while a pimply faced young man of 20 or so got out from behind the steering wheel. The woman walked up to the tavern door and entered.

She went directly to the bar and motioned for Tooger Mahone, the bartender and owner, to come over.

"Is Mayor Jim Bradley here? I was supposed to meet him at this place." She looked around the room, a disdainful expression on her face.

Tooger turned and waved at Bradley. "Hey, your honor, this good-looking woman here wants to see you."

Jim walked slowly to the end of the bar and said, "Knock it off, Tooger. How do you do, ah, Miss—?" He stared at her with open admiration when she turned to face him.

"I'm Melissa Berkley from Channel 39 in Dubuque. Tell me more about this scam you said you've uncovered."

Bradley quickly repeated everything he'd told her on the telephone and then added a replay of the conversation he'd had with Rob LaMotte earlier.

"You're contending then, Mr. Mayor, that the LaMottes acquired the property in question in some illegal way, is that right?"

Bradley nodded, a gruff look of satisfaction on his fleshy face.

"And you say you have the proof, is that right?"

Again he nodded. "It's in the county court-house. The current owner claims he knows nothing. The clerk I talked with in the court-house seemed as puzzled by the transaction as I was. Now I'm no genuis, you understand, but I know right from wrong, and this appears to be as wrong to me as I don't know what."

"Well," Melissa said, "I'll want to get you on tape, giving the same answers to the questions I just asked you. We can do that outside some-place."

"Hey," Tooger said, "do it in front of my place. I can use the free publicity."

Bradley turned, staring at Tooger in a way that made the man first look down and then turn around and go to the back of the bar. Facing the reporter once more, he said, "Sorry about that. It ain't every day a TV reporter comes to Nowaupeton."

"Will it be possible to get a shot of the mansion? And do you think this Rob LaMotte will allow me to ask him some questions?"

"Don't know about that. You can take pictures of his house from the county road though. I know that much."

"Well, I'll try to interview him."

"I'll show you the way after you're done with me," Bradley said. "Maybe you might get farther along with him if I ain't there. He ordered me out of his house. Hah! *His* house, my eye. We'll see about that. Nine chances out of ten, the other businesses involved were probably got the same way."

Bradley followed the woman out of the tavern when she didn't reply. Once the camera was ready, Melissa began her questioning with an introduction.

"We've been called here to Nowaupeton, Iowa, by Mayor James Bradley, Jr. who believes that a house and surrounding property may have been transferred illegally by the county to a family by the name of LaMotte. Is that right, Mayor Bradley?"

"Yes, it is. I discovered it in the county courthouse this week. I'll say this much—it was by accident."

"Can you tell me what happened? How does an illegal transfer of property come about?"

Bradley repeated the story for the benefit of the TV camera up to the point of implicating the county itself.

"Are you saying the county could be at fault here, Mayor Bradley?"

"I'm not saying anyone or anything could be at fault. I'm merely saying that something wrong took place over thirty years ago and it should be straightened out somehow."

"It could go deeper than you've implied here?"

Bradley smiled and smoothed his thinning hair over his bald spot. "Yes, it could go very deep. I'm going to pursue this to the last word to keep greedy manipulators out of Nowaupeton. We don't need people like that around here."

"Thank you, Mayor Bradley."

After Bradley led the TV man into the countryside, he parked out of sight of the

LaMotte mansion. He directed the truck down the road several hundred yards and then turned his bike around and headed back toward Nowaupeton.

Shooting several minutes' worth of scenery as well as the mansion on top of the hill, Melissa directed the cameraman to drive up to the front of the house.

Rob stormed out the instant the van stopped and the woman got out. Before he would order them off his property, he waited for the woman to approach him.

After she introduced herself, she said, "Mr. LaMotte, Mayor Bradley has stated that there is some legal question as to whether or not you actually own your property here. I'd like to give you a chance to answer that charge on camera."

Rob studied the young woman for an instant. It might be wise to take her up on her offer if he didn't want to lose any ground in any forth-coming legal battle. "All right. Where do you want to do this?"

"You have a lovely home, Mr. LaMotte. Why don't we film you right here on the front porch?"

"Very well," Rob said and adjusted his shirt front.

Frank pushed at Sherry's body as he neared his climax. When he achieved it, his sperm gushed into her as she continued threshing about beneath him, fighting to climax herself.

Finally her senses exploded, and she spiraled down from the heights she and her lover had climbed.

"I better get dressed. Jeremy will be home soon from that meeting at school. It's a little past six already."

Frank got off the bed and said, "I'm going to take a quick shower. I've got to get back to the restaurant before seven." He walked by the small TV set on the dresser and turned it on.

Once he was in the bathroom, Sherry got off the bed and slipped into the negligee Frank had bought for her. She paid little attention to the newscast that was on the screen. Turning around, she fixed her attention on it for no reason other than to have something to do until Frank got out of the shower.

"This story was filmed by our sister station in Dubuque, Channel 39, and concerns a suspected property scam of some sort. Melissa Berkley is the reporter."

The screen blinked and a heavy-set, bearded man stood in front of a bar.

"We've been called here to Nowaupeton, Iowa, by Mayor James Bradley, Jr.," the reporter said from off camera, "who believes that a house and property may have been transferred illegally by the county to a family by the name of LaMotte."

Sherry's attention was riveted to the TV set when she heard the name. She listened intently for the name to be repeated, but it wasn't. Had she heard right, or had she imagined it? She didn't know.

Just then, Frank stepped into the bedroom and said, "What's the matter?"

"Shhhhh," she said, pointing to the screen when the image of a large mansion filled it.

The voice of Melissa Berkley continued over the picture. "We're here on the front porch of Rob LaMotte's magnificent home outside the northeastern Iowa town of Nowaupeton."

"Rob's house?" Sherry squealed, disbelief etched on her face.

" . . . claims there's some illegality in the past history of the LaMotte mansion ownership. What do you know of the Mayor's charges, Mr. LaMotte?"

When Rob's face filled the screen, Sherry squealed again. "It's Rob. For Christ's sake, it's Rob. No wonder he hasn't been coming around to pester me. He's not in town."

"Be quiet for crying out loud," Frank said.

" . . . came to my home shortly after lunch today and said something crazy about the house not being mine or some such tripe as that."

"Therefore, you claim the house is truly yours?"

"Of course it's mine. I inherited it from my grandfather, Emil LaMotte."

"Was your grandfather a wealthy man?"

Rob hesitated for an instant, and Sherry opened her mouth to say something. Frank clamped a hand over it and whispered, "Not now."

"He was very successful from what I know of him," Rob said, "and he left me his entire estate."

"What kind of man was he?" Melissa asked.

"I didn't know him. I never met him."

"Well," the reporter said, dropping her voice to add an air of mystery, "this situation will continue to unfold in Nowaupeton and Channel 39 will be right here to keep you informed. Be sure to watch all of our newscasts for further developments in this strange story."

The screen went dark for an instant before a commercial came on.

Sherry sat back on the bed. "I don't believe it."

Frank pulled on his shorts and sat down next to her to put on his socks.

"What do you make of that, Frank?"

He shrugged. "You got me."

"It was Rob, all right. He looks good on TV. But what the hell were they talking about, Frank?"

"From what I heard, it sounds as though he's inherited something that may not be his."

"That dumb sonofabitch can't do anything right, can he?" Sherry got off the bed and went to the TV set, turning down the volume. "Did he say how much he was left by his grandfather?"

Frank looked up. "No. Why? You interested in making up with him?"

"I don't know. It might be worth it. What do you think?"

Frank shrugged and pulled on his pants. "You might be smart if you checked it out."

"It's gotta be a bunch of bullshit. I don't believe it."

"Yeah, you're probably right. He's a phony."

"You got that right."

"He'll probably get into a mess of some sort." Frank put on his tie and stepped closer to one of the mirrors.

"I think I'm well rid of him."

Frank turned around after finishing with his tie and said, "Still . . ."

Sherry looked up. "Still what?"

"What if it's all on the level? What if he really is worth a bundle?"

Sherry looked away. "Did you think about how to check up on him? You said you would."

"I know I did. I just haven't had the time."

"What should I do?"

"He might be worth a lot of dough, Sherry."

"What should I do?" she repeated.

"I think you should go there and be your tender, loving self. That's what I'd do."

"I can't. I can't stand him anymore. He's such a worthless wimp."

"A wimp maybe, but maybe not worthless."

"You know, he looked different somehow, and he even sounded different. More in charge. Do you know what I mean?" Sherry looked past Frank and caught sight of her own reflection in the mirrors and quickly looked away.

"Having money can do that to a person. You better go. You should be available to help him if he needs you. Be the dutiful and sorrowful wife."

"Sorrowful?"

"You bet. Sorry that you walked out on him the way you did, but you've seen the error of your move. You still love him. You want him. You've got to be with him."

"He'll see through it. Besides, what if he *is* crooked?"

"What if he isn't?"

"You're probably right, Frank. It's better to be there and be available, like you said. I see what you mean."

"Tell you what. I'll rent a car for you tomorrow. Then you can go to this place, whatever it's called."

"Yeah. I think you're absolutely right, Frank. Now isn't the time to walk away from Rob, not if he's worth a lot of money." She watched Frank's reflection in the mirror stand up and come toward hers. He embraced her and they kissed.

CHAPTER SEVENTEEN

Rob lay on his back, staring into the darkness. Had he made a mistake? Had he been wrong to talk with the television reporter? What had he said? He mentally replayed the questions the attractive woman had asked and immediately recalled his responses. He'd said nothing that was out of line. Surely he hadn't said anything derogatory about Mayor Bradley. Even if he had, the mayor was a public figure and should expect comments of a critical nature from time to time. Bradley seemed to be attacking Rob on a personal basis. Why? What could the man possibly have against him?

He thought of James Bradley, Sr. crashing head-on with the other councilman. Of course Emil had wished for them to be dead, and both of his grandfather's adversaries had died. But did James Bradley, Jr. know of that? How could he? If the cause of death was an auto accident, nothing could be suspected other than mere happenstance. If that were truly the case, then what did James Bradley, Jr., Mayor of Nowaupeton, actually want?

Rob shook his head. The mayor's attitude, his visit that afternoon and his vindictive summoning of TV reporters and newspapers made no sense to Rob at all. At least, as far as he knew, none of the newspapers had shown up. That in itself was good. TV had a way of slipping news by viewers if they weren't paying close attention, but a newspaper account could be read and reread. Maybe, if Rob were lucky, the whole incident would soon be forgotten.

The thought of Bradley's motivation continued to bother Rob. What was he up to? What did he want from Rob? What did he actually know? And if he did know something, why did he wait until now to confront someone with his suspicions? Were they only suspicions, or had he actually uncovered something? He'd said something about records at the county courthouse. What could be there that would incriminate Emil or Rob?

Throwing back the covers, Rob sat up and turned on the light. Pulling on his robe, he went to the hall door. He had to think.

He made his way along the hall toward the wide staircase and hurried down. When he reached the first floor, he went to the library.

After he had turned on the lights there, he crossed the room and reached up for the book. When he held it, he felt a certain calm wash over him, and he relaxed. He leaned back in the easy chair and clutched the book to his chest.

He refocused his thoughts on James Bradley, Jr. What did the man want?

A humming sound in Rob's ear went virtually unnoticed as words began forming in his mind.

"Your wealth."

Rob's eyes widened. It was the voice from his dream. Had he imagined that answer or was he actually hearing something? Still, the idea made sense. Why wouldn't someone who might be jealous want that which wasn't his? Was Bradley simply jealous of Rob's wealth?

"Yes."

If that were so, was there anything to be concerned about Bradley suspecting foul play in the matter of his father's accidental death?

Rob blanched, his eyes widening as a dry, hoarse laughter filled his head. Of course the deaths hadn't been accidental, had they? Emil had willed it, but did the younger Bradley know of this?

"You worry yourself over nothing," the sultry voice whispered. *"Bradley can do nothing to you. No one can. You have a power that comparatively few have had. Use it. Enjoy it. Don't bother with inconsequential people such as this idiot, Bradley."*

Rob felt relaxed. Instead of worrying, he tried to analyze the voice that had spoken in his head. Had it actually been a voice, or had he imagined the whole thing? Was hell the source of the book's power? Or was the book the source itself? He concentrated for a long moment on what the book had said or what he had imagined the book had said. *"—a power that only a few have had."* What did that mean? Who other than his own grandfather had had possession of the book?

He looked around the room. At night the library took on a warm glow that none of the other rooms had, and he felt comfortable there. Perhaps all he should do is put the book back on the shelf and go to bed. He moved to get up but found he couldn't.

"Don't you want to solve the problem of the mayor?"

Hadn't the book or the voice or whatever said that the mayor was no problem and that Rob shouldn't worry over it? Why then should he solve the problem if there was no problem?

"Do you enjoy a fly buzzing around your head? Do you enjoy a mosquito trying to bite you?"

Rob automatically shook his head.

"Then do something about this brainless idiot. He'll only serve to pester you like a pebble in your shoe."

Rob focused on the words. Brainless idiot? That was an apt description of the man he had recently met for the first time. Do something? What? What could he do? For the most part, Rob usually let bygones be bygones, but now he was experiencing the desire to create havoc. He'd never been one to fight with or without reason. He preferred turing the other cheek in the Christian tradition.

But the wish for violence and revenge now surged to the peak of his consciousness. It would serve this Mayor Bradley right if something dreadful did happen to him. But what? What could Rob wish for that would satiate his suddenly awakened lust for blood and vengence?

If he had Bradley there right then, he'd bash his head in. He'd pound him senseless. He'd beat the mayor to death with his bare hands.

Rob's eyes widened and his head jerked up when he heard the dry, hoarse laughter of before ringing in his ears. He looked about the room. The sound was too real for him to be imagining it. Where was it coming from—who was laughing?

More laughter answered his unspoken question, and then it stopped.

Rob felt uncomfortable. Reaching up he found his forehead wet and became aware of the fact that his pajamas and robe were damp as well. He had to go back to bed. This was foolish. When he stood up, he felt a weight on his lower body and looked down. He had an erection. When had that happened? Could thinking about what he'd do to Bradley have aroused him sexually?

He went to the shelves, returned the book to its place and retraced his steps to the hallway.

The library was plunged into blackness when he turned off the light and hurried up the stairs.

Tricia!

The thought of the woman, lying in her bed, loomed in his mind. Should he go to her now? Would she accept him under circumstances such as this? He had no reason to go there other than to ask her to have sex with him. Sex? Yes. It couldn't be called love. They didn't know each other. Didn't two people have to know each other well before they could call it making love? At one time he and Sherry had made love, but that was long ago.

Tricia's face hovered in his mind's eye. She was beautiful. She liked him. He knew that. And he found her more than attractive. Perhaps . . .

He passed the door to his room and hurried toward the back of the house.

"Give me a beer, Tooger," Bradley said, leaning on the bar. The aroma of draught beer, salty pretzels and stale cigarette smoke filled the room. Bradley didn't notice the smells, nor did the other patrons.

"Sure, Mayor. It ain't every day I get a TV celebrity in here." Tooger said as he drew the beer. He scraped the foam off the glass with a wooden spatula before setting the mug in front of Bradley.

"Yeah, Jim, were you nervous?" Spider Timmons asked.

"Nothing to it. All I did was talk." Bradley lifted the glass and sipped the beer.

"You always was good at talking, Jimmy," Charley Franklin said in his high-pitched, chirping voice.

Everyone laughed.

Tooger leaned over the bar and said, "Tell us, Jim. What the hell's going on?"

"Well," Bradley said. He lifted the glass and emptied it in one long swallow. "I think the Newton place was stolen by old man LaMotte back in the early fifties. He . . ."

"Hellsfire," Joe Morrison said, picking up his glass of beer, "he didn't have brains enough to pound sand in a rat hole. I knew him pretty good."

Everyone turned to look at Morrison, who was in his 70s.

"How well did you know him?" Bradley asked, motioning to the bartender for a refill.

"Well, I'd say as good as anyone did."

"And how was that?"

"Well, I—that guy—he—"

"That's what I thought," Bradley said, lifting his head in a gesture of superiority. "How old are you, Joe?"

"Seventy-five my last birthday." Morrison winked and clicked his false teeth.

"You know how old Emil LaMotte was when he died?" Bradley drained half his mug and set it on the bar.

Morrison screwed his whiskered face up and shook his head.

"I'll tell you," Bradley said. "According to his 1955 driver's license record, he was in his nineties, and as I remember him, he looked like he was about fifty or so. Right, fellas?" He finished the mug of beer and called for another.

Everyone nodded, mumbling about their own recollections of Emil.

"What difference does that make?" Tooger asked. "You jealous 'cause you look like hell and you're only in your forties?"

Everyone roared, and Bradley held his hands up for quiet. "I'm telling you he got the mansion and the land that went with it for less than one thousand bucks and then he started buying up most of the businesses in town here."

"He also helped turn Nowaupeton into a pretty nice little resort town, too, didn't he?" Digger O'Dadish asked.

"You didn't lose your old man, Digger, not the way I did," Bradley said, lifting his fresh beer and downing most of it.

"You ain't gonna try to say old Emil had anything to do with that, are you?"

Before Bradley could answer, Artie Cushing stepped forward. "I was on the church fund-raising committee the year old Emil gave the Father ten thousand dollars. Would a crook do something like that?"

Bradley turned to face Cushing. "He might do it to make himself feel better about fucking the whole community."

"I think you're wrong, Bradley," Cushing

said and strode toward the door. " 'Night, Tooger."

"Night, Artie."

The rest of the men milled around for a moment, settling back to where they'd been before Jim Bradley had come in.

Bradley downed the rest of his beer. "Well, I gotta get home, Tooger. Behave." He threw a five dollar bill on the bar and adjusted his white billed cap as he walked to the door. When he stood outside, he inhaled the crisp, fall air and went to his motorcycle. When the Harley-Davidson kicked over, he revved the motor a couple of times before roaring away into the poorly lighted business section of Nowaupeton.

Rob hesitated at the door. Was he doing the right thing? Where had the question come from? He pictured the woman inside the bedroom. Tricia Woodless. Very attractive. Very nice to look at. Should he go in? Should he run the risk of turning her off completely? True, he had said they'd do something soon and he had meant it, but should it be at his demand? Shouldn't she have something to say about it? He'd noticed the hunger in her eyes, recognized it as a reflection of his own need. Whenever he and Sherry recently had indulged in sex, it had been only biologically functional, never resembling the exchange of love as in the earlier years.

He stepped back and jumped when the casement clock began striking the hour of midnight.

There seemed to be something special about Tricia, and he didn't want to upset any chance he might have with her in the future. He grinned wickedly. Some kind of millionaire he turned out to be. He could have just about any woman he wanted, and he was opting for his cook and housekeeper. It might be better to wait and try when the opportunity presented itself. If he moved too quickly on her, she might decide to quit, then he'd be without any sort of help at all. Not that he couldn't hire whoever he needed, but Tricia knew the house.

Shaking his head, he turned away. There seemed to be as many reasons not to go in and be with her as there were to go ahead and do it.

Suddenly Allan Weipert's warning sounded loudly in his mind. He shouldn't even be thinking about doing anything like this if he wanted to cut Sherry off with nothing more than a minimal settlement. Of course he would take care of his son in the best possible way, but he wanted to hurt Sherry as much and as deeply as possible for the hurt she had caused him. If he stepped out of line and it became known, his soon-to-be-ex-wife might have a weapon to use against him in a court of law.

It was better to do nothing and protect himself at he same time.

The thought of the book came to him. He always could use it to get rid of Sherry, but he didn't want to do something like that. He didn't hate her that much. If she stayed away and they had a reasonable divorce, he'd be happy. She could go her way and he'd go his. They could share their son if Rob couldn't get full custody of him, but he would never again worry about Sherry Paulson LaMotte. He didn't ever want to see her again.

He strode down the hall to his room.

Jim Bradley wove his bike through the streets toward his home and his wife, Carla. Since she'd be in bed by the time he got home, he could sneak in and climb into bed without waking her. The fall air washed over him and helped clear his foggy mind. He'd had one too many beers and should have left Tooger's sooner. He wondered if he'd be able to sneak in the house and get into bed without disturbing his wife.

Maybe he should go for a quick ride through the countryside and clear his head completely. After all, if she would say anything, he could always say he was on official business for the town and the time just sort of slipped away from him. But if he slurred one word or burped just once or made a misstep of any kind, she'd know in an instant that he'd been drinking and that he'd been lying about the official business as well.

Carla wasn't necessarily a shrew, but she didn't like being left out of any fun times. She often went riding with him on the motorcycle, and the two of them had attended rallies at different places over the years. She backed him in every way, even when it came to not wearing helmets when they went biking. She agreed with him that the state had no right to tell them to wear a piece of clothing or safety equipment. Jim loved her, and that was all that mattered as far as he was concerned.

He turned the Harley-Davidson around and roared back in the direction from which he'd come. It wouldn't take more than 15 or 20 minutes to clear his head, and then he could go home and face her without worrying.

He blasted past Tooger's Tavern and raced into the countryside after passing the church. The air felt invigorating and wasn't nearly as cold as it could have been for that time of year. Little by little, he could feel the wispy alcoholic cobwebs clearing from his mind. He felt good and twisted the accelerator further open. The bike leaped forward.

When he approached the tight turn before crossing Mill Creek, he squeezed the brake handles, but there was no resistance. The brakes were gone. As the bike careened into the curve, Bradley leaned into it, almost instinctively in an effort to keep his balance.

The road straightened and he found he'd made it through the sharp bend. The concrete bridge abutments glared in the headlight. All he had to do was go between them and he'd be able to let the bike coast to a stop.

The motorcycle suddenly hurtled forward, the accelerator twisting of its own volition in his hand. He tried to turn it back and looked down to see what was wrong. The bike swerved to the left, then to the right. His attention on the accelerator, Bradley didn't see the right-hand abutment looming in front of the bike.

Just before he rammed into it, he looked up and screamed. The front wheel struck first, collapsing like a child's toy, then the back of the bike reared up, throwing him into the night.

Bradley turned over once and plunged into the cement bridge wall, head first. His skull cracked open, the brains gushing onto the concrete floor of the bridge. His neck telescoped into his shoulders and the upper vertebrae smashed together, fusing into one misshapen mass of bone.

His body flip-flopped once, landing on its back. Bradley's eyes stared at the bright, twinkling stars overhead without seeing them. A trickle of blood ran down from the corner of his mouth, and the split in his head continued oozing grayish white slime onto the roadway.

CHAPTER EIGHTEEN

Rob scanned *The Des Moines Register* over the rim of his coffee cup. He'd slept well the previous night and felt rested. While staring at the printed page, a thought suddenly struck him. Where was the mayor? Had something happened to him? Why had the idea of Bradley suddenly come upon him? He'd had a few wishful thoughts yesterday, where the man was concerned, but— The idea grew. Something must have happened to him. Why did he feel like that? Could he know the future, too? Could he possibly know what was happening elsewhere? Rob frowned.

He didn't like Bradley. He'd made no argument against that. Bradley had come to him, threatening him in outright as well as veiled ways. Why shouldn't Rob be able to protect himself? But did he have to go to such extremes? Extremes? What extremes? He wasn't even certain that anything actually had happened to the mayor.

Rob almost dropped the coffee cup when the doorbell rang, echoing raucously through the large house. He didn't move. Let Tricia answer it. He didn't feel in the mood to talk with anyone at the moment.

The bell rang again, and when Rob looked through the window at the end of the dining room, he could see his housekeeper walking away from the back of the mansion toward a small shed.

Folding the paper and laying it next to his place setting, he stood and hurried to the front door. Just as he was about to turn the knob, the bell let out another ring. He threw open the door and stared for a moment at the uniformed man standing on the front porch.

"Rob LaMotte?" the man asked, taking a small step forward.

Rob automatically stepped back. "Yes? What can I do for you?"

"I'm Sheriff Olly Sothern. Can I come in?"

Rob didn't move for an instant, trying to understand why the sheriff was calling on him. Then, realizing the uniformed man had asked him a question, he stepped back and said, "Won't you come in? It's a little chilly out there, isn't it?"

"Thank you," Sothern said, striding into the

front hall.

"Would you like to come into the library, Sheriff?" Rob indicated the room to his left.

"No, this is fine right here. I just have a couple of questions to ask you. Before I do though, I want to explain that it isn't necessarily my idea to be here, asking you anything. Do you understand?"

Rob look puzzled. What could the sheriff mean? Didn't he run his own office? Who could have told him to come here to ask questions? The sheriff appeared to be a strong-willed person from what Rob could see. His slightly graying blond hair was neatly combed, and he appeared to be in good shape although his age wasn't readily evident based on his overall appearance. He could have been in his late thirties or early fifties, but Rob couldn't tell.

"I . . . I guess so, Sheriff. What can I do for you?"

"Where were you last night around midnight or so?"

"Why, here, at home. In bed—or I almost was. Why are you asking?"

"I said it wasn't my idea to come here and ask you these questions."

"Whose idea was it then?" Rob felt more confident. If the sheriff had to be told what to do, Rob felt he didn't have anything to fear. Anyway, why should he have anything to fear?

"Some of the townspeople thought it would be a good idea to ask you where you'd been last night."

"The townspeople? I'm afraid I'm not following you at all, Sheriff."

"The Mayor of Nowaupeton died last night. He—"

"Mayor Bradley." Rob did his best to keep from showing any emotion other than surprise or shock. "What happened?"

"He ran into a bridge abutment outside of town last night. He'd been—"

"Excuse me, Sheriff. How could I possibly have anything to do with something like that?"

"That's what I said. But those people who'd been with him at Tooger's Tavern seemed to think there might be suspicious play involved. Did you and the mayor have some bad blood between you?"

Rob turned, leading the man into the library. He wanted to sit down. He felt he had nothing to fear, but he decided if he sat down, he'd better be able to control any nervous fidgeting or prancing about from one foot to the other. He understood enough about body language to know that signs like that might be misinterpreted by the sheriff as signs of anxiety or apprehension. He indicated a chair for the sheriff.

"No, thank you. I'll stand," Sothern said, fixing his unwavering stare on Rob who sat down heavily in the leather easy chair. "Did you?"

"Did I what?" Rob asked quietly.

"Did you and the mayor have an argument or feud going?"

"No, I wouldn't say that."

"That's not what the boys at the tavern said. They seemed to think you might be real angry at Bradley for the things he said on TV about you and the fact that he was trying to prove something where you and your property were concerned. You want to change your story now?"

"No, why should I? I'm not denying that Mayor Bradley came here and accused my grandfather of something or other. As far as I'm concerned, I only inherited the property and his estate quite recently. I'm not aware if what the mayor said could be true or false."

Sothern nodded. "I see. I tended to pooh-pooh the idea when they brought it up, but they insisted I come here."

"I guess I'm sorry to hear that the mayor's dead. I didn't know him at all, other than meeting him yesterday."

"I believe it's an open and shut accident case. I just had to humor some of Tooger's customers. They were friends of Bradley's."

Rob laughed, short and sarcastically. "They thought I had something to do with it?"

Sothern nodded.

"How could I? What could I have done if it was an accident like you said? Better yet, why?"

"I suppose they thought ˈyou might be holding a grudge against the mayor for what he said. Did you have anything against him?"

Rob smiled inwardly. The sheriff was coming

at him from several different angles but always with the same question, just worded differently. "No, Sheriff, I didn't. I tried to convince him that I knew nothing of what he was telling me, but he wouldn't listen. I finally had to order him out of the house."

"I see. Were you angry?"

"Yes—but not that much."

"How much?"

"I wasn't angry enough to try to hurt him, if that's what you're saying. If there was mechanical failure with his motorcycle or car or whatever, how could I have managed that?"

"Funny you should say motorcycle first, Mr. LaMotte. Why did you?"

Rob glared at the sheriff. The man was being ridiculous. "Because I saw him on one yesterday when he came here. I just thought of it first, that's all."

Sothern nodded slowly. "You say you were here around midnight, is that right?"

"Yes. Can we go back to the accident? What happened?"

"Well, apparently the mayor and some of his buddies had been at Tooger's, and after talking about you he left and said he was going home. But we found his body and wrecked motorcycle by the Mill Creek bridge outside of Nowaupeton around one o'clock this morning. He apparently lost control and smashed into the abutment."

"Wasn't he wearing a helmet?" Rob asked.

Sothern shook his head. "You'd have to have

known Bradley. He didn't believe in them. In fact, he'd written a couple of letters to different newspapers around the area and even went to the state capitol to picket that law one time."

"So what you're saying is that he lost control of his bike, crashed and probably had his brains spread all over the place in a manner of speaking. Correct?"

The sheriff nodded.

"And his friends want to pin it on me? Christ, that's really funny. A man who didn't believe in helmets when riding a motorcycle does himself in, and then his friends try to pin it on the new kid in town."

"Now that you put it that way, it does sound pretty stupid, doesn't it?"

"You bet it does."

"I suppose you can prove that you were here around midnight if push comes to shove?"

Rob's eyes widened. "You don't believe me, do you?"

"I didn't say—"

"I can verify that he was here."

Both men turned to face Tricia, framed by the oak doorway.

"Who are you?" Sothern asked.

"I'm Tricia Woodless. I'm Mr. LaMotte's housekeeper and was his grandfather's housekeeper as well. Who are you?"

"Sheriff Sothern, ma'am."

"Of course, Sheriff," she said, crossing the room to stand on the far side of Rob's chair, keeping it between her and the lawman. "You weren't sheriff when Mr. LaMotte's grand-father disappeared, were you?"

"No. I remember the investigation that went on. There was quite a manhunt but no trace was ever found, was there?"

Tricia shook her head.

"You were with him at midnight?" Sothern motioned toward Rob.

"No, sir, not as such, but I did hear him in the hall outside my room when the downstairs clock struck midnight."

Sothern turned to Rob, waiting to see if he'd say anything.

"I'd been downstairs and came up at midnight."

"Well," Sothern said, "that gives you an alibi, I guess. Anybody else here?"

"No."

Sothern took a quick look from Tricia to Rob and then said, "I knew I shouldn't have come here. Sorry for any inconvenience, folks."

After showing the sheriff to the front door, Tricia closed it behind him and returned to the library where she found Rob standing by the fireplace, waiting.

"Thanks for the alibi."

"I did hear you, you know." Crossing the room, she approached the table.

"I'm sorry if I awakened you."

"I'd not been sleeping yet." She stopped at the library table.

Rob stepped toward the barrier separating them and he stared deeply into her eyes. The hunger was still there. Could his needs be as blatant as well?

Tricia leaned on the table and said, "By the way, what *were* you doing in the hall at midnight?" A twinkle of mischievousness settled in with the longing.

Rob blushed. He couldn't tell her. "Another time. All right?"

Tricia bowed her head just a bit and smiled knowingly. "Of course, sir." She turned to leave and when he called out to her.

Rob hurried around the table and approached her.

"Yes sir?"

Rob wanted to reach out and embrace her, to kiss her and hold her tightly. He could see in her everything that had been missing in his relationship with Sherry. His stomach knotted at the thought of his wife. He had to start thinking of her as his ex-wife. That would put a different light on their rapidly dying marriage, and as soon as he had Weipert dissolve the marriage, the better he would feel.

But he had to control himself where Tricia was concerned. Rob wasn't a very good liar under stress, and if he had to go into court, he didn't want to lie under oath or run the risk of being caught lying. As badly as he wanted Tricia, he had to keep her at a distance for now.

"I . . . I just wanted to thank you again for backing me up where the sheriff was concerned," he said, looking away.

"My pleasure, sir." She turned and left the

room.

Though Rob could sense the woman's frustration, he had to think of his whole future, not just the next few minutes or a brief period of physical gratification. Where was he getting the moral fortitude from? He wondered what his reaction would have been had he met Tricia while he and Sherry had been on good terms? He wouldn't have done anything. Maybe Rob LaMotte wasn't a success where life was concerned but he had never cheated on his wife. He would wait until he was free of Sherry to make his feelings known to Tricia, though he felt she already knew.

Turning back to face the shelves, he caught sight of the book and shivered. The mayor was dead. Now what would happen? At least the sonofabitch couldn't bother him anymore. His stupid friends had almost caused some problems, but at least the sheriff was a reasonable man and hadn't thought that Rob could have had anything to do with the accident.

Rob's hands shook. A film of sweat formed on his forehead, and he trembled. Had he been the one responsible for Bradley's death? What had he thought? That the man's brains should be bashed in or something of that nature. Rob felt sick for a moment.

The power within his grasp was unbelievable, and it was all his. He didn't have to share it with anyone unless he so chose. The book gave him power over other's futures and destinies where he himself was concerned. If someone crossed him, all he had to do was wish the sucker dead and the deed would be done but never reflect on him. The fact the tavern customers had sent the sheriff to him had been just a shot in the dark. They were blowing hot air when it came to suspecting Rob of anything.

A dark expression crossed over his face. He'd have to be careful where his wishes and desires were concerned if he elected to use the book again. He could never voice in front of anyone what he wanted to happen to a person, unless it were good. Anything bad, he'd have to keep to himself. That way no one would ever link him with a death or accident or anything that might profit him in some way.

Hurrying to the shelves, Rob reached up and pulled down the book with the golden pages. He reflected on the dreams he'd had wherein the contents and meanings of the writings had been made clear. He still wondered who had written it and how old it was. How had his grandfather come to possess it? From what he knew of the book's immediate past history, which had been revealed to him in miniscule bits and pieces, the book had not been used to its fullest by his grandfather.

Rob hugged the book to his chest and felt the prickly sensation of energy flowing into his body from it.

His eyes widened. Why didn't he simply wish Sherry out of existence. That would be the easiest way out of the marriage. What was he thinking of? What was happening to him? How could he think such things? Still, if she weren't around, he wouldn't have to feel paranoid where his wealth was concerned. As soon as she found out about it, she'd be down on him, for what she'd consider her fair share.

And what of Jeremy? He wanted nothing but the best for his son. Sherry would be an obstacle to his providing for their son, but Rob had already decided he'd take care of Sherry in his own inimitable way.

Clutching the book, he suddenly felt light-headed and nauseated. His stomach heaved, and he reached out to steady himself. He'd felt something like this yesterday when Bradley had called on him. Was someone else planning an attack against him? Had the sheriff gone back to the tavern and told the mayor's friends to forget about trying to pin Bradley's death on him? Would they accept that, or were they on their way ready to lynch him from the nearest tree? If they were, they'd be sorry. What could Rob do to them? He'd think of something. With the book in his possession, he felt completely safe and out of harm's reach. He felt absolutely invincible.

Rob began pacing about the library. The sense of doom was drawing closer, but he'd be ready. When the doorbell rang, he jumped and stared at the door. He hadn't even heard them come up the driveway much less onto the porch. How many were there? What should he wish for? How would he make these idiots pay?

The doorbell grated through the quiet once

more. He felt surprised that Tricia hadn't answered it yet. Perhaps he should go and get it over with. He peered out but couldn't see who was at the door from the library window. He saw a new car standing in the driveway—a small Chevrolet. There couldn't be too many of them if they all got into one car.

Confident and assured, Rob walked to the front door and threw it open. He stared, his mouth dropping open.

Sherry, holding Jeremy's hand in hers, smiled up at Rob.

CHAPTER NINETEEN

Rob stared. It couldn't be. Not now. How the hell had Sherry found him? His mental turmoil ended when he looked at Jeremy. Dropping to his knees, Rob held out his arms and the boy leaped into his father's embrace. For a long time they hugged, unmindful of Sherry's presence or her attempt to smile lovingly.

Holding Jeremy at arm's length, Rob said, "Hi, son. How are you? I've missed you."

Jeremy's voice cracked when he said, "I've missed you, too, Dad." Tears welled in his eyes and ran down his cheeks. He wiped them with his coat sleeve and smiled broadly, crying at the same time.

Rob got to his feet and fixed his attention on Sherry. "Well?"

Sherry looked away and then back to him, taking in the front of the mansion. "Well what?"

"Well, how did you find me?"

"You were on television, remember? I happened to see you. It didn't take a mental giant to figure out where you might be. A couple of questions in town and here I am. That is, we're here." She smiled down at Jeremy. "Aren't we, son?"

Jeremy nodded and slipped an arm around Rob's waist.

"Aren't you going to ask us in?" Sherry leaned to one side, trying to see past Rob into the front hallway of the house.

Rob ground his teeth. His anger seethed below the veneer of happiness he felt at seeing his son once more. Why had she come? The answer was all too obvious. She'd seen him on the news program all because of that bastard Bradley. Well, Bradley had paid dearly for his actions.

The sudden realization that he'd committed murder overwhelmed Rob again for an instant. Had he actually committed murder? He shook his head imperceptibly. No. He could rationalize the opposite just as easily. He'd merely wished that Bradley would die. Even that wasn't quite right. He'd wished for the opportunity to bash the man's brains out and beat him to a pulp. That had been his wish. Just because the mayor had been killed in a motor cycle accident was nothing more than coincidental.

"Come in," he said quietly, stepping to one side and allowing his wife to enter. Jeremy's sudden presence made him long for the father/son relationship he wanted and knew they could have, now that he had money and security. He'd thought of Jeremy different times and wondered how he could possibly get him away from Sherry without a long drawn-out court battle that would leave scars not only on their son but on them as well.

He closed the door behind him and leaned against it.

"Wow," Sherry whispered softly. "This is really something." She crossed the hall to the mirror and ran a fingertip over the smooth gilt frame. A cast bronze statue caught her attention and she went to it, again caressing it with her fingers. "How much is all this stuff worth?" she asked breathlessly.

Rob shook his head. That was typical of her, to think of the dollar value up front, but he wasn't really being fair to Sherry. Despite the fact that he no longer loved her, he couldn't deny that he'd reacted the same way when he first entered the mansion, nor could he ignore their past together. They'd had absolutely nothing other than their clothes and a few pieces of junk furniture they'd managed to buy.

"Let's go in the library," he said, motioning toward the open double doors. Jeremy obeyed instantly and went ahead. Rob waited for Sherry to pull herself away from one of the paintings.

"How much, Rob? How much is all of this stuff worth?" She stopped next to him and reached out, running her appraising fingers over his cheek. "How much are *you* worth, darling?"

He shook off her touch and gently pushed her toward the library. Jeremy had taken the leather easy chair and Rob pointed to the couch for Sherry.

When he walked to the fireplace instead of sitting down next to her, she looked at him and then at Jeremy. "Come here, Jeremy honey. Let your daddy sit there."

Jeremy obediently went to her but sat at the far end of the divan, out of her reach. A frown crossed his face and he looked away.

Rob didn't move. He'd sit down if he felt like it, not because Sherry suggested it.

"All those books," Sherry said quietly. "They must be worth a fortune. Aren't you going to tell me anything about your inheritance or who left it to you or—or anything?"

"If I thought you were interested for my sake only, I might consider it." Rob looked over her head without actually peering into her face. He knew she thought he was looking at her. He thought she looked awful, and still, when he did peruse her without her being aware of it, he knew she hadn't changed at all. She looked the same now as she had when he last saw her in the restaurant. Sherry looked like Sherry. She was the same. It was Rob's perception that had changed. She looked sleazy and cheap.

Tricia's face suddenly formed in his mind, and he shook his head in an effort to dislodge his housekeeper from his thoughts for the time being. He had to contend with his wife first. What could he do? Off in the distance, he heard someone speaking to him. "I'm sorry. Did you say something, Sherry?"

Concealing her frustration at not being able to command his attention and at having to repeat her question again, his wife said in a controlled voice, "I asked you if you thought you could handle all of this alone? Are you deaf or daydreaming? And what have you done to yourself? You look ten, fifteen years younger. When I saw you on television, I thought you looked better but thought it was the camera flattering you. What gives?"

"Don't bother yourself wondering if I can handle this. I can. I'm sorry if I seem to be daydreaming, but I'm a little shocked at seeing the two of you. That's all." Rob turned away.

"So what's your secret for growing younger?"

Rob stepped away from the mantle but retreated almost instantly back to where he'd been standing. "I haven't done anything. Maybe you just never noticed before."

"Notice what? Your paunch? Your graying hair? The worry lines on your face? They once were all there, but now they're gone. What did you do? Dye your hair and buy a girdle?" She laughed at her own joke but stopped when she saw it hadn't affected Rob.

"Don't worry yourself about me. I thought you were going to see an attorney. What about the divor—?" He motioned to Jeremy and mouthed the words, "Does he know?"

She shook her head.

"Jeremy?" Rob said, taking a step toward his son, who was gazing about the room. "Would you like to go outside and play for a while? The yard is really big. It's not that cold out and you'll be able to go exploring."

"Do I have to?" Jeremy stared at his father, his eyes wide.

"I wish you would, son. Your mother and I have some things to talk over. Don't go too far. I wouldn't want you to get lost."

"I won't get lost," the boy said, a note of irritation in his voice.

"You've never been out in the country alone before. Just keep the house in sight all of the time. Will you?"

Jeremy stood and scuffed a shoe on the thick oriental rug. "Yeah." He slowly walked to the hallway and opened the front door.

When it closed, Rob turned to Sherry. "What about the divorce? You are going through with it, aren't you?"

"What divorce? Are you crazy?"

"You were going to file, weren't you? You told me your attorney would be in touch with me. You said it in front of witnesses."

Sherry's voice rose as her anger increased. "I know that. I know what I said, but that

wouldn't hold up anywhere. I was mad at you
that day. I've simmered down. I've had time to
think, and I've decided I was wrong to walk out
on you like that. All right? I'm admitting it. I
was wrong."

"What changed your mind?" Rob asked, a
hint of sarcasm in his tone. He knew only too
well what had brought about the change in
Sherry. She was a determined woman. Once
she made up her mind, she seldom changed it.
It would be highly uncharacteristic of her to
have changed it now. But the chance to live like
a millionaire would change just about anyone's
mind, most especially someone like Sherry.

"I acted hastily, that's all. Aren't you going
to forgive me? I made a mistake."

"Damned TV news report," he muttered.
"Where'd you get the car?"

"I rented it. Rob? I'm still in love with you.
Don't you realize that?"

"You rented it?" he asked, choosing to ignore
her amorous overture for the time being. "You
must be doing pretty good on your waitress
job."

"All right, already. My boss rented it for me."

"Ah-hah. I'm beginning to understand now.
What stake does he have in all of your
retractions and change of heart? Plenty, I'll
bet."

"He doesn't. Really. It was my idea to come
up here and see you and try to make up. All he
said was that I might be making a mistake if
I went through with the divorce."

"And now that you've seen the house and a little of the inside, you've come to the conclusion that you'd be making a big mistake to turn around and leave me. Am I right?"

She shook her head and turned away.

"Come on, Sherry. Tell me. What're your plans?"

"I'm here. That's all that counts."

"I hope you're not planning on moving in here."

"And why not? I'm your wife. This is as much Jeremy's and my home as it is yours. We were willing to share that dumpy apartment with you. Why wouldn't we be willing to share in all of this as well?"

"Yeah, you were willing to share the apartment right up until the time you walked out on me." Rob raised his voice. "Well, let me tell you something, Miss High 'n' Mighty. I'd broken the jinx that was holding me back from selling the day you walked out. I'd come home that night to celebrate with wine and flowers for you. Don't you think I knew how tough you'd had it? I'm not that insensitive. But when you had Frank throw me out of his restaurant, you fried any chance of reconciliation right then. I'd told you about the inheritance but you made shit out of it and me. I—"

"I did not have Frank throw you out," she said loudly. "You were disturbing his place of business, and he thought he had every right to throw you out. Rob, I still love you."

"Bullshit! You love my money."

"I suppose you quit your job?"

"Of course. I don't need it anymore."

"You've got that much? You don't even have to worry about working?"

"That's none of your business. You said you didn't want any part of me anymore. Remember?"

"Sir?"

Rob whirled about to face the doorway and found Tricia standing there. She must have heard them arguing. "Yes, Tricia?"

"Who the hell is this?" Sherry asked, turning around on the couch to appraise the housekeeper.

"Are you all right, sir?"

"Yes. Ah, Tricia, this is my wife, Sherry LaMotte. Sherry, this is Tricia Woodless, my housekeeper."

Tricia bowed slightly toward Sherry, while a look of bewilderment crossed her face.

"Housekeeper? Hah! Bimbo, you mean. She'll have to go, Rob. I won't have another woman in my house. I can take care of it just as good if not better than she does. After all, it's our house, not hers."

"That's enough, Sherry. Get out of here now! Go alone. Leave Jeremy here with me."

"Are you crazy? I wouldn't think of leaving him here in this house of sin. Don't think for an instant that I can't see through your little setup here."

"That'll be all, Tricia. I'll call if I need you," Rob said, his voice shaking as his rage built.

"Are you sure, sir?"

He nodded and turned back to give Sherry his full attention. "How dare you? How dare you come into my home and make accusations like that?"

"You think I'm stupid? I know what's going on. You've got a nice little deal here, Rob. Big house. Nicely furnished. Built-in sex partner whenever you need it. Tell me, does she object to your early morning bouts? I'm taking Jeremy and getting out of here. I—"

"Why, Mom?" Jeremy asked from the doorway.

Rob and Sherry spun about to face their son. Neither had heard him enter the house and both stood frozen, unable to think of a reasonable explanation for whatever the child might have heard.

"Why what, Jeremy?" Sherry asked, fighting to control her embarrassment and forcing a smile at the same time.

"Why should we leave? I don't think Daddy's doing anything that you and Frank Yearnall didn't do. You did things with him, didn't you, Mom?"

"What?" Rob choked. "Are you telling the truth, Jeremy?" He turned, fixing an icy stare on his wife.

"What's he know?" Sherry said, putting up a front. "He's only a kid."

Rob took several steps toward her. "Get out of here and get out of here *now*."

When Sherry saw the look of utter hatred on

Rob's face, she jumped behind a chair, keeping it between them. "Stay there, Rob. You'll do something we'll both be sorry for. Don't touch me. Don't look at me like that."

"Get out of here and don't ever come back. I'll have my lawyer contact you. I'll be filing for divorce now. I've got grounds. With what I know from Jeremy, you'll be lucky if you get a red cent settled on you. Get out!"

"But—"

"Go. Now. Don't make it any more difficult."

Sherry turned to leave and swept past Jeremy who turned away when she hurried by him.

Rob bit his tongue. The bitch! The whore! Doing something like that in front of Jeremy. He shuddered. How could she have done something so stupid?

Concentrating on his wife, he suddenly saw a bed, surrounded by mirrors and Sherry lying on the bed with Frank Yearnall. But where were they? In his apartment? As far as Rob knew, Frank was married but didn't live in an apartment. Then his thoughts clarified and he understood the situation. Sherry had paid for the apartment with sex with her boss. The sonofabitch! He'd see to it that Frank Yearnall got his just comeuppance as well. Mayor Bradley had gotten his just desserts when he crossed Rob. Now Yearnall would get his.

How could Sherry have done it? Had she been that desperate to get away from their marriage? It didn't matter. He hated her. He wanted nothing more to do with her in any way, shape or form. They were through. Still, he would have enjoyed throttling her to show his superiority just once. He'd have choked her until her neck snapped and only then would he have had his fill of revenge.

Maybe he could still get one more shot at her before she left. He ran after her.

"No. Don't, Daddy!" Jeremy grabbed at his father as he ran by, stopping him for an instant.

"Let me go, son."

"No. You'll hurt her. I don't want you to hurt her. Let her go. I want to be with you anyway, Daddy." He looked up pleadingly at his father.

Rob stopped just as the front door slammed shut. Looking down at his child, he picked him up and hugged him tightly. "Oh, Jeremy, I'm sorry. I didn't want to hurt you by having you see us fight like this. I'm sorry, son. I really am."

"I want to stay here with you, Dad. I really missed you. I didn't like living with Mom alone. Besides, that creep Frank was around a lot of the time."

The scream from outside sounded far removed from the front hallway. At first neither Rob nor Jeremy knew what it was. The thudding sound of something falling down the steps froze both for an instant before Rob leaped for the front door, dropping Jeremy at the same time.

He threw the heavy door back, crashing it into the wall, and stepped out onto the wide front porch. He could see nothing. Half-turning to face his son, he found Jeremy with a puzzled look on his face that Rob thought reflected his own sense of bewilderment.

"What's wrong?" Tricia ran up behind them.

"I don't know," Rob said, walking slowly across the porch. When he reached the top of the steps, he stopped and peered down. He sensed more than realized that Tricia and his son were coming up behind him.

Sherry lay at the bottom of the steps, her head bent to one side in an unnatural position. Her eyes stared sightlessly up at Rob, and he looked away.

He grabbed Jeremy when the boy stepped around him and whisked him into his arms, turning his son's face away from the sight of his dead mother lying at the foot of the steps.

CHAPTER TWENTY

Rob stared at the chalk marks, outlining the position Sherry's body had assumed when she fell down the steps and broke her neck. He felt badly that she had died in that manner. They had loved each other at one time, but she had seen to it that their love had been destroyed. Still that same love had produced Jeremy, and for that he was grateful. And of course Jeremy had loved her. He shuddered. For that he felt the most remorse. He'd killed, by willing it, his son's mother.

Staring out over the yard, he jumped when the sheriff tugged on his sleeve. "Wh—what?" He turned to face the lawman.

Sheriff Sothern stepped closer to Rob. "I asked you if you'd like to finish talking with me inside—away from the scene?"

Rob turned. "Yes, of course. Where's Jeremy?"

"I believe your housekeeper took him upstairs."

Rob led the lawman through the front hallway and into the library. When they were seated Rob said, "Where were we?"

"You'd just told me that you and the Missus had argued and you ordered her out of the house."

Rob quickly finished telling him what happened and how no one had been anywhere near Sherry when she tripped and fell.

"You believe she tripped?" Sothern narrowed his eyes and studied Rob.

"Either that or she twisted an ankle or something. What do you think happened?"

The sheriff sat up straight when Rob asked him for his opinion. "What I think as far as conjecture is concerned don't matter much. I have to go by what you and your housekeeper tell me and the physical evidence. I can deduce anything I want, but it has to go along with all the other aspects. You say your boy was with you, is that right?"

Rob nodded. "We were out in the hall."

"And your housekeeper?"

"She was right behind us, a little ways back in the hall."

"Well, if their stories match yours, the whole thing will end right here."

"Do you have to talk with Jeremy?"

"Of course. He's a witness same as you and the Woodless woman."

"I wish he wouldn't have to talk about it."

"If you want this cleared up, he'd better talk. I know it's tough for the kid losing his mother and all, but don't worry about it. I've got kids of my own. I'll be kind."

Rob looked away from Sothern. He had no reason to think the sheriff would be anything else. Poor Jeremy. To see the body of his mother lying at the foot of the steps, her head and neck bent back at a grotesque angle, would stay with him for years to come. Perhaps, if Jeremy talked about the trauma with the sheriff, he'd take the first step in handling the problem.

"All right, Sheriff, you can talk with him. I'll get him and Tricia."

After Rob had brought them into the library, the sheriff asked him to step out into the hall, and try as he would, he couldn't hear the conversation. Leaning against the far wall, he could see Tricia, a somber expression on her lovely face as she spoke with the sheriff. At one point she indicated the back of the house with a motion of her arm and then settled back. Shortly thereafter, he saw her look toward the hall to where he was standing but concluded she was telling the sheriff something and hadn't even noticed him.

She suddenly got to her feet and was walking toward Rob. Taking a step toward her, he fought the urge to take her in his arms. When she stopped several feet away from him, he said, "How was it?"

"There was nothing difficult about it. I simply told the truth."

"How's Jeremy?"

They both turned to see the boy sitting down opposite Sothern.

"He was out of earshot while I was talking. The sheriff asked me to hold my voice down so he wouldn't hear what I said."

Rob turned away and looked up the staircase. How long would it take for the boy to tell the sheriff what had happened?

"Mr. LaMotte?"

"Yes?"

"I'm sorry about your wife's death."

"Don't be, Tricia. You didn't know her. And I won't be a hypocrite and accept condolences for it. I am sorry for Jeremy. Sherry was his mother, but I didn't love her anymore and she didn't love me."

Tricia stared at Rob, aghast at the brutal statement.

When he saw her expression, he quickly added, "Don't think I'm cold or heartless. A month ago—hell, two weeks ago—I would have been devastated by this, but she made a decision that ended any feeling I ever had for her. I hope you don't think too harshly of me."

"I think nothing of the kind. I only—" She stopped when the sheriff came up behind them.

"Well, Mr. LaMotte, your son's story more or less checks out with yours and the house keeper's. That ends it right here. Accidental death. That's the way it'll read in my report and the coroner will concur, I'm sure." He fixed his attention on Rob, ignoring Tricia."

"Excuse me, sir," she said and turned to retreat to the kitchen.

"I'm glad she's gone," Sothern said. "I want to say something to you, and I want to say it to you in private."

"What's that, Sheriff?"

"You're trouble, LaMotte. I don't think I like you. You come into the county, and before you're even settled, the Mayor of Nowaupeton is killed in an accident. He and—"

"Are you trying to say I had something to do with that?"

"Let me finish, LaMotte. You and he had an argument—a difference of opinion. He claimed there was something fishy about the way you and your family came to own this property and gain your wealth. He made a public statement yesterday and then he died last night. Now your wife, who apparently was fighting with you, conveniently falls down the steps and breaks her neck and won't figure in any divorce decree or settlement. I can't prove—"

"Sheriff, I'm no lawyer, but I know circumstantial evidence when I hear it and so do you. If you don't like me, that's no loss as far as I'm concerned, but I won't have you suggesting something about me you can't prove. If you're finished, I'd appreciate it very much if you got the hell off my land."

Sothern turned to leave the house and stopped when he opened the door. "Just don't leave the county. Stay put, just in case I've got more questions I want you to answer. Got it?"

Rob glared at him, brusquely nodding.

"If you got a lawyer, it might not be a bad idea to contact him."

"Hey, wait a minute," Rob called, following the sheriff onto the front porch. A brisk October breeze whipped around the corner of the house, sending a chill down Rob's spine.

Sothern stopped halfway down the steps and turned to face Rob. Looking up, he said, "You got nothing to worry about, LaMotte. You're clean—for now. I'd just tell my attorney, if I were you, that there have been people turning up dead—people who don't seem to see eye to eye with you. That's all. Like you said, there's nothing but circumstantial evidence and that's flimsy at best." He turned and hurried down the rest of the steps and got in his car, which was parked behind the rented one in which Sherry and Jeremy had arrived a few hours earlier.

Rob watched him back up and pull around the Chevrolet. He sped out of the driveway and down the hill.

"Daddy?"

Rob spun about to find Jeremy standing in the doorway. He looked so small in the large opening. Rob hurried to him, taking his son's hand in his and went inside. "What is it, son?"

"Is Mommy dead forever?"

Rob dropped to his knees and embraced him. "I'm afraid she is. That's what happens when people die. They leave forever."

Jeremy whimpered and hugged his father. "Are you glad she's dead?"

"Oh God, no. I was angry but I didn't want to see her like that, Jeremy. You have to believe me. Your Mommy was a good woman. She—"

"Why'd she yell at you all the time if she was a good woman? Is that the way good people are?"

"She wanted me to succeed, son. I guess she didn't know how to help me and felt frustrated when I wasn't doing too well on my job."

"What's frus-trated mean?" He looked up at Rob, wide-eyed.

Rob smiled inwardly at his son's innocence. "Remember the time you were making a model airplane and there were a couple of parts that didn't seem to fit together?"

Jeremy nodded.

"Remember how angry you got when they wouldn't fit and you tried and tried without getting them together?"

Jeremy nodded again.

"Well, that's how your Mom felt. She knew I could do better but didn't know how to help me. So she got mad and yelled a lot at me. Understand?"

Jeremy brightened a bit and nodded.

Rob hugged him again. "It's just you and me now. We'll have to help each other and work together. Can you do that?"

"Sure, Dad."

Rob felt an ocean of relief sweep over him. Jeremy was his alone now. One day he'd be successful in some field of endeavor, and all of the LaMotte wealth would be his as well. Their lives had done a complete about-face, but a nagging dread lurked at the bottom of Rob's soul.

A noise behind him brought Rob to his feet, and he found Tricia standing in the shadows, a smile on her mouth.

"Yes, Tricia?"

"I'll be preparing the evening meal, sir. Is there anything I can do for you?"

"No, that'll be fine, Tricia."

"If it's all right with you, I'll take your son upstairs and get him settled in a room. Then I'll start dinner."

Rob said nothing and stepped toward the library when Tricia took Jeremy by the hand and led him up the stairs.

Rob felt uneasy and restless. He was disturbed, but not by what the sheriff had said. Sure, the mayor had died less than 24 hours ago and now Sherry had fallen and broken her neck. There wasn't anyone in the world who could connect Rob with either death in a suspicious or accusatory way. He wanted to yelp with glee when he thought how easy it was for him to gain retaliation against someone who displeased him. He didn't even have to purposely think of a punishment. All he had to do was think of what he'd do if he himself had the chance.

Now, with Sherry dead, he had no obstacle to overcome as Jeremy's full-time father. He frowned. He was a murderer in a way and still wanted nothing but the best for his son. Was he a monster? Should he be condemned because he had his offspring's best interest in mind?

He wanted nothing more than all of the LaMotte wealth to pass intact to Jeremy. He smiled. A month ago, he'd have left his son his name and nothing more. Now he could and would leave him millions of dollars.

Rob sobered. And there was the book. The book was part of it, wasn't it? Why didn't he simply destroy the book? Throw it away. Heave it into the Mississippi River? Better yet, melt it down to another shape. That might be a good idea. If he tried to give it away or throw it away, it would probably come back. Somehow it had managed to get from the library to his bedroom and back without anyone's help.

He dropped into the leather easy chair and slumped down. He'd do it. The first thing tomorrow, he'd devise a way to destroy the book.

Before he could form another thought, a piercing agony ripped through his head. Never had he experienced such pain. It seemed to bore a hole from the forehead to the back of his skull. Cold sweat poured from his body, and he trembled as if afflicted with a severe chill

Pinpoints of light bombarded his closed eyes and he felt faint. As a sensation of swelling filled his mind, he thought his whole body was distorting. Then the pain and the bloating seemed to localize and center in his head. The ideas poured in, filling his mind.

Suddenly he knew what had happened to Emil. His grandfather had paid the price without ever knowing the book's full potential power. Because Rob had slept on it, much of the content had transferred to his brain, but Emil merely had his own wishes fulfilled because he lacked the knowledge as to how to really manipulate matters with the book.

The book was the *Book of The Dead!*

Now Rob understood the meaning of the phrase that had hammered at him when he had had the nightmares. The Dead. There were people who were of The Dead. What did it mean? What was the difference between being of The Dead or simply being dead?

Members of The Dead had been the owners of the book at one time or another in the past. They'd gathered in riches beyond their wildest dreams, but when their allocated time was completed, their price for having owned the book and reaping the harvest of wealth was to become a member of The Dead.

Rob opened his eyes and stifled the scream he felt building. The library was gone, and he stood on the black shore of his nightmare. The fiery ocean lay in front of him, and all around he could see the black shapes shuffling about, just as they had in his dreams when he'd rested with his head on the book. The black shapes were The Dead. He ran up to one and reached out. His hand passed through, and he felt the same cold clamminess as before.

New thoughts bombarded his mind. The Dead could not communicate with one another, nor could they see one another or speak with one another. They existed in their own plane and were never aware of anything or anyone. They were in a state of complete solitude. Theirs was a solitary existence for the rest of eternity without contact with anyone or anything.

Rob shut his eyes and held his breath. What could he do? Was he doomed as well? When he could stand the lack of oxygen no longer, he let his breath rush out and he opened his eyes. He was back in the library.

His shirt was soaked with perspiration and his hands still trembled. What had he gotten involved with when he claimed his inheritance? Had he seen a glimpse of his own future? Could he somehow turn away from it? His heart grew heavy when he thought of Jeremy, his son and heir, becoming involved in the same way.

Not Jeremy. He couldn't allow that. Somehow he had to change the course of events that would lead to his son's involvement. He had to destroy the book, and the sooner the better. If he didn't, he would perish and so would Jeremy. Rob had already killed twice.

He liked the sense of revengeful justice involved, but had it been justice or merely his own ego being salved and his wishes fulfilled? Still, he didn't want Jeremy owning the book or killing anyone because he'd been crossed in some way.

How could any of this have been prevented? None of the events of the last week or so might have taken place if Sherry had been home when Rob had returned with a bottle of wine and flowers for her. If she'd been there, perhaps the two detectives working for Zwotney would not have been there to tell him to call on the attorney. Or if they had, he might have completely forgotten about it, if Sherry and he celebrated his success.

But she hadn't been there, and he'd paced about, worrying for his wife and child's welfare. Then, when he discovered the clothes were gone and his despair set in, he'd found the card and called the attorney the next day.

And whose fault had it been that Sherry had left? To some degree it was Rob's. He knew that. Sherry was the sort who would remain in a situation as long as necessary and not leave for any reason. That much credit he had to give to her. She had hung in there as long as there wasn't any outside interference, but finally there had been outside interference—Frank Yearnall. It was his fault that Sherry had left. Rob understood that now as well. Because of the book, he knew Yearnall was merely out to satisfy his own needs and didn't give a damn about Sherry or how much she or her family might suffer. Yearnall had convinced her to move out and into his apartment. Rob visualized it and tensed when he saw the mirrored bedroom. The bastard was sick—and Sherry had gone along with everything he suggested. It was all Frank Yearnall's fault.

Leaping from the chair, Rob paced about the library. If he had Frank there right now, he'd pulverize the bastard. He'd beat him to a pulp with his bare hands.

"I'll be back in a few minutes, Barb," Frank said, walking toward the back of the kitchen. "You take over the cash register 'til I get back, okay?"

Barb smoothed her uniform and adjusted her small apron. Thrusting her large breasts out, she nodded. "Hurry back." She left the kitchen, and Jack Kolman, the dishwasher, flicked his cigarette ash toward Frank when he passed.

Frank didn't notice the gesture and opened the door. The cool October air rushed into the warm kitchen, and he closed the door behind him. Walking to his car, he fumbled for his keys and suddenly doubled over as if someone had punched him in the stomach.

He gasped for air, clutching the side of the car to keep from collapsing.

"What th—?"

Another blow cut short his question, and his head flew back as a third unseen blow connected, straightening him up.

"Get away from me!" he cried. "Here. Take my money. Don't hit me again." He looked around, shocked at not seeing anyone.

Then, as if the request had infuriated the invisible attacker, the assault was renewed viciously. Blow after blow rained on Frank's head and body. His mouth puffed up, blood trickling from the corner. Both eyes swelled shut as they were struck simultaneously. The pounding continued until he collapsed in a heap on the ground. Without warning, he was lifted and his coat torn off, spinning him about like a clumsy top. His shirt followed. Then his pants and underwear were shredded. He stood naked, vainly attempting to cover his nudity, a bewildered expression on his swollen face.

The unseen fists pounded at him, raising red welts along his back and front as he tried desperately to protect himself.

"Stop! Stop it!" His cries went unheeded as he was thrown against the brick wall of the building on the far side of the alley. Frank stood for a moment, then slowly slid to the ground. Again he was picked up and hurled against the wall of his own restaurant. This time, his head struck first and his skull cracked open from the force. Bits of brain and blood showered the ground.

His motor instincts still working, he struggled to stand and fell under a torrent of blows that slowly tore away the skin from the flesh and the flesh from the bones. Frank had long since died by the time his skeleton was ground into dust and mixed with the bloody soup that had been his body.

Nothing remained. The wind capriciously rolled his torn clothing toward the street half a block away, and a heavy silence filled the alley.

A pair of red eyes scanned the area before the owner stuck out its nose. It twitched, reading the air. Then another pair of eyes and then another poked out, searching the early evening dark. Soon hundreds of rats congregated, feeding on what remained of Frank Yearnall.

Rob sat stiffly in the easy chair. Cold sweat still ran down his face. His body felt clammy, and he shivered from the unnatural chill. He could hear Tricia and Jeremy coming down the steps. He had to get control of himself.

Forcing himself to move, he sat up enough to pull out his handkerchief. Dabbing at his brow when they entered, he said, "Well, son, did Tricia find you a nice room?"

"Uh-huh. It's really neat."

Tricia stepped close. "What's wrong, sir? Are you ill?"

"It's nothing. I'll be all right."

"You look awfully pale, and you're sweating. Something is wrong." Tricia moved even closer.

"I . . . I don't know. I might be sick. I felt really strange there for a moment."

"I think you should go to bed right now. You look terrible. If you're not better by morning,

I'll call the doctor in Guttenberg."

"What about Jeremy?"

"I'll take care of him. I'll fix his supper and bring you a tray if you want to eat."

"Just fix Jeremy's meal. I'll be all right. I'm sure of it."

Jeremy moved toward his father. "Daddy?"

"What is it, son?"

"You okay? You look sick, like Tricia said."

"I'll be fine, Jeremy. Do what Tricia says and go to bed when she tells you. I'll be fine in the morning."

"Promise?" Jeremy asked.

"I promise."

The boy hugged his father around the waist and said, "I love you, Dad."

Rob returned the embrace. "I love you, too, son. Now, get away from me in case I have something catching. Go with Tricia."

"Come on, Jeremy. I'll fix you a super supper."

Jeremy forced a smile and took her hand as they walked from the library. He liked the woman and he loved his father. He knew it would be better here than it had been with his mother.

Rob stood alone in the library for a moment. He knew too much about the book. All of the past owners had been murderers of one type or another. If a person who happened upon the book was good, changes would take place and a maniacal power would hold them in its grasp while they accumulated wealth and eliminated ny person who stood in their way.

Rob was frightened. His grandfather had illed. He had killed. He didn't want the same hing happening to Jeremy. If Rob had to pay he price of becoming one of The Dead, he'd do t, but only if he could assure the fact that eremy wouldn't be so cursed. Still, if Rob illed everything to Jeremy, there'd be nothing e could do. He suspected the book probably ould never be destroyed. It came from a time o distant that its origins were beyond the omprehension of man. And it would go on orever, condemning its owners to a fate worse han hell.

Hell? Rob blanched. In the second dream the armth he felt from the light overhead had een so comforting. The figure in the brilliance ad wept when Rob looked up. What had any f it meant? Who was the figure? The figure nd the warm light had disappeared, and lthough at the time he hadn't noticed, Rob had elt colder and alone. He felt the same way now, nly more so.

He didn't want to hurt Jeremy by giving him nything that could harm him. He had to get ut of the predicament he found himself in and omehow destroy the book. Rob had to save eremy and break the spell of the damnable ook to save himself.

But how?

CHAPTER TWENTY-ONE

Rob ran a hand through his hair. How could he get rid of that goddamned book? How did one destroy something made of gold? File it into dust? Melt it into a puddle? Of course, he'd melt the damned thing. Destroy it completely as it existed and change its form. He knew he had to destroy it or his son would pay a heavy penalty for inheriting it. What about himself? Wouldn't he have to pay a price for his gains? He didn't know. His grandfather had obtained wealth and money and power with the book. He'd also removed certain people, who represented obstacles to his own end.

Rob blanched. He'd done the same thing. He'd been directly or indirectly responsible for the deaths of Mayor Bradley and Sherry—and

Frank Yearnall in all probability. He had wished for the opportunity to pulverize his wife's boss with his bare hands. If the norm held true, Frank Yearnall was more than likely dead, or would be soon. Rob had killed three people by wishing them dead. Did that make him as guilty as his grandfather? He knew what had happened to his grandfather. He was the only one who did know, and he couldn't tell anyone for fear they'd think him mad.

Perhaps his own fate would be changed if something happened to the book. Could he succeed in destroying it? He had to try—not for himself but for Jeremy. He couldn't stand the thought of his son being a murderer, no matter how indirectly, nor did he want him to know the vengeful killer his father had been. Was Rob mad? He didn't know. Maybe he was imagining the whole thing. Maybe he was putting too much importance on coincidence.

But he knew he had willed them dead, and his will had been satisfied. Now he had to get rid of the book. If it meant his own life in doing so, he'd happily give it up to save his son from the same fate.

The first thing he had to do was get Tricia and Jeremy out of the house. He had to send them someplace until he finished.

He hurried to the kitchen and found Tricia sitting at the round table with his son. It looked to Rob as if they were getting along famously. He smiled. Tricia had a calm, likeable personality. He wished Sherry had been more like that. If she had been, she would probably be alive, and the three of them would be together and happy. But she was gone, and Rob felt no pangs of regret or guilt concerning her.

"Tricia?"

She jumped at the sound of his voice, unaware he had entered the kitchen. "Yes sir?"

"I'm feeling much better, and I'd like to talk to you for a moment—alone."

Jeremy looked up at his father and smiled. "You gonna eat, Dad? This is really good soup."

"After a while, son. Right now I've got to talk with Tricia for a moment." He stepped aside and waited for her to pass him. Then he followed her to the library.

"You're sure you're feeling better?"

The hint of concern in her voice was evident and Rob renewed his vow to destroy the book and begin his life again. He'd had a taste of the good life and he wanted more, but he wanted it in a normal way.

"I'd like you to do something for me, Tricia."

"What's that, sir?"

"I want you to take Jeremy into Nowaupeton and go shopping."

"Shop? At this hour? The stores aren't open much longer, if they're even open now." She studied him, a quizzical look crossing her face.

"If they're closed, then take him for a ride through the countryside. Use the car my wife came in."

"But . . ."

"Don't ask any questions now. I've got a job

to do here and I don't want either of you
around. It might be dangerous."

"I—I don't understand."

Rob pictured himself melting the book. How
could he do that? He didn't have the tools for
a job like that. Suddenly, the red-hot pain
similar to the one he'd had before, pierced his
head and he spun about, almost falling to the
floor.

Tricia leaped forward, grabbing him and
helping him to a chair. When he was upright
he held his head and rocked back and forth.
Melting the book wouldn't work. The book was
telling him he couldn't destroy it. Nor could he
throw it away or bury it. It would come back
to him until The Dead claimed him as one of
their own.

The book gave the power and still it held in
reserve the ability to annihilate the source of
that power. Still, if he had power, perhaps—
perhaps he could . . . The pain lessened and
disappeared. He sat up, a crooked smile
twisting his face.

"Come with me, Tricia." He leaped to his feet
and went to the stairs, running up two at a
time. She followed him as quickly as she could.

"Don't run. You'll fall," she called after him.

When he reached the second floor, he went
to the master bedroom. The room looked
inviting and he vowed that if he survived his
ordeal, he'd move into it at once. After she
entered, he closed the door and leaned against
it.

He felt far enough removed from the book to formulate his plan. He'd use the power the book had given him in an attempt to destroy the blasted thing. He didn't know what would happen if he tried but he knew he didn't want Jeremy or Tricia around when he did. No matter what he tried with the book, he wanted to be alone.

"Tricia, I want you to listen to everything I tell you. Don't think I'm mad and run away from me. I need your help and I need it now. Jeremy needs your help as well. You must take him away from here and don't come back until tomorrow."

Tricia nodded. "But why? What's going on? What are you going to do? I don't understand."

"Sit down. I'm going to tell you what's been going on around here. I'll tell you about my grandfather and why he looked so young when he was actually very, very old. I'll tell you things that will absolutely defy understanding."

Her eyes widening, she sat down on the bed.

Rob paced about the spacious room and said, "It began when my grandfather found a strange book and brought it home with him."

Tricia's mouth hung open. When Rob finished the story, accounting for Sherry's death, he stopped for a moment.

"Now I've got to try to destroy it. If I don't and something happens to me, Jeremy will inherit the land and the house and the bus-

inesses and that goddamned book. I don't want
him to be involved, do you understand?"

"I think I do. But why can't I help you destroy
it?"

"I don't know what's going to happen. It's
probably going to be very dangerous, and I
wouldn't want anything to happen to you." He
looked away and felt a rush of color rise to his
face.

Tricia got off the bed and walked toward
him. "I've only known you for a short time, not
even a week, but in that time I've grown quite
fond of you. I don't want to see you get hurt
trying to do this."

Rob looked back at her. "I'd like to tell you
some of the feelings I've had about you, Tricia,
but time won't permit. After I get rid of this
book, I'll tell you how I feel about you. You see,
I'm fond of you, too."

Tricia stepped closer. "I could even say I love
you." She looked directly into his eyes and saw
the turmoil and frustration there.

"I do love you, Tricia. I have since the first
moment I met you."

They blended into each other's arms and
kissed, their tongues meeting as they explored
the hidden recesses of each other's mouth.

"Please, let me help you," she pleaded.

"You'll be helping me by taking Jeremy out
of here for tonight. Once the book is gone,
things'll be fine."

"But what if something happens to you?"

"At least I'll know that Jeremy's safe with

you. If I'm successful, we'll all be together tomorrow. If I'm not . . " His voice trailed off.

"If you're not successful, then what?" She grabbed him by the arms and turned him to face her. "Then what?"

"Then you'll have to take care of Jeremy. Will you?"

Instead of answering, she threw her arms around him. "Nothing will happen to you. It can't. Promise you'll be careful?"

"I promise."

"Then I'll go. But remember that I don't want to. I'm leaving to please you. I feel I should stay here with you, but I won't." She turned, walking slowly to the door. When she reached it, she stopped and turned to face him once more. "Where are the keys?"

"In the ignition."

"I love you." She turned before he could answer and left.

"I love you, too, Tricia," he said softly after the door closed.

A few minutes later he heard the front door open and close. He ran to the window overlooking the driveway and watched in the darkness as his son started to get into the car. He stopped and looked up. When he saw Rob, he waved, a puzzled almost frightened look on his face.

Rob waved back. When his son was in and the door closed, he heard the motor turn over, and after the headlights went on Tricia eased the car away from the house and around the horseshoe driveway.

He watched until the taillights disappeared. Then he turned back and faced the matter at hand.

He had to concentrate. He had to dwell on the power the book had given him. The more he thought about it, the stranger he felt. He could feel the power flowing through his body, something he'd never before experienced. The surge of strength amazed him, and he knew he could do almost anything he wished.

A crackling sound filled the room, and he knew it came from within him. A small statue, standing on a table near the door, caught his attention. He pointed at it, wishing for it to be destroyed. A blue bolt of energy shot from his fingertip, straight at the piece of statuary which disintegrated.

Unable to control the laughter he felt mounting within him, he gave it vent and his mad cackling filled the room. Now he could destroy the book. He ran to the door and threw it open. Dashing down the steps, he stopped when he reached the bottom. In the library he could see a strange greenish, yellow glow filling the room, undulating, rising, dying as if a living thing were in there, breathing in such a way as to make the motion visible.

The book floated from the shelf to the table and stayed there as if waiting to see what Rob's next move would be.

He stepped toward the double doors and entered. As the book's glowing intensified, Rob could feel his own power building to a fevered pitch. Perhaps he should try once more before attacking the book. He pointed to the fireplace and instantly a blaze danced upon the logs that had rested there. He was ready.

Gathering his courage, he stepped closer to the book. His thoughts centered on destroying the book, atomizing it, making it vanish from his life. Then he pointed at it.

"How come we're going shopping now?" Jeremy asked, turning to Tricia.

"Your daddy wanted us to go now," she said wistfully. She never should have agreed to leave. Her place was there with him. Of course she agreed that Jeremy's safety had to be taken into consideration, but if she loved Rob she should be with him and help him somehow.

"Do you like my dad?"

"Of course I do, Jeremy. Why do you ask?"

"How come he's changed?"

She turned from the lane onto the country road. "Changed? How?"

"He looks different."

"How do you mean different?"

"He looks younger than he did. He had a few gray hairs by his ears. They're gone. And he had some little lines around his eyes. They're gone, too."

The book! Tricia now understood that Emil had looked like he did because of the book. She'd never thought of it before Rob came to the house, but now that he'd told her of the

book and its power, she understood a lot more
than she had. It didn't bother her that Rob had
wished his wife or the mayor dead. She'd had
thoughts like that at different times about
different people as well. Of course she didn't
have anything to do with the book, so her
thoughts were merely idle ones that passed and
weren't thought of again.

"Does that bother you?" she asked.

"Heck no. I think he looks great. How long
will we be gone?"

Tricia suddenly realized that what she was
doing was wrong, not because of Jeremy but
because she felt as if she were deserting Rob
when he needed her. She slammed on the
brakes.

"What's the matter?" Jeremy asked, bracing
himself on the dashboard.

"We're going back. I've got to do something
for your father."

"Now?"

"Now." She pulled into a farm lane and
turned around, flooring the accelerator.

The Chevrolet roared back along the country
road toward the mansion's driveway. When she
pulled into it, she slammed on the brakes once
more.

"Oh, my God!" she cried.

"Daddy. Daddy!" Jeremy's wailing cry filled
the car as she floored the accelerator once
more.

Rob's frustration boiled over. Nothing

happened. He stared at the book. "Goddamn you! Be destroyed!"

Why hadn't anythng happened? He focused the power on the book as he had on the statue and on the logs. Why hadn't it worked? Was the book too powerful for him to destroy?

He hated the book now. He hated so intensely that he felt the hatred grow and multiply within him, building alongside the power which also intensified. He concentrated his full will on the book, the cause of his hatred.

Overwhelmed by the sensations within him, Rob pointed once more at the book and a gigantic blue lightning bolt leaped from his hand and fingers, straight at the leather-bound volume of golden pages on the table in front of him.

The bolt struck the book, ricocheting off and sizzling its way into the hall where it hit the mirror. It reflected back into the library straight at the books lining the shelves. The books exploded, bursting into flames that spread about the room, landing on the drapes and the rug and the furniture. In seconds, a raging blaze filled the room, and Rob stood rooted to the spot, unable to move.

The fire roared out of control, racing from the library, into the hall, capriciously kissing the wallpaper, engulfing the paintings and apping at the wooden balustrade.

Then Rob thought he heard a voice. It couldn't be. Jeremy? Had they come back? Then he could hear Tricia's call.

"Mr. LaMotte! Rob? Rob?"

"Daddy?"

Transfixed, Rob couldn't move. The fire inched its way across the rug toward his feet, reaching up to ignite his pants' legs. Why couldn't he move? He willed it. He demanded his body to move but it wouldn't respond. The searing pain of the flames burning his legs reached his brain and he screamed.

"Daddy! Come out!" Jeremy screamed at the top of his voice.

"Jeremy, get back. You'll be burned," Tricia called.

"Jeremy! Jeremy, son! Go back. Run."

"Dad!"

Rob heard the one word and realized Jeremy was no longer outside but inside the house. He peered through the flames and could see his son standing in the hallway, trying to reach him, to help him, to save him.

"Run, Jeremy, run! Save yourself!"

Jeremy stared for a long moment at his father standing in the library, more a pillar of fire than a human being. Then he turned and ran for the front door. When he reached it, he stopped and shouted into the flames charging toward him, "I love you, Dad! I love you!"

Tricia reached through the doorway and grabbed the boy, yanking him to safety. They ran down the steps, both stopping at the bottom when they heard Rob shout.

"I love you, Jeremy!"

The fire raced through the old house

consuming it as the woman and child backed away.

When Jeremy turned and ran toward the door, Rob concentrated on attempting to move. He had to get out of the library. Realizing his son was going to be safe, he yelled once more, "I love you, Jeremy!"

The fire ate at him, devouring his flesh. What would happen to him now? Was he going to simply die, or would he become of The Dead? He didn't know and he didn't care. The pain had numbed his mind, and he could think of nothing coherently.

Then the truth struck him. He was already dead. He was of The Dead. He could see the black shore and the fiery ocean. When he saw Sherry coming toward him, he wondered why he could make out her face and not those of the others who were approaching him. Sherry paid him no mind and turned, waiting for Frank Yearnall. Rob concluded that they were merely dead and not of The Dead. When he looked again, Sherry and Frank were nowhere to be seen. The shadowy figures were coming for him.

He called out to them but they ignored him. Then he realized the enormity of the curse. Forever and ever, he would never communicate with another being, nor be aware of their presence. In a short time he wouldn't be able to see those with whom he was cursed to spend eternity. The forms wavered for an instant before disappearing. Then the flaming ocean and the shore of black sand vanished.

He was alone—forever.

Once the trauma of the fire and Rob's death had been faced, Tricia and Jeremy returned to the ruins of the mansion a week later.

They sat in the rented Chevrolet for a long time before either ventured out. Without speaking, they walked slowly to the charred remains of the front steps. Both realized the utter destruction the fire had caused. Most of the structure had collapsed and fallen into the basement.

They walked slowly around the perimeter of the house, trying to identify something, anything. The volunteer fire department had arrived but too late to save anything of the building itself. Rob's body had been found charred to a small pile of ashes, which had been gathered up by the county coroner.

When Tricia and Jeremy came to the fourth and final side of the foundation, she stopped and pointed, "Look, Jeremy. What's that?"

Thy boy followed her outstretched arm and shook his head. "I don't know. Do you?"

"It looks like a . . . a book." Her hand flew to her mouth. Even though Rob had only told her of the book, she'd never actually seen it. She probably had looked at it hundreds of times without realizing the book's power. If that were the book lying in the middle of the rubble, she wouldn't have been surprised. Rob had been taken from her and from Jeremy because of it. She hated it. She loathed it.

"Come on, Jeremy," she said. "Let's go."

The boy started toward the car and she followed, only to stop for an instant to take one more look.

The book was gone.

EPILOGUE

Chicago, Illinois

Davey Maghee staggered along the alley that emptied onto State Street. His head hurt. He'd drunk too much muscatel, but what else was there to do? If he could scrounge up the price of a bottle, he'd buy another, just to soothe the pain and get into his little, fuzzy world.

He'd given up teaching because the kids got on his nerves, and the day he slammed one up against the lockers he'd been fired. Then his wife left him and he turned to alcohol for companionship.

Right now he needed a little rest before he continued toward State Street. He'd have to be careful if he tried panhandling there. The cops would come down on him like a plague if they caught him begging. But hell! All he needed was a couple of bucks and he'd be in good shape.

Slumping down along the wall next to a garbage pail, he laid his head against the cold bricks. He'd have to start looking for shelter pretty soon or he'd freeze to death one night when it got real cold. It might be a relief if he died. But if he did, he couldn't have any more wine.

Enough rest. He had to get going and get a bottle soon or the worms and rats would start climbing all over him again.

As he tried to push himself up, his right hand closed on something. Picking it up, his eyes widened when he saw it was a book. It seemed disproportionately heavy.

His eyes widened even more and he blew his wine-sodden breath out heavily when he opened it and saw the golden pages.

Davey grinned. He could hock it for a few bucks and maybe buy a case of muscatel.

Standing up, he staggered down the alley toward the bright lights of State Street.